DESCENT INTO FURY

THE DAYS OF ASH AND FURY VOLUME FOUR

AN EPIC FANTASY BY

SEAN HINN

BOBDOG
BOOKS

Descent into Fury is a work of fiction. Names, characters, places, events and incidents are either the products of the author's imagination or used in a fictitious manner. Any resemblance to actual persons, living or dead, or actual events is purely coincidental.

© 2016, 2017, 2018 by Sean Hinn

Published in the United States of America by Bobdog Books.

ISBN 978-0-9980960-8-7

First Edition

Published July 2019

10 9 8 7 6 5 4 3 2 1

www.seanhinn.com

http://www.facebook.com/TahrSeanHinn

Email the author at sean@seanhinn.com

TABLE OF CONTENTS

To all who have ventured
Into the dark places
And have again found the door...
And to those who will.

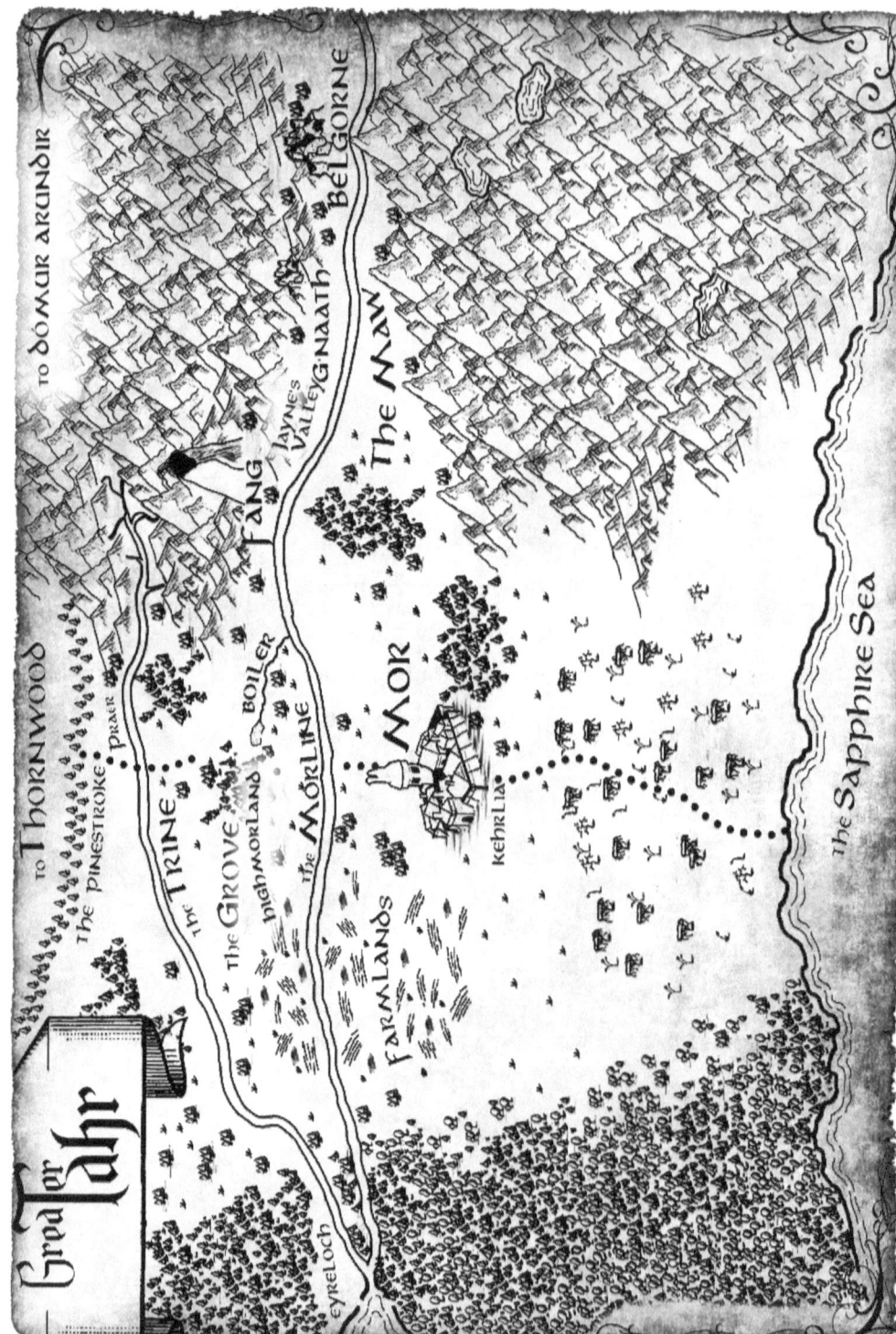

THE DAYS OF ASH AND FURY

PART SEVEN

CONTINUED FROM
SPAWN OF FURY,
(OR ASH: ACT ONE)

I: THE MORLINE

IR BARRIS OF THORNWOOD tore west along the Morline astride the great black stallion Phantom, the pair only just failing to outpace the dawn. On any other morning, the familiar harmony of speed, power, and grace might have been a joy, but on this day, the First Knight carried only dread in his heart.

Barris had seen the pillar of light. He had sensed the battle ahead, caught the scent of evil on the winds... the scent of death. Men of Mor had died today, he knew, though the cause of his dread was less abstract, more personal. In his deepest heart, Barris knew he had lost something dear to him this dawn. Some*one*. He knew in the way a twin might know her sibling is in danger. He knew in the way a wife would wake suddenly in the night, knowing her husband had faced his end in some far-off war. He knew in the way an estranged daughter might sense a chill at the passing of her mother.

Or how a father might know, upon losing a son.

Phantom broke free of the tree line and the trail widened. The pair accelerated, cold wind pulling tears from the corners of Barris' cobalt eyes as the carnage before him came into focus. Torn and smoldering bodies lay strewn on either side of the great river. The Morline Bridge was just... gone.

Phantom needed no guidance, nor could the aggrieved knight have provided any. Barris shut his eyes against what he knew they would soon see, sobbing freely as Phantom came to a halt beside Mikallis' torn and burnt body. Triumph greeted Phantom with a nudge and a whinny. Phantom stamped and snorted as Barris slid from the saddle, one hand remaining in contact with his horse, the other trembling as he knelt beside the young, broken captain and reached to close his lifeless eyes.

Mikallis had suffered. The tracks of his movement told the story of his end; he had crawled through the ash and snow as his flesh melted away, dragging himself towards something, or someone. *A vile acid did this,* Barris imagined. An excretion of the dragon, certainly, for the signs of its rage were everywhere... deep gouges in the muddied ground, burned and shredded bodies wearing the robes of Kehrlia. Barris sobbed and prayed and mourned over Mikallis' body for a time that might have been a turn or an hour before noticing the faint glow emanating from beneath the fallen elf's shirt. *The Mark.* Mikallis had made a great sacrifice this day, and the knowledge filled Barris with both breathless pride and even more profound regret at the loss of the elf he would have named son. The sight of the Mark called to mind Barris' own duties, and the heart-spent knight finally wiped his eyes. He stood to survey his surroundings in more detail.

A few paces away lay Redemption, the sword he had carried most of his life until he released it into the care of Lucan not-Thorne. Barris turned, searching among the dead for the young man. He saw instead his mount, Hope, huddled nearby beside Sera, Spirit, and Osraed. The knight released his Bond with Phantom and made his way to the four horses but froze as he neared them and saw: there on the ground lay his oldest friend, Trellia Evanti, Vicaris of the Grove. Barris reached to touch

Osraed, Bonding with her grey mare. Images flashed in his mind; he saw her death clearly through the mare's memory, Trellia cleaved in two by an enormous dragon scale that still jutted from the ground between her two halves. He saw the battle with the dragon through their eyes, saw Mikallis' heroic sacrifice in a vain attempt to save his friends, saw the four inexplicably vanish as Kalashagon bore down on them. He knew some magic must have whisked them away and could only hope they were safe, somewhere.

Returning to the present, Barris eyed the dragon scale. Its presence was an affront he could not abide. He paid no heed to the black, viscous sheen as he snatched the great plate from the ground, screaming, and flung it a hundred paces across the Morline as if skipping a stone. It stuck a foot deep in the far bank and Barris fell to his knees once more, weeping again from eyes he had thought bereft of tears.

A tingling in his hands became an intense, burning pain as the acidic residue from the scale ate at his palms. He made no sound, believing that to cry out against the pain would diminish the far greater suffering he knew Mikallis had endured. He made his way down the bank to dunk his hands in the icy water of the river, muttering a prayer that he knew would not hasten his healing but would, at least, prevent the burns from deepening. Large, fluid-filled blisters had begun to form, but his wounds would not worsen.

A cry from across the river drew his attention. *Someone still lives!* Barris stood, searching for a way across the Morline, but there was none. He recalled the trick Nishali had taught him and in a few bounds skipped his way across the frigid water of the

Morline and onto its southern shore. He climbed the embankment.

"Who calls? Where are you?"

"Here! Oh, Father please help me! Here!" A young man's voice cried out, weak and tortured.

Barris ran through the ashen slush to the man's side. A glance told him there was nothing he could do for the dying Incantor.

"Please. Help me."

Barris knelt beside him, placing a hand on his shoulder. "Peace, friend. Tell me your name."

The man met Barris' eyes. "This is my fault. All my fault. I'm... so sorry."

"Shh, now. This cannot be your—"

"*It is!*" The man coughed as Barris surveyed his wounds. His lower half was mangled, his spine bent at an unnatural angle. The stench of burning flesh brought a gag to Barris' lips. "I *knew!* Father forgive me, but I knew! *He is a monster!*"

"Who, friend? Who is a monster?"

"SARTEAN! He's not dead, you know. Not forever! Kal will call him!" The man coughed again, blood gurgling from his mouth. He grasped at Barris' cloak as the light in his eyes began to fade. "He is indebted. *He will return!*"

Barris blanched. He sensed a power in that word... *indebted.*

The knight stroked the man's forehead. "Tell me your name, sir, so that I may pray for your peace."

The man laughed; a mirthless, choking sound. "Jarriah. My name is Jarriah. But there will be no peace for me." The hand grasping Barris' cloak went slack, and Jarriah died.

Barris muttered a short prayer and closed the man's eyes. He stood.

Sartean D'Avers is dead. The thought chilled the knight, knowing what power the Master of Kehrlia possessed, marveling at what might have killed him. Barris began checking the bodies, one by one, offering prayers, closing eyes. *Why?* he wondered, not for the first time in his long years. *Why do we trouble to close eyes that no longer see?* He found Sartean D'Avers' body near to noon. The condition of the corpse puzzled him. No injury was visible whatsoever, aside from a hole the size of a fist that went clean through the back of his head and out his mouth. Some projectile had lain him low, but it was nowhere to be found. The accurate placement of the wound implied it was deliberate, and surely not caused by the dragon.

An Incantor, Barris surmised. *A rival. While he was distracted, certainly.*

Barris made his way back across the Morline to Phantom and the other horses. With painstaking reverence and profound sorrow, he wrapped the remains of Mikallis and Trellia in horse blankets and tied them to Triumph and Osraed. He wept as he completed the grim task, considering where Aria, Lucan, J'arn and Shyla might have gone. He decided their most likely destination would be the Grove.

Barris spoke to the horses. "You must take them home. Home to the Grove." Barris sent images of the Spring through the Bond to the horses. "Follow Hope, she will lead you. Will you not, Hope?" The chestnut mare snorted in reply. Barris tied Redemption to Phantom's saddle and climbed atop the stallion. He looked over his shoulder to the eastern skies, seeing the plume of smoke and ash from Fang had slowed, though thick rivulets of lava ran from its mouth. He gave Phantom's neck a gentle pat. "We must again make haste, my friend." The declaration brought a choke from deep within the First Knight, but he managed to suppress the sob as he urged Phantom north at a gallop.

I will not cry twice.

But he did.

II: THE DOORS OF NYR AVI

*MUST NOT open my eyes. Ever. I must not.*

"You may, Mikallis Elmshadow. Do not be afraid."

The deep, clear voice bore an ageless quality, its soothing words carried along on currents of truth. Yet Mikallis did not dare heed them.

If I look, I will know. I do not want to know.

"Truth need not be seen, brave elf. It simply is, as it must be."

I do not want to know.

"But you do. You know where you are.

I do not want to know.

"You know how you have come here."

No.

"And you know my voice."

I do.

Father.

"Of a sort. Come now. Open your eyes. They will only confirm that which is true."

Mikallis could not resist the gentle, urging voice. Cool white light replaced the dark gloom of death as his eyelids parted. His eyes quickly adapted but saw nothing, for there was nothing to see. Only light. He could not tell if he was in or out of doors. The air was not warm nor cold, humid nor dry. He knew he could stand if he chose, but not upon what, for he floated in place in that sea of luminescence and sensed no floor beneath him. He simply *was*.

"May... may I see you?" Mikallis asked, trying his voice, surprised at its strength.

"You may prefer not to, Mikallis, for you have a choice to make now, and once you have seen me, not all paths will remain open to you."

Mikallis frowned, confused.

"Some truths belong only in their place, young elf. Tell me, where would you go?"

A warmth spread across Mikallis' bare chest. He felt at it with his hand, knowing immediately its source and thus understanding the question. *The Mark.* All his life he had recited the next words he would speak, never knowing if he would be given the chance to speak them.

"I would go where you will me, Father."

"Would you?" The voice laughed gently, a father's laugh. "I suppose you would, though your heart yearns for a more specific path. Yes?"

Mikallis stood, nodding.

"You have earned your choice, Mikallis Elmshadow. Your sacrifice was great. I am sorry for the pain it caused you."

Mikallis recalled the last moments of his life, but, mercifully, he could not recall the pain. He understood that to be a gift, and he sensed the words of sorrow the First Father spoke were sincere, yet they begged a question. *The* question.

"Why?" Mikallis somehow knew he need not be more specific.

"Choice," came the response, and Mikallis understood. He remained still and quiet for a time.

"I choose to go to Aria, Father. If it is possible. Forgive my selfishness, but I—"

"There is nothing to forgive, dear Mikallis. Your love is true, and there is no greater thing. But I cannot give you what you ask. Aria... she is lost to me, for now. To us. There is no door."

Mikallis had no time to bemoan the thought as five distinct doors suddenly surrounded him, each slightly taller than he, each wide enough for two elves to pass shoulder-to-shoulder. It was not so much as if they had appeared from thin air, but rather that they had been there all along, somehow beneath his notice.

Immediately before him stood the first door: a wooden door with a large iron knocker carved in the shape of an elm. It sat within no jamb nor threshold; there were no hinges. As he drew near, he could almost, but not quite, make out the sound of children laughing. To its right stood a stone door, an imposing slab of solid rock, the relief of an axe expertly chiseled into its center. Next stood a thick iron gate, quite nondescript but for a brass latch that seemed embedded into some cloud, holding it fast. Tall grasses leaned through wide gaps in the grille through which Mikallis could not see beyond. The fourth door was a thing of beauty, a glowing crystalline design with intricate cuts and facets refracting every conceivable color of light. It might have been diamond or glass, Mikallis could not tell, but it was the most beautiful thing he had ever seen.

He turned to his right, to the fifth door. There he saw a huge boulder, perfectly spherical, at least on the side that faced him. Thick, damp moss hung from the stone in clumps and strips. The scent emanating from the door was the first aroma he had noticed since his awakening; an old smell, ancient even. If Mikallis were to name it, he would call it the scent of time.

An empty space stood between the fifth door and the first, and while Mikallis could see nothing there but empty whiteness, he knew there *should* be a door, and he knew that had there been one, he did not want to go through it. A sickly whiff of sulfur filled his nostrils as he stood before the empty space, and he instinctively turned away. He spoke his fear aloud.

"There is no door."

Silence.

"I must reach her, Father."

"Yes," the voice replied. "You must. Much depends on it. Perhaps all. Your world is in peril, Mikallis Elmshadow, and your Aria is one of only a few who might save it, but she is lost now, and she must find her way back. When she does, if she does, she will need you, and on that day, you will need to be more than what you are. There are those who might teach you, but as they guide your path, so you must lead them."

"I... I do not understand."

"No. You would not. Yet it is as it must be, and you must choose, young Mikallis. I can tell you no more, only that you must have faith, and you must choose wisely. Goodbye for now, brave elf. We will meet again."

"No, please! Tell me how to choose!" The Mark on Mikallis' chest warmed again briefly. When the warmth faded, he knew he was alone.

III: FURY

 HYLA GREYKIN HAD never known such pain. A moment before, the young gnomish woman had cowered before the might of Kalashagon's murderous flame, fearing a horrific, blistering death. Now a new sort of fire seared her from within, intensifying with every vain, excruciating attempt at breath as she knelt upon the rough ground. She could not see. There was no light, not even enough for her keen G'naari eyes to function. She could not speak. She could barely cough, the acidic atmosphere too thin to power her voice. A pitiful croak was all she could manage as poisonous fumes dulled her senses and consciousness began to fade.

~Yeh must will the air clean! I canna do it for yeh, I be helpin' Wolf!~

Shyla recognized the thought as belonging to Lady Cindra.

~Imagine it, and yeh can make it be!~

Shyla struggled to make sense of her grandmother's conveyances, but the burning... there was only burning... *oh please make it stop it hurts! Please oh please it hurts it hurts it—*

A strong, calloused hand grasped her by the neck, pulling her close. Hot, dry lips covered her own; wiry hair mashed against her face. She would have screamed, but there was no air.

And then there was.

Shyla threw her arms around J'arn Silverstone's neck and pulled him tight as he shared his breath with her. The dwarf sent his thoughts to the frightened gnome.

~Breathe with me, Shyla. Ye can do it. Think about sweeter air. Think about the Grove.~

Shyla could scarcely think at all, but through her embrace with J'arn, she sensed what she must do.

~Breathe with me, girl. Breathe now, 'tis all right.~

Shyla taught herself how to breathe again, but it was most certainly *not* all right.

~Where's Lucan? Where's Aria?~

~We are here,~ Aria conveyed. Lucan's thoughts remained his own, though Shyla could sense great sorrow from the young man, and regret.

~But... but where—~

Cindra replaced J'arn's hand on Shyla's neck as he withdrew. *~Be still, child. We are safe for now.~*

~Mawbottom, we are!~

Wolf nuzzled up against Shyla. She ran a trembling hand through his fur... *too hot, too dry....*

~Use yer Bond, Shyla,~ conveyed Cindra. *~He needs yeh.~*

She did, and Wolf's fear was palpable. He was not in pain, not anymore, but he had been. His paw had been cut badly; Cindra had healed it. His lungs had burned like Shyla's; Cindra had fed him a drop of her own blood, and he had quickly learned to breathe. He was well physically, for now, but Shyla did not need to feel his heavy panting and trembling to know he was afraid. The darkness was too dark. He did not belong here. No one belonged here. This was not a place of life. This was not a place at all. This was noplace.

Shyla hugged Wolf close as she tried to make sense of it all.

She had used her ring. She had named Cindra. They had all been taken up again into the empty space between moments, but it was not like before. They had crossed through something, a membrane of sorts, a chasm, and something in Shyla's very soul knew: she did not belong on this side of that boundary. Shyla had resisted and thus arrived later than her companions. She wished she had resisted more.

This is the Mawbottom.

This is Fury.

"We hafta to get outta here! Now!"

~Silence, girl! They will hear you. Do not use yer voice!~

Cindra's stern warning multiplied Shyla's terror.

They?

~Aria, use yer ring! Get us outta here!~

~I cannot, Shyla.~

~What? Why? Never mind, Luc, you do it! Hurry! We canna stay here!~

Cindra replied for him. *~They canna do it, Shyla. Such magic does not work here. Listen, now. There is much yeh must know, and little time before they come again.~*

~It hurts to breathe, Lady!~

~I know, child. Yeh will need to get used to it. Yeh have come to Fury, a bit later than yer friends, and Prince J'arn here told me much of what yeh faced on Tahr—~

~How much later?~

~A bit. Now listen, Shyla! There be things down here that yeh ain't never seen, things yeh ain't never thought of, big things, all tooth and claw. We ain't supposed to be here, and they sense us. They can see yeh in the dark, and they wanna bring yeh to 'im. ~

~Him?~

~The Hand, child. They almost had me more'n once, but I... well, I bested 'em. But he sends more every time, and soon as he knows yeh all be down here, I s'pose he'll send 'em all.~

~What are they, Lady?~

Cindra remained silent for a moment. Shyla pulled Wolf closer, listening to the labored breathing of her friends, waiting.

~Dead ones, Shyla. Mostly. Evil in life, worse in death. Dead as they are though, they still feed, and they still breed. I seen little ones, too. But never mind that. What yeh need to know is this: yeh canna fall asleep alone, or yeh'll die. Someone needs to keep yeh breathin'. And yeh don't wanna, anyhow. They sneak up on yeh when yeh rest, and then they get yeh.~

~But Lady, how did yeh get here? When?~

~I dunno when, Shyla. Many days. Maybe half a cycle. And I came through G'naath. The Elders opened a door, and I walked through it.~

~But... how have yeh survived? When do yeh sleep?~

~Hush now, child, I got more to tell yeh! Now this part is gonna frighten yeh, but yeh need t'be strong, hear?~

Shyla suppressed a cough as she shuddered. *This* part?

~Yes, Lady. I'll be strong.~

~He can hear yeh think. Just like we can hear each other. He ain't always listening, but sometimes he is, and he'll speak to yeh. Yeh canna trust a thing he says! Not ever! Do yeh understand?~

A deep, malevolent voice replied in the minds of the companions.

~WHY MUST YOU SPOIL THE SURPRISE, WITCH?~

Wolf barked loudly in fright and snapped at the air. A chill crept up Shyla's spine into her mind, freezing her good sense. She cried out, as did Lucan.

The voice laughed; a hateful, mocking rumble. Shyla tried to shut her mind against the intrusion. *No! Yeh canna hear me!*

~OH YES, I HEAR YOU, WITCHLING. AND NOW MY LEGION HAS HEARD YOU. WE WILL MEET SOON.~

The voice withdrew. Cindra spoke aloud.

"They know where we are. Prepare to fight!" Cindra cast a glowing orb before her and allowed it to rise several feet above their heads. Shyla gaped in awe as her surroundings came into view. The companions, Wolf, and Cindra rose to their feet within a medium-sized cavern, perhaps two dozen paces in diameter. The walls were nearly solid iron, as was the floor, aside from blackened, jagged chunks of some other stone that jutted out here and there. They were surrounded on three sides by the walls of the cavity. The orb barely illuminated a large opening on one side from which two tunnels ran, left and right. Shyla looked up, seeking another means of escape, but found none. She could not tell how high the ceiling was.

She lowered her gaze to her companions. Each were covered head to toe in ash and soot. Twin streams of pale flesh lined Aria's face, eyes to chin, channels washed clean by unwiped tears. J'arn stood at the ready, axe in hand, eyes darting left and right. When he met Shyla's gaze, he quickly looked away. Lucan did not. He winked at Shyla and offered a crooked smile as he lit his own orb, adding more light to the cavern. Odd as his expression was, it was nothing compared to the sight of Lady Cindra.

As grandmother and granddaughter regarded one another, bright, young, silver eyes gleamed impossibly from within the elder gnome's face... eyes that had been old, set in an old face. Eyes that had been red. Lady Cindra now looked to be Shyla's age, aside from two streaks of white hair that cut through the red and framed her cherubic face. The expression on that face, however, betrayed her true age. Here was wisdom. Here was ferocious determination. Here was rage. Here was *power*.

Aria's voice cut through the silence.

"How do we fight them, Lady?"

Lucan drew his dagger.

"No! Not with blades! If they bleed, yeh'll burn!"

"How then?" demanded J'arn.

Shyla immediately understood. They were like the dragon.

"Fire. Ice. Wind."

"Just so, Shyla," replied Cindra as a skittering sound echoed throughout the cavern. "Quiet, now. They come."

IV: WESTMORLAND

ILA RAN deeper into the forest.

She had been running for hours, sustained by her magic. The chill and the miles and the fear had begun to take their toll, yet she could not stop, for Kalashagon sought her, and he would not suffer her to live.

~I will find you, little witch. You flee me in vain.~

The voice of the dragon tormented her, taunted her, dared her to convey a reply. She could sense its source—somewhere to the west and south, a dozen miles, perhaps. If she could sense him, he could sense her... if she were to reply, Kalashagon would find her, and she would soon die burning.

Mila harbored no illusions as to whether she could defeat the great beast alone. Her power was not limitless. Nothing was. The best she could hope to do was hide, to find shelter where she could think up a plan. As it was, she could barely think at all. The dragon had begun harrying her at daybreak, and between his derisions and her own haunted thoughts, the sorceress could barely reason, certainly not well enough to formulate a strategy.

Kalashagon had been true to his word; he did not kill her the day before. Mila had been left alone to contemplate her actions, and she did.

She had killed Sartean. Avenged her parents. Achieved her life's purpose.

In doing so, she had doomed countless others.

More children would be without mothers.

More would be without fathers.

The devastation of Kalashagon would, no doubt, exceed any evil ever committed by the Master of Kehrlia.

Yet, until Kalashagon had pushed his way into her mind at dawn, Mila had felt no remorse. No regret. Only satisfaction that Sartean D'Avers' sins had finally come back to drown him.

It had been easier the night before, as Mila lay within her tent, to assuage any feelings of guilt with the knowledge that such an evil had been removed from the world. She had not lied to herself: allowing Kalashagon to live was a horror. But the dragon was not a horror of her making. Neither was Sartean, but *she* had committed horrors at his behest, all in the name of someday being able to destroy him. If she did not do so when the chance arose, how could she justify all she had done?

The question of whether such justifications were sufficient had not mattered to Mila as she had lain in darkness, fatigued in body and spirit. Sartean was dead. She turned the sight of his demise over and over in her head, watching it unfold again and again until exhaustion finally claimed her for the night. Her last thought of the day had been her first regret: the wizard's swift death had been far too merciful.

The grey dawn, however, brought with it a sense of emptiness. Yano was lost, as were many of the Incantors of Kehrlia. She had little love for her peers—Kehrlia nurtured few friendships—but he had been an ally, and the loss of life was disturbing, if not exactly saddening. Mila did not often indulge sorrow, and the sorceress would not allow herself to do so over the deaths of a few dozen of Sartean's lackeys. She did, however, know sorrow that morning, and its name was Earl.

Mila knew the burly wagon loader would have seen her kill Sartean, subsequently freeing Kalashagon. He would have seen the wizards die in dragonfire. He would know Yano was dead, and he would know what havoc Kalashagon would still wreak on the world.

And he would hate her for all of it.

That, and only that, gave Mila pause, for she had known only one good man in all her life, besides her father, and that man was Earl.

If he hates me, I am truly lost.

Mila did not have much time to consider the idea when she awoke that morning. She had only just awakened and pulled on her boots when the voice pierced her mind.

~You die today, little witch.~

~I am no witch!~

She knew her mistake before the thought was complete. Her foolish reply had alerted the dragon to her location.

~Oh, but you are. Did you not know? Surely you knew. From where does such power come? You are cursed, Mila Felsin. Your blood is as vile as my own.~

There was no time to pack. Mila grabbed her pouch of gems and shoved them into her cloak. She broke east and ran flat-out for an hour as Kalashagon taunted her.

~I sense your fear, little witch. But why do you run? You cannot outpace me. I am the very essence of speed. You will only die exhausted. Why not face me? Why not die well?~

Mila ran, unwilling to die this day, well or otherwise. More than once Kalashagon flew overhead. The first time, she hid behind a fallen tree, but her hot, labored breath in the still forest air blew a thick cloud around her head. She knew the dragon would find her soon enough. When he had gone, she ran again, in the direction he had gone, assuming he would not double back over the same path. She was wrong. On his next pass, Mila concealed herself with magic. She regretted it immediately as the dragon pulled up near her position, hovering.

~You are near, little witch. I smell your magic. Such a sweet smell. Not unlike... burning meat. Perhaps it is your blood... does your magic burn you from within, Mila Felsin? You will burn from without soon enough.~

Mila watched through the canopy as Kalashagon circled her position. Discerning his pattern of flight was no difficult task; he flew mostly in circles to the left, his head cocked towards the ground. On one such pass, however, he changed direction, and Mila discovered why he flew as he did: a gaping, oozing hole sat where the dragon's enormous, black right eye had once been.

The elf and her company! They must have harmed him somehow!

Mila took heart and quickly broke towards the northwest, in the direction he would be least likely to glimpse her. She ran on through the afternoon, making certain to stay on Kalashagon's right side whenever possible. Eventually, he lost her scent and doubled back towards Mor, but Mila did not stop running. Only distance could protect her from the dragon, and she clawed at the trails she ran with animal desperation.

The day wore on. Mila tired. Her mind kept returning to the dragon's declaration as she ran.

You are cursed, Mila Felsin.

Perhaps she was. Perhaps some vile blood did run in her veins. *What other explanation could there be? I am not like others. Even my parents knew.*

Yet Mila was disinclined to believe that blood could determine the course of a person's life. *Do not evil men sometimes father good children? Do not good, loving mothers give life to moral abominations?* Above all else, Mila wondered at her own lineage: if her blood was tainted, from where did that taint come? Her memories of her mother and father had greyed over the years, but she recalled who they *were*. How they loved her. How they loved one another. No, whatever foulness coursed through her body, it had not come from them.

But there is *a foulness within me*, she admitted silently.

She had spent all her life blaming her sins on Sartean. But what had Darrin once said, the man who had taken her in after her parents' death? Mila recalled the day she had first taken a life:

He leered at her. "You are unclean," he said, the darkness in his tone reminding her of Sartean's voice that terrible night. He reached around her, fingers grasping at the ties to her nightdress.

Mila's magic had not suffered from misuse. Darrin died before taking his next breath, his heart imploding as if Mila had reached into his chest and squeezed the life out with her own fingers.

She climbed over Darrin's corpse, stood, and dressed. She was not angry. She was not afraid. She felt neither guilt nor remorse. But that realization—that she had just taken a man's life without a second thought—that idea horrified her.

"What am I?" she asked herself aloud.

Over the years, Mila had reasoned that she was justified in taking Darrin's life; he had, after all, intended to violate a young girl he had taken in as his own daughter. When, in her musings, that excuse wore thin, she reminded herself of the loss she had endured at Sartean's hand. Surely his evil deed had scarred her... who could find fault with her instinct to defend herself against evil men?

Yet as Mila ran deeper into the forest, Darrin's ever-haunting final words mingled with the dragon's observations—

> *...unclean...*
> *...cursed...*
> *...vile...*
> *...little witch...*

—and the strength of her justifications gave way to a growing realization: she could not recall a time when she could call herself *good*.

And then, of course, there was the magic.

Mila ran on, her heart and mind dueling for the right to name the color of her soul. While the war inside the sorceress was an old one, neither side ever truly managing to gain ground against the other, the events of the previous day had tilted the scales. Her foe was dead, but in its place, another had arisen, one who breathed fire, one who spoke into her very mind with revolting intimacy. Mila could not decide which she dreaded most about the mighty Kalashagon—his fire or his familiarity—but there was no doubt: he would be dead and gone but for Mila's appetite for vengeance.

The ash of Fang was less thick in the forest where Mila found herself, but the snow was not. Only a widening gap between the trees on either side of her gave clue that she had run onto a path, one that had become a trail. Overcast skies made it difficult to tell direction, but Mila realized she had been going mostly uphill. As Mor sat within a deep valley that extended west past the farmlands but rose steadily in elevation as one traveled north or east, her climb could only mean that she had turned north at some point.

The trail was not well-traveled; it had not snowed here recently, but only a single rider's wind-swept tracks were visible. *A rider returning home,* she reasoned. *No man with a choice would ride into Mor these past days.* She was not excited about the prospect of meeting strangers, but she was quickly becoming exhausted. Her gems could sustain her body at a run almost indefinitely while her concentration was strong, but it most certainly was not. The sorceress needed shelter and rest, preferably before nightfall. She dared not camp again. A fire might warm her bones, but it would also attract attention, particularly from a flying beast with an overhead view.

An hour later, Mila stood before the door of a small cabin in a wooded cul-de-sac. Lantern light shone through filmy glass. She decided against knocking; an unwelcome knock would seem far more threatening than a young woman's voice.

"Hello? Is there anyone there?"

Mila heard shuffling noises and a bar thrown against the door. A woman's face peered through the small window.

"Who goes there? What do you want?"

"I am alone, ma'am. And cold. I mean no harm."

V: THE TEMPLE OF KAL

AUGHTER NIA REMOVED HER crimson robe and laid it across the foot of her cot. The cool, damp air of the temple raised bumps on her exposed skin. She glanced at the grey shift hanging beside the entrance to her stony chambers. The woolen cloth was terribly uncomfortable; better to be cold, she decided, than to suffer the incessant itching caused by the hateful garment. The very thought of it made her skin crawl. She repressed the urge to scratch herself; a Daughter of Kal would not indulge such trivial wants of the flesh, lest she face the Mother's wrath. Not that it mattered today.

She had done her duty well. Well enough, she had hoped, to at least avoid punishment. It was an honor, the Mother had said, being trusted to carry the amulet to Sartean. Certainly, many of her sisters agreed, jealous twisting warping their faces when Nia had been chosen. Yet, even on that day, Nia suspected the true reason for her selection: she alone among her sisters would not be tempted to steal it. The magic would not work for her. She had not given herself wholly to Kal, and she suspected the Mother knew it. Now, as she awaited her summons after three days' solitude and fasting, she had no doubt. She was not due to recite her second Oath for two more years, yet the Mother had called her. Her deception had been discovered. Soon she would be exposed... and punished.

Nia crossed the small room to the table opposite her bed and pulled out the wooden chair. Not *her* wooden chair; she owned no possessions, besides her two garments and a pair of wooden sandals. In her chamber she was allowed only a cot, the small wooden table, the chair, a decanter and a glass. Not even a chamber pot; if she had need to relieve herself, she would be required to venture outside. Not until a Daughter took her second Oath would she be granted more.

Presently she poured herself some water and took a sip. Her stomach rumbled. A high, narrow window cut into the stone wall allowed in just enough light for her to sense the time of day. It was nearing dusk, which meant she would, on an ordinary day, soon be allowed one of two daily meals. She recalled how she often dreaded the walk to the dining hall. The other acolytes would know better than to speak to her, communication among the Unordained being forbidden. The Ordained she encountered, however, never failed to torment her. Today, she longed for something as ordinary as such banes.

They *knew*. Somehow, they all knew. Becoming a Daughter granted no special powers of telepathy. Only a sorcerer was capable of seeing into another's mind, but Nia had no doubt: her second secret was no secret at all.

On the day of her first Oath, she had omitted one word. She could not bring herself to say it. Something in the deepest part of her, her soul perhaps, cried out against it. She had coveted the power, of course... none alive could surpass the magic of the Daughters, perhaps save Sartean himself. She had earned the Mother's favor through her deeds at Kehrlia. She had been ruthless in her studies, more so in competition against her peers.

And above all, she had taken a life. Such an act was not a requirement for admission to the temple, but it guaranteed one's acceptance if they chose to seek the life of a Daughter.

Yet this was her *first* secret: she had not done so deliberately. The young man she had killed in her fourth year at Kehrlia was not her enemy. She bore him no malice. In fact, she believed she had loved him, at least insofar as a young, foolish woman could genuinely love someone. It was simply a spell gone wrong, one intended to enhance their pleasure while in one another's arms. They mistranslated the incantation, and instead of increasing their desire, it turned it to rage. When the smoke cleared, she was alive, and he was dead.

She could not, of course, admit her failed spell to Sartean. It would have meant her instant expulsion. Instead, she concocted a tale. The two had argued, she had said. A lover's quarrel, nothing more. But he became enraged, jealous... he attacked her, she defended herself, and she prevailed.

Her status among her peers improved considerably after that day. The story took on a life of its own, and by the time it had reached the temple, she was rumored to be a most powerful and merciless wizard indeed.

As was so each year, on the day she graduated Kehrlia, the Daughters were present. Two women had graduated that year, and when the ceremonies concluded, the trio of young Daughters approached Nia. They told her of the great and boundless power she could one day possess. They spoke of the sorority of their sisterhood. She must come with them, they said. All her questions would be answered. All her desires would one day be fulfilled.

For a child born into servitude on the shores of the Sapphire

Sea, she had come quite far. Her father, a fisherman whose voice she could not recall, had loved her, if memory served. The scent of brine and blurry recollections of a brown-skinned man with leathery hands and sad, soulful eyes were all she had left of him. In those days she saw him only in the offseason, as the heat of summer peaked and the fish swam too deep for nets to reach, and then only once or twice when he was given leave to visit with his family. Any hope of a deeper connection had been lost when her mother sold her to Kehrlia. For this, Nia carried no hatred for her mother.

She recalled her last night in her family's hovel by the sea, lying awake, drenched equally in sweat and her mother's tears before the Incantors came for her at dawn. Her mother had no choice. Nia, barely eight years old, was already known to be possessed of small magics. She had thus caught an Incantor's eye, and Kehrlia spared no coin in obtaining its newest candidate for apprenticeship. Her four younger siblings, Miano, Pito, Ethiria and Lanidae, two boys and two girls, would be loosed from the bonds of generational servitude with the gold of Kehrlia. Nia would be given a chance to become something more than some sea lord's waterwife.

Even at such a young age, Nia had understood. Her magic was the gift that would save her family from a meager life of hunger and labor. She did not, however, understand why she could not see her father one last time before she was taken. He would have been home within a cycle. She had begged her mother. Begged the Incantors. Surely there was no hurry? Surely a few days would make little difference? It was to be the first of many hard lessons about the way things worked at Kehrlia: sentiment had no place in an Incantor's heart, not under Sartean D'Avers' rule. To be admitted to an apprenticeship would be to silently suffer many things, and to succeed in graduating would be to become as ruthless as those who had pulled her from her mother's arms that humid summer morning. She was no wealthy son or daughter of Mor. Coin would not ensure her path. She was the crownless daughter of a nameless sea clan. She would toil in the halls of Kehrlia until she came of age, thus, hopefully, earning her entrance to the academy. She would be tested for apprenticeship. To fail to please her masters, to fail her entrance examination, or to dare escape would bring the wrath of Kehrlia to her family's house.

She had succeeded in all. Her family's security had been assured. *Yes,* she thought, *I have come far, but I will go no farther.*

The sound of a gong reverberated throughout the temple, bringing Nia from her reveries. For the Ordained, it was time for supper. For the other Unordained sisters, which numbered fewer than a dozen, it was time for an hour on their knees in supplication to Kal. They would be allowed to eat what the Daughters left over while they washed their bowls and cups. Nia would not join them in the kitchens today.

For Nia, it was the moment of her reckoning. She pulled her woolen shift over her head, slipped calloused feet into worn sandals, and made her way to the chapel. Her eyes kept to the floor, the sweet, foreboding scent of incense sufficient to guide her way.

The Mother stood in flowing brandywine linen before the wooden altar, her severe visage scantly lit by oil lanterns hung on the chapel walls. Once nearly bereft of hue, the altar now stood darkened and stained, nearer in tone to the Mother's gown than to the pale, petrified maple from which it was long ago carved. On either side stood three Daughters, gowned in white, eyes downcast. The Mother's dark eyes, however, bore into Nia's own.

Nia lowered her eyes.

The Mother's voice bore the chill of winter. "Shall you kneel? Shall we proceed with this charade then, Daughter?"

Nia looked up, glancing briefly into the Mother's voracious gaze, then higher, toward the soaring ceiling of the stone chamber, craning her neck to peer through its slender windows, straining, one last time, to make out the light of the Twins that just then crested the horizon.

I will see you in the next world, Father.

"I am prepared, Mother."

"To take your Oath? Which would that be, your first, or your second, Nia of the sea?"

Of course. She knew. She had known all along.

Nia took a breath and straightened her spine. Her face remained impassive, though her knees belied her fear.

"I suppose neither."

The Mother smiled coolly.

"Good. You have found your courage. Though, do you think it will avail you, at this late hour?"

"Does it matter?"

The Mother stepped down from the dais and approached, delicate fingers tracing the hilt of the ceremonial dagger at her waist. Nia took an unsteady breath.

"It does, my daughter." The Mother's tone warmed. Nia

blanched, the Mother's uncharacteristically kind manner somehow more terrifying than the dagger at her waist.

"You resist the teachings of Kal. You, and only you, among your sisters. Knowing what you forsake. Is this strength, I wonder... or weakness? I have not decided."

Nia blinked, but did not reply.

"Perhaps both," the Mother continued. "Or neither. Perhaps you yourself do not yet know."

Nia cleared her throat. "I know I will not speak the words, Mother."

"Ah, Nia." The Mother drew a fingernail across Nia's chin. "Have I mistreated you so? Surely you understand, the poverty and sacrifices of the Unordained are necessary."

"I have no quarrel with the ways of the temple, Mother."

"Only with our god."

Nia nodded. "Only that."

"But why? Look around you. Was this not all foretold? The coming of the beast. The defeat of the Master of Kehrlia at the hands of his own pupil. The fires, the quakes, the collapse of kingdoms... do you think Kal responsible for these things? Do you lay the blame at his feet?"

Nia frowned. "Who else?"

The Mother sighed and returned to the dais. She ran a hand across the altar slowly, with reverence. "You blame the messenger, Nia. It is given to us to know what will come, we who devote ourselves to Kal. It is given to us to carry his power within us, so that we might withstand such times." The Mother turned again to face Nia. "Do you no longer seek his power? Surely you once did."

Nia nodded. "I did. And... and I suppose I still do. But I will not devote myself to his cause. I will not hasten the fall of Tahr."

"Ah, my dear child, but you already do. You brought the amulet to Sartean, did you not?"

"Only to please you, Mother, and to preserve my own life. Had I not, another would have in my place. My actions made no difference."

The mother nodded, a gesture that struck Nia as both benign and spiteful. "Perhaps you begin to understand, then. Tell me, do you blame the lapping sea for the worn stone, Nia?"

"I... of course not."

"No. Is the falling branch to blame for the lame horse? Or is it the wind? Or the storm? Or perhaps the season? Would you fault the darkened leaves for the coming of autumn? You are but a dying leaf, dear child. As are we all. There is but one choice open to you... a choice only our lord Kal can grant. Shall you be the first to fall, or the last?"

Nia moved to speak. The mother held up a hand.

"Do not answer, Daughter Nia. You are conflicted. I can see it in your eyes. What of Lor's power, you wonder? What of the power of life? You have much yet to learn, not the least of which is this: life is a beginning. Death is an end. All things must die... all things must end. The truest power, my child, lies not in clinging to the fragile tendrils of life, but in embracing the ultimate, final power of death. It is Kal who commands this power. None other."

"So you say, Mother. Yet I still will not give myself to him."

The Mother sighed. "No, I suppose you will not." The mother withdrew her dagger and placed it on the altar. The six Daughters present raised their heads. "Not today, at least."

Nia's eyes widened.

"You are a leaf, Nia. No more. But a spark to a dry leaf can ignite a flame to consume kingdoms. You will serve Kal as the winds decide. As *I* decide. I *am* those winds. I *am* your spark, Daughter Nia. Your life will not end today, Oath or no. We have much work to do, and before the end, *you will serve us well.*"

VI: THE MAW

S O NOW YEH HAVE a mind to fight then, elf?" Oort spat at the ground before Nishali's feet. "Now that yer own beloved's been lost?" Nishali clenched her fists but did not reply. The diminutive gnome looked every bit the Wolfslayer as he glared up into the First Ranger's reddened eyes.

"Not lost," Sir Marchion corrected, gently. "Killed. Killed in cold blood, along with my knights."

Oort turned his glare to the Second Knight of Thornwood. "Yup. Like Dohr woulda done to my Thinny, given the chance. Have yeh seen her this morning, knight? Have yeh seen her purple, swollen face? Well, have yeh?"

"Enough." Nishali's tone belied the inferno raging in her heart. Her narrowed eyes made clear she would brook no further dressing down from the gnome. "Your wife will be avenged, Wolfslayer."

"Do as yeh please." Oort turned to his left, eyeing Lux briefly. "But so help me, not one dwarf will set foot in G'naath while I live." From the corner of his eye, Oort saw Argl peeking out from behind a tent. "Argl, what are yeh still doin' here? I thought I sent yeh with Rak—"

Rak stepped out from behind Argl. The two gnomes bore identical sheepish expressions.

Rak replied for Argl. "Ah, thing is, Wolfslayer, we thought

maybe yeh might need—"

"I don't give a wet snot what yeh thought! Get a sled made up for Thinny. We'll be goin' home!"

Lux spoke up without hesitation. "I'll see ye there, Oort. T'was my fault—"

"Did yeh not hear me, dwarf? I said not a one of yeh will set foot in G'naath. *Not a one!*"

Lux took a knee before the gnome. "Aye, I heard ye. And soon as ye be safe in G'naath, I'll turn back. Let me do this, Wolfslayer. Ye need a strong back for the journey. I can pull a sled far as ye like. I owe ye this debt. Let me pay it."

Oort thought for a moment before nodding. "Yer damned right yeh owe, dwarf. But not me. Yeh owe my Thinny. And I'll let yeh pay. But when we get to the tunnels, yeh'll not be welcome. When I see yeh after, if I see yeh, know that I'll not call yeh friend." Oort turned to Sir Marchion. "Might as well make it known, knight. G'naath be at war now. If my people see yer elves in the company of dwarves, they'll be liable to end up with an arrow between the eyes. Choose yer friends carefully." Oort stormed off after Argl towards Thinny's tent.

Lux turned to Nishali.

"I've no right to ask this of ye, ranger, but I'll ask anyways. Will ye see to it that Nova is healed, and treated fairly? She's done ye no harm."

Nishali's jaw clenched.

"Please. I can't be in two places at once."

"No," Nishali replied. "You cannot. King Dohr will see Nova as a traitor, yes?"

Lux nodded. "Aye, already does. Woulda had her hanged if I

didn't rescue her."

"Can she fight? *Will* she fight?"

Lux frowned. "She can. Hard as a hammer, that one. But if ye mean to ask her to fight her own people—"

"I mean to allow her to choose, when she is healed. And I will see her restored. But I warn you, if she intends to take up arms with Dohr—"

"She won't. That she won't do. Leastways I don't think she would."

Nishali nodded. "I will see her healed and release her. If I see her on the battlefield, however, know that her fate is sealed."

Lux sighed. "Aye. Fare ye well, First Ranger."

Nishali watched silently as Lux followed off after Oort.

Sir Marchion busied himself with the fire, waiting for a turn before speaking. The afternoon light, such as it was in the deep, pervasive overcast, began to fade.

"We should contact our queen, Nishali."

"I have sent word along the Winds. She will soon know my intentions."

"I meant that we should await Trellia's instructions."

Nishali leveled a gaze at Marchion. "I know what you meant. You may do as you please. My rangers and I will attack before dawn. You will not sway me in this." Nishali looked away, towards the south, towards Belgorne. "Neither will Trellia."

"She is your queen, Nishali."

"Queen of what? Of Thornwood? Thornwood is no more."

"That is not true, and you know it. The Citadel will be rebuilt."

"Foolishness. It will fall again. Look around you, knight. The world ends. The land cries out, and none can answer. You know what this is. It was all foretold."

"I know more than you think, ranger. I cannot sense the pain of the land as you do, but I have carried the secrets of Ya Di all my long years. As has your queen. As has Barris. There are things you do not—"

"*You have your duties!*" Nishali screamed, tears again welling in her eyes. Elves around the camp turned to listen. Nishali pointed to the sky, towards Fang. "Your enemy flies above us! It roils beneath us! *My* enemy camps to the south. Defend the dream that was Thornwood if you like. Defend Tahr. Defend your family, and your queen. I'll not oppose you. But this false king of Belgorne is at this very moment devising a strategy to protect his false crown. He will recall his army, the dwarves he sent north. We wait for Trellia to dither and politic, and his position strengthens! I will not wait until he has fortified himself before I end him!"

Marchion looked down, frustration clear on his features.

Nishali quieted, a bit, though she did not soften. "It is a tactical matter, Second Knight."

"Only that?" asked Marchion.

Nishali took a breath. "No. Not only that."

Marchion placed a hand on Nishali's shoulder, who seethed at the gesture, but did not withdraw. "For all we know, when Hatchet and his army returns, *if* they return, they may depose Dohr on learning of his deeds. We may not *need* to take action. We may not need to lose more elves."

Nishali batted Marchion's hand away. "Listen to yourself! You are a warrior! Your knights have been slain! My Second, my Kade..." her voice trailed off. She wiped at her eyes. "No. I will not dishonor them by *cowering* while we hope that Hatchet takes up arms against his own king for the sake of a few dead elves and a defiled gnome." Nishali turned from Marchion to see two crowds of elves gathered around them, listening. The rangers and knights of Thornwood clustered in their respective groups. Nishali could see lines being silently drawn. The disciplined knights would not speak out. They would follow their Second. Her rangers were donning leather.

"Elves of Thornwood!" she cried. "I assault this false king at dawn! You may join me if you choose, but I will do so myself if I must! I will avenge our fallen if I must slay every dwarf of Belgorne with my own bow and knife! I swear it on the waters of the Grove!"

"You will not do so alone!" a ranger cried in response.

Nishali sought, and found, the source of the voice. A youngish ranger, no more than fifty years. She knew this woman, had trained her. Lithe, fearless, stoic. Not unlike herself. Nishali moved to stand before her. The two locked eyes as Nishali silently vowed to remember this moment of fidelity, to someday return the grace.

The First Ranger took a knee.

"*Nü glahr ni*, Lanna Arbarri."

Every ranger in earshot answered in refrain.

"*Nü glahr ni.*"

Nishali stood and turned to face Marchion. She watched as he met her eyes, the two sharing a brief, silent exchange over the duration of a single breath before Marchion turned his attention to his knights. Nishali turned as well, watching their faces. Jaws clenched. Hands tightened on sword hilts. The knights of Thornwood straightened their spines, widened their stances. There was no mistaking their hearts. These elves wanted to fight, but they would do as their Second commanded.

Nishali understood Marchion's position. He *did* have other duties. Duties passed on to the knights of Thornwood over the course of generations. The world *was* ending. If it was to endure, Marchion's knights would play an irreplaceable role in the battles to come. Marchion was right—she did not fully understand that role. The secrets of Ya Di were only recently revealed to her, and only in part. Yet, Nishali hoped he understood that if they did not put down the threat of the Belgorne king, and soon, they would be facing hardened enemies on too many fronts. Whether the great winged menace could be defeated was a question she dared not attempt to answer, but she knew this: if the elves had to face the beast, the looming perils of Ya Di, and an organized Belgorne, they would surely be lost. Yet Marchion was also right in his accusation: her own heart's motive had nothing to do with tactics.

Marchion ran thick fingers through his greyed locks. Exasperation and anxiety deepened the lines in his aging brow. His voice, however, carried the authority of his station. "Knights," he began. "What has been done to your kin is an abomination." Murmurs and nods of assent in reply. "King Dohr must be put down. *In time.*" Nishali's shoulders drooped. Marchion paused, offering her a glance, before continuing. "But the people of Belgorne are no threat to us. They are starving. Freezing. Turned out from their home. We were ordered by our queen to confront the threat of G'naath. By all accounts, that threat is no more. The Elders are dead and gone. Those who have begun this terrible chain of events are no more. But this was all foretold. The fall of the Citadel. The fall of Belgorne. The fires, the quakes, the awakening of Fang, and yes, even the beast. *That* is our true enemy, and not only *our* enemy. It is the enemy of Belgorne, of Mor, of even G'naath. All the peoples of Tahr. We will not see the other side of this threat if we make war amongst ourselves." Marchion paused again. Nishali read the expressions of his knights. There was no question, they would obey his order, whatever it might be.

Marchion faced Nishali and her rangers. "I grieve for your Second. I will grieve for my knights until my dying day. But, in the absence of orders to the contrary from our queen, I will not commit us to war."

Nishali's manner darkened. "You will not impede my rangers, Sir Marchion."

Marchion shook his head. "No, I will not, Nishali Windwillow. In fact quite the opposite. Knights! You will provide the rangers with anything they might ask of you. You will assist them in preparation for the attack. And we will await orders from our queen while we fortify our position here in the valley."

"Sir!" a knight protested. "With respect, sir, we cannot stand idle while our brothers and sisters go to war!"

"I did not command you to stand idle, knight! And the elves do not go to war! Nishali, you wish to bring Dohr to justice, yes?"

Nishali nodded. "I do. And I will."

"That, and only that?"

Nishali hesitated but nodded again.

"There are perhaps a hundred starving soldiers guarding him. Young, inexperienced dwarves, if our reports are correct. Not a combat-hardened veteran among them. They are led by a coward. Do you require all the knights of Thornwood to apprehend him?"

Nishali smiled. "No. I most certainly do not."

Marchion nodded. He did not return her smile. "I did not think so." He addressed the elves as a whole. "This is a ranger operation. It should be conducted in stealth, if possible. Dohr Silverstone is the target, not the innocent dwarves of Belgorne, nor his misguided soldiery. Knights, you will assist the rangers in any way their First commands! Rangers... Thornwood counts on you to see this done. Bring the coward to us alive, so that he might face justice for his crimes. *That* is the law. But... if he forces your hand—" Marchion gave Nishali a knowing look "—then he has sealed his own fate. On behalf of our fallen, rangers, we thank you for carrying out this duty. *Nü glahr ni!*"

The knights roared as one. "*Nü glahr ni!*"

Marchion walked towards an empty tent, inclining his head towards Nishali. She followed him into the tent.

Nishali spoke first. "Thank you. That was well handl—"

"What in Fury is wrong with you?"

Nishali was taken aback. "Excuse me?"

"I swear to you Nishali, if you ever address my knights without my permission again, I will arrest you on the spot. What in Fury's name would you have done if I hadn't found a way to support you?"

"My second is *dead*! I require no permission—"

"To lead your rangers? No. To rally my knights, while I stand there with my arse in my hands? *You damned well do!*"

Nishali bowed her head. She had overstepped, shaming Marchion. And herself.

"You grieve. I understand. But put your head together, *First Ranger*, or you'll be leading your elves to their deaths."

Marchion threw back the flap and stormed from the tent.

Nishali stood alone for a turn, shaking in rage and humiliation. Marchion was right. She must collect her thoughts and set aside her grief. She would bring Dohr to justice. She would do her duty.

Dohr. The cowardly wretch.

You will die tomorrow, King of Nothing. I swear it.

VII: THE LANGUID LADY

CREAMS ECHOED throughout the empty brothel. Kalindra reached for her sister, offering a comforting hand. Maris recoiled, shaking. Half a day had passed since Vincent Thomison's agony had begun. The screams had not diminished. Maris was at her end.

"He should just let him die," Maris croaked, not for the first time, the declaration whispered like a prayer. "This is... this cannot go on."

Kalindra replied, her unsteady voice as soothing as she could make it. "Trust Gerald, sis. Trust Chaneela. They are skilled—"

Another scream.

"Oh, yes, quite skilled!" Maris shot her sister a dark glance through red-rimmed eyes. "Does that sound like a man being healed to you, Kalindra? They are torturing him to death!"

Eriks Lane quietly entered the living room. He sat on a plush scarlet velvet chair across from the two sisters. Kalindra looked up, hope and fear balanced in her expression. Maris would not meet his eyes. Her shoulders heaved as another horrid cry split the silence.

"They're nearly done," said the soldier.

Maris looked up, managing a reply. "And?"

Eriks paused, seeking words. "There will be... scarring."

Maris looked down again.

Kalindra prodded the soldier. "And his sight?"

Eriks offered a half-shrug. "Couldn't save the eye. The other... well, we'll know when he comes to."

"Comes *to*?" Maris replied, aghast. "If he's not awake, who in bleeding Fury's doing all the screaming?"

Eriks stood, understanding there were no words of comfort he could offer. "He's not going to remember this, Maris. He's not conscious, not in the way you or I would think. He's... well, it's just a reflex. I've seen it before..." the soldier trailed off and his gaze changed, hazel eyes now staring intently through the wall, backwards in time.

Kalindra stood and embraced the soldier. "Thank you, Eriks." She kissed his cheek. "How are you holding up?"

Another scream, quieter and more pitiful than the last.

"I'm fine. Need to see about my soldiers, though."

"Speaking of," Kalindra added. "Could you recommend any who might be in need of gold? One or two?"

"Every soldier in Mor is in need of gold right now. But they're all on alert. I can't spare any, and I know Slater can't. Why?"

"Well, we're going to close up shop until this beast is defeated."

"Closed shops invite trouble," Eriks replied.

"You see my point."

"Hmm." Eriks looked around, noting the rare empty interior of the Languid Lady. "I would think you'd be drowning in business. Not today, obviously, but generally. War usually keeps brothels full."

Kalinda took Eriks' arm and led him toward the door, away from her sobbing sister. "But this is no typical war, is it? Like you said, there's no coin to be had. Even if there were, half the soldiers have abandoned Mor."

Eriks nodded. "Those without families."

"Exactly. I think the Lady has had her last fling, for a while at least. I'd hate to see her ransacked, though."

Eriks turned and glanced towards Maris. He lowered his voice. "It's inevitable. I give it another day, maybe two. People will run out of food. There's no wagons coming, not from the west at least."

"Not from anywhere. We won't see merchants from the Sapphire again until spring."

"If then," Eriks said. "With General Fallon's army heading south, I doubt there will be anything left to sell."

Kalindra leaned in, resting her head in against Eriks' chest. "What will we do?"

Eriks cradled Kalindra in his arms, resting his chin on her head. He ran his fingers once through her dark, silken hair. The two old friends stood quietly together for several breaths.

"We're working on something, Kalindra. Gerald has a plan to grow food, but we need the elves and any wizards we can find. It will take some time."

"And in the meantime? We've got enough in the cellar to last Maris and I a cycle, but not if we can't protect it."

Eriks nodded. "I'll see if I can find a man or two. I assume you'll be staying here?"

Kalindra nodded.

"Chaneela?"

"She'll stay."

"Good, maybe one man will do, then. The four of you can

trade keeping watch. You'll need to pay in food, though. Gold has little use these days."

"That'll cut our rations by a quarter."

"Assume a third. A guard will eat more than you three will, and you won't want to be stingy. Not if you don't want to wake up one morning to empty stores."

"You're full of good news, aren't you?"

"You know people's nature better than I ever will, Kalindra. I doubt I'm telling you anything you don't already know."

Kalindra nodded. "Yeah, but I was hoping you'd tell me I'm wrong."

Eriks shook his head. "You're not wrong. It's going to get bad, and soon. I'd tell you to just head south and follow the army, but—"

"Not with that dragon thing flying around. No, thank you. I'd much rather starve than die as that thing's breakfast."

Eriks nodded, though the look on his face made clear he could not decide which manner of death he would prefer.

Kalindra leaned in, whispering. "Do you hear that?"

Eriks listened. "I hear nothing."

"Neither do I. I think Gerald is finished."

~

Gerald wiped a layer of sweat and blood from his brow. Chaneela offered him another handkerchief. He did not bother taking it. The wizard fell back onto the sofa, exhausted.

Chaneela sat beside him, the two silently watching Vincent Thomison's chest rise and fall in the meager lantern light. Gerald reached for Chaneela's trembling hand, noticing for the first time in all his many years how truly frail the human hand is, how thin and bony and insignificant. *Such delicate things,* he considered, *from which all the great and terrible things of life are wrought.*

As if in reply, Chaneela squeezed his fingers. "You saved him, Gerald. I'm proud of you."

"*We* saved him. But... Fury, *to what end?*"

Chaneela took a moment before responding. "It is not a man's face that makes his measure."

Gerald scoffed. "Maybe not. But that's barely a face at all anymore. You think Maris will still want—"

"Maris is more woman than *that*, Gerald Longstock. And it doesn't matter anyhow. Vincent..." She trailed off.

"Go on."

Chaneela took a breath. "I never thought I would say such a thing. I'm a practical woman, you know."

"Oh, I know," Gerald teased.

"Lucky for you. But Vincent... so help me, I believe he is meant for something more."

Gerald frowned. "More? More than what?"

Chaneela rolled her eyes. "Don't be daft, Gerald. Or funny, or whatever it is you're being. You know full well what I mean."

"Say it anyways, dear. I want to hear how you see it."

Chaneela shifted in her seat to face Gerald. "Well, look at his life. Look how he's changed. You've known him as long as I have. He was a bratty, self-entitled little aristocrat before Anie."

"That is certainly true," Gerald agreed.

"Then... well, there were the dark times, of course, but then he becomes The Merchant. Comes to lead all of us. You ever notice how easily we fell in step with him? All these years, all of us... every single one of us would have died for him."

"That's easily enough explained. He saved all of us, from one devil or another. Some more than once."

"Not you, though. He never saved you, did he?"

Gerald considered the question before answering. "Not in the way you mean, no."

"But you followed him. All these years. I can't imagine it was for the money."

Gerald laughed. "No, not that. A wizard hasn't much need for gold, as you well know."

"Well, it wasn't for power. Any of a dozen influential families would have retained you."

"Several tried."

"Exactly. But you followed Vincent. Why?"

Gerald had pondered this very question more than once over the years. He knew the answer. He had always known. But he could not yet say it aloud.

"Like you say, I suppose. Something more. But enough about the mighty Merchant. What about you? You've served Maris and Kalindra for two decades. Why?"

Chaneela offered a mischievous smile. "Isn't it obvious? All those virile young men coming and going?"

Gerald laughed. He leaned in and kissed Chaneela on the forehead.

"And you could have had your pick, my dear."

Chaneela placed a hand on Gerald's chest, leaning him back in the sofa. She rested her head on his shoulder and closed her eyes.

"I did, you old fool."

Gerald smiled, closing his own eyes, listening to Vincent's rhythmic breathing. By the time that breathing had stopped, the wizard had already drifted off to sleep.

~

The pain came in endless waves, crashing against Vincent's mind like molten lava. Consciousness would fade, giving way to the unbearable agony, only to be ignited again by Gerald's ministrations. Vincent was no stranger to pain. He knew what pain was: his flesh warned his mind. *You must flee! You are on fire! Run, find water, you burn! Run now now NOW YOU MUST RUN NOW!* Knowing made no difference. There was only the terrible, constant emergency, the insatiable urge to escape from within his own skin as Gerald scrubbed and prodded and cut... until it was too much. Then his mind would flee on its own, to a dark place where the pain was not gone, nor even diminished, but a place where his mind could say "Thank you, pain, but I am occupied at the moment," and close the door. The pain knew the back way in, of course, and would not be kept out long.

Every breath was a horror, his lungs seared by dragonfire. Vincent knew his eye was gone. He knew one side of his face was gone, burned to the bone, teeth and tongue exposed. He could sense the dry heat in his mouth on the right side. Even the wizard's breath as he tended to Vincent's wounds brought agony... nerves never before exposed to air sent currents of strange, unfamiliar agony into his head. A ringing, whistling sound in his right ear would not cease; surely his hearing in that ear was gone forever.

Burns ravaged the rest of his body. Some were minor, he could tell. These Gerald and Chaneela ignored. Others... Scrub. Rinse. Cut. Sew.

Finally, after what must surely have been days, Gerald began to chant and the pain began to recede. This, above all else, told Vincent how near he had been to death. He had seen Gerald heal men before. He knew that to withhold relief was to keep the mind functioning... his pain had been, quite literally, the only thing keeping him alive.

Gerald's voice carried a heavy hint of resignation. "That's all we can do for now."

It was not until then that Vincent considered the dragon. A part of himself had refused to acknowledge how he had come to suffer as he was, not until he felt he might survive it. Now, however, he could think of nothing else. *How can such a thing come to be? What drives it? Who controls it? How can we kill it? Can it be killed? Are there more? Will there be?*

Conscious thought faded, giving way to exhaustion. Scenes and recollections of the dragon's attack flashed in Vincent's mind, fragmented images of fangs and fire. A terrible, inhuman scream... *no, Steelwind!* His faithful, constant friend these many years... gone. A young female soldier, whose name he did not know... gone. The scenes faded to grey, then to black. Vincent stood dreaming in a sea of nothing. He cried out, to everyone, to no one. *What can stop such an abomination? Nothing! Nothing at all! It is our doom, and if it is not, then its creator surely is! Damn you both! Damn you to Fury!*

Nothing gave answer. Despair overcame Vincent then, his anger shoved aside by a sense of both emptiness and panic. The emptiness grew, smothering all fear and pain, but the absence of these things was no comfort. Some small, nagging splinter of reason lingered, warning the Merchant that his body was failing him, that he must breathe, that if he did not, all would end, all would be lost.

Yet he could not. Or, he did not. And it shamed him.

What was black became white.

"Vin, my love." The voice was everywhere.

Anie!

Vincent called to her in his thoughts, but no words came.

"It is as before, my love, remember? You may only listen."

Vincent remembered. He had been here before. The secrets he had been hiding from himself since his death in the throne room came flooding back. Secrets he had learned on his last visit to this place between places, timeless truths that gave answer to the great mysteries of life. Yet even these meant nothing when compared to the sweetness of the voice that delivered them.

Oh, I love you Anie! Please, let me tell you... let me hold you...

"You must return again, Vin. It is not time."

A soundless scream vainly sought escape from Vincent's being.

"Do not fear, my love. She loves you—"

But I love you. Only you. Always, forever you.

"—and you must love her in return. And above all, you must love Tahr, my brave, sweet man. For without your love, she will be lost forever. As will all things."

I miss you, Anie. Sweet wife, I miss you so.

"Go now, love. Do not fear. I will see you again, but only if you succeed."

How? What do I do? Tell me, please, I will do anything for you. But I am lost—

"Do not fail me, my love. Do not fail Tahr. Upon your deeds, all things rely."

Please, let me see you! Just once, please...

"Goodbye, sweet husband."

No! Please, no!

Vincent's mournful cry carried him back to the world of the living.

~

"Maris."

Chaneela gently shook her shoulder.

"Wake up, Maris. He wants to see you."

Maris shot out of bed, making for the door before Chaneela grabbed her.

"You need to dress, dear."

"Oh. I, um... tell him I will be right there."

For the three days since his visit with Anie, Vincent had refused visitors. He would only see Gerald, and only because Gerald would not leave his side. He would sleep, scream, wake, and sleep again. The wizard offered what comfort he could, when he could, but mainly his efforts were dedicated to the grisly task of rebuilding what he could of Vincent's face. Only that morning, when Gerald assured Vincent he had done all he could do, did he again permit Chaneela into the room, and only then to gauge her reaction.

It was as Vincent had feared.

Chaneela entered with a cup of tea on a saucer. While, to her credit, her face did not betray her reaction, the clattering of the cup and saucer did.

"That bad?" Vincent asked dryly.

Chaneela set the saucer down on the table beside the bed. She swallowed, glancing at the hand mirror Gerald had left Vincent. It lay face down on the bed. "Haven't you looked yet?"

Vincent shook his head. "Can't get up the nerve."

Chaneela reached over Vincent's legs for the mirror. She placed it in his hand.

"Gerald says you're getting stronger. How is the pain?"

Vincent did not reply.

"Maris wants to see you."

Vincent scoffed. "She *thinks* she wants to see me."

"Well, how would you know? You won't even look at yourself."

"It's not so simple, Chan—"

"It's exactly that simple. Or did you injure your spine as well?"

Vincent glared darkly. Chaneela was unfazed.

"Gerald's work is done. He says you can walk, and if you can walk, you can ride. You can't stay here forever." She stood. "I'm going to get Maris. Look at yourself first if you want, or don't."

Chaneela left the room without further comment. Vincent stared at the back of the mirror in his hand. He was not ready, but Chaneela was right—they could not stay there forever.

Vincent turned the mirror over, keeping his good eye closed for just a breath longer. He steeled himself and opened it, peering at his reflection. The left side of his face appeared normal, for the most part, aside from a missing eyebrow. The right side was partially obscured by a towel Gerald had loosely secured in place, the eye and much of his jaw fully covered. The horror began at the cleft of his chin. Somehow, Gerald had rebuilt a cheek for him, closing the open wound that exposed his teeth and bone, but the flesh there was closer in appearance to ground meat than to a man's face. Pink, raw, mottled... he knew what lay under the towel would be no better; worse, certainly. He could not look.

Vincent resisted the urge to weep. Anie's warning resounded in his mind...

"Upon your deeds, all things rely."

A knock at the door. Vincent set down the mirror and adjusted the towel, covering a bit more of his face. He reached to the lantern on the nightstand, turning down the flame.

"Come in."

Maris entered as if walking on glass. She lifted her eyes in Vincent's direction, barely, then turned, closing the heavy door behind her. She did not immediately turn back around.

"It's all right, Mare." A quiver in Vincent's voice betrayed the fiction.

Maris turned and walked to Vincent's bedside, pausing for a moment at the foot of the bed, then turning to choose the chair to his left. She sat and reached for his hand. Vincent grasped it and looked up, into her face, but her eyes remained focused on their intertwined fingers.

"Gerald tells me the worst is over," she said.

"He tells me the same. My wounds are closed, and he no longer fears infection. He is—"

"He is very skilled. You are lucky to have him."

"I am lucky to have you as well."

Maris looked up, into Vincent's eye. She held his gaze firmly for a time, her own eyes filling with tears, but she refused to blink, refused to focus elsewhere. After a long moment she did blink, releasing a cascade of tears down pallid cheeks. She let her eyes wander across his face, slowly. Her breath caught when her gaze settled on his lips. There, the towel did not conceal.

"The pain..."

"It is tolerable now. And it will fade."

Maris released Vincent's hand, reaching towards the towel. He moved to stop her.

"Maris—"

"I have to see. Please."

Vincent took a steadying breath. "All right. Go ahead. But—"

Maris removed the towel in one quick, fluid motion, as if she could frighten away what lay underneath.

"Oh!" she yelped, jumping to her feet.

Maris covered her mouth with her hand. Her brow creased and furrowed, revulsion reshaping her features. Vincent reached for her hand. She pulled away and took a step back, gagging.

"I... I'm sorry, Vincent, I can't..."

Maris ran from the room.

Vincent picked up the mirror, his hand shaking, recalling Anie's words...

"She loves you."

He glanced into the mirror.

Oh, my sweet wife. Not even you could love this.

VIII: THE NORTHERN ROAD

LL WAS GREY; the road, dusted in a miserable blend of snow and ash; the sky, obscured by a single colorless cloud extending infinitely in all directions. The trees, the brush, even Phantom's majestic coat... the world had descended into a cold, drab, boundless purgatory, and Barris rode through it.

Phantom carried the knight slowly north, the elf and horse each lacking the heart to ride at speed. For the first time since the day many years ago when Terrias wed another, the First Knight of Thornwood fell to despair. He had known, then, that his heart would one day heal, or, if not heal, at least beat again. He had known the time would come when he could again find the strength to eat, to train, to ride, perhaps even to laugh. On this day, he knew no such thing.

It had been Mikallis, then, whose innocence and joy had lifted Barris' heart from its desolation. Now, the boy he would have called son was no more. Barris knew that somewhere, perhaps near, the abomination that took his life flew over Tahr, stalking its next prey. Soon, if the lessons of Ya Di proved true, he and his knights would face it.

But the outcome of that battle may be of no consequence, Barris considered. *Without the Five, we cannot stand against what comes after.*

When he was young, Trellia had once told Barris that he had

missed his calling, that his should have been the life of a Ranger. Few elves could match Barris' skill with a sword, however, even in his earliest youth, and thus his path had been decided. But fewer still could equal his tracking instincts. *"You will see what has been, Barris,"* she had said. *"You will see through the eyes of the beasts. You will read the land. You will sense its breath, its story."* Barris had ignored Trellia then; the call of glinting steel had long before captured his heart.

But she was right, as was Nishali many years later when she echoed the sentiment. *"If you had been a Ranger, I would not be First,"* she had said. Barris' ability to read the land, to see past events in his mind's eye, to coax memories from the minds of beasts and interpret them, even days after they had taken place, was unrivaled. The evidence had left no doubt: Aria, J'arn, Shyla and Lucan—along with Wolf—had vanished into thin air. For this, there were few explanations, and the more Barris pondered the matter, the more his despair took hold.

His first, instinctive analysis was borne of hope, he knew: some magic had whisked the companions away, protecting them from the dragon. But in truth, Barris knew of no such spell, and he knew as much about magic as any elf. Certainly, they *had* been whisked away, as he had seen through Triumph's eyes and memories. But by what? By whom?

The dragon was enormous, and for such a great beast to fly, to breathe fire, it must, Barris imagined, be possessing of great magic. If such a spell existed, certainly the beast carried enough innate power to invoke it. But why would it? It had been bearing down on the companions, ready to strike; no, the beast did not cast them away.

It was known that Redemption, the ancient sword Barris had given Lucan which he now again carried, was capable of great magics, but the sword had lain beside Mikallis' body. No, this was not the answer.

Some time had passed since Barris had seen the companions. It was possible that they had come to gain some token, some artifact capable of protecting them, hiding them, even transporting them in a moment of great need... this still seemed most likely to Barris, but the idea begged other ominous questions: where did they go? Did they survive the spell? Would they ever return? *Could* they ever return?

Phantom started, throwing his head. He stood pat, refusing to ride further, stamping. Barris returned his attention to the present, looking ahead. The knight listened.

A rustle in the brush, perhaps a hundred paces ahead. Something closed on their position. Barris let himself slip into the Bond, sharing his consciousness with Phantom, sensing the ground through the great stallion's hooves. Whatever it was that came, it was large.

The knight slid from the saddle, grasping Redemption but leaving it sheathed. He could feel the cold of the hilt through his glove; a sensation Barris found comforting.

A grey mass bounded onto the trail then, thirty paces ahead. It made for the elf. Barris recognized the beast to be a bear, but a terrible, emaciated example of what was once certainly a great beast. *She should be hibernating*, Barris thought, but understood: she had not stored enough fat to survive the winter. Now she was starving, as were her cubs, most likely.

Barris tried the Bond. "Easy, Mother. I mean you no—"

An ear-splitting roar emitted from the bear. Barris expected her to rear up, to threaten, but instead she tore ahead. He barely unsheathed his sword before she had reached him. Barris swung Redemption mightily, but at the last moment the bear lunged left, for Phantom.

Phantom reared. Barris screamed and leapt to his right mid-swing, carving a red line across the bear's gaunt thigh, but not before its claws raked Phantom's belly. The black stallion went down emitting an awful, painful cry to match Barris' own. The bear turned on Barris and lunged, through the air toward the knight, its right paw wound to strike.

Inhale.

Barris dropped to a knee. Redemption danced in his hand, an extension of his will, its tip carving the bear's neck open on the first stroke, right to left. He reversed his grip and slashed to the right, opening the beast's chest. The knight spun on his knee, the sword's momentum carrying him in a full circle, his left hand coming up to reinforce the next stroke, cleaving the bear's hind leg. The dying bear's hindquarters were still aloft as Barris propelled himself upwards, turning, lunging into the air after the animal. He landed with his full weight on the hilt, burying Redemption into the bear's ribs from behind, piercing its heart.

Exhale.

"Phantom!" Barris left his sword in the bear and scrambled to reach the great stallion, who lay panting on his side in the snow and ash. He lay a hand on Phantom's shoulder, his friend's pain and fear conveyed instantly, terribly, through the Bond.

"Shh, easy now, friend, easy..." Barris sent what comfort he could through the Bond, with little effect. He examined the wound.

Deep, parallel gashes gouged across Phantom's flank and barrel. Blood leaked freely from the wound, but evenly. Barris felt sure that no major artery had been severed, but the wound was terribly deep. If not for the saddle strap catching a claw, Phantom would surely have been beyond help. Any stress, even standing, even the weight of Phantom's own organs, could open his belly completely. The wound would have to be sewn shut, and quickly, and if Phantom fought him...

Barris had needle and leather in his saddlebag, but Phantom lay atop it. He would need to remove the saddle and slide it out from under the horse.

Barris let himself slip deeply into the Bond.

~Hear me, friend. You must trust me.~

He moved to unstrap the saddle. Phantom kicked weakly.

~No, you cannot kick, great beast. You must be still. Trust me, please. I will save you, but you must trust me...~

The procedure took the better part of an hour. Barris first packed the wound with snow, hoping to dull Phantom's pain, and perhaps he had succeeded, to some degree, but not nearly enough to still his friend. Phantom had bitten Barris twice as he sewed the gash shut, the second bite opening a wound in Barris' thigh that nearly required its own stitches. Hooves battered the knight, leaving his upper body a purple, bruised mess before he tied the last knot.

Phantom understood that Barris had finished and wanted to stand. The wound still oozed blood in places, and Barris feared the stiches would not hold, but there was no more he could do, not to heal his friend nor prevent him from rising.

Barris kept a hand on Phantom's shoulder as he stood,

sensing his pain as if it were his own, testing it, feeling for internal damage through the Bond. He felt none, but what he did feel alarmed him anew. Phantom's right hind leg was badly strained near the stifle, a deep tissue injury that would have slowed him to a walk, gash or no. There was no way to know if it would aggravate or heal on its own; only time would tell.

"I am so sorry, my friend. Let us get off the road and rest for a day. You will feel better tomorrow."

Barris pulled Redemption free from the dead bear, wiped it clean it on its fur, and sheathed it. He gathered the saddle and bags; he would carry them himself.

Barris led Phantom from the road into the trees, thick droplets of blood leaving a trail in the snow as the grey day darkened to black.

IX: THE DOORS OF NYR AVI

IME PASSED, presumably. Mikallis could not tell. Perhaps, here, time moved differently. *Perhaps not at all.* No, that seemed unlikely. Certainly, time marched forward elsewhere. Aria needed him, or she would. What had He said?

"... she will need you, and on that day, you will need to be more than what you are."

What I am is dead, thought Mikallis. *What I need to be is alive, or I am good to no one.*

Yet of course there was more to it. He had a choice to make— not *whether* to return to the world of the living, but *how*.

Mikallis turned, examining his illuminated surroundings. These were the fabled Doors of *Nyr Avi*, of new life. Mention of the Doors was made sparingly in the old texts. Overwhelmingly, the elven scholars familiar with the lore believed such references to be no more than parable, representative of the choices available to one after death. Growing up in the Evanti household, where knowledge and study were prized above all, Mikallis had been among few in his generation to have viewed the original writings, and while he recalled very little, he knew there should be a sixth door.

He also knew, or at least now began to suspect, that his

understanding of the texts had been insufficient, if not erroneous altogether. To this, the first two doors held what he believed were obvious clues. *This one... the knocker in the shape of an elm. That one... solid stone, the relief of an axe...*

The first would have to do with Eyreloch, Mikallis reasoned, perhaps its ancient elms. It would make sense for such a door to be available to an elf. But he felt strongly that the second door led to Stonarris, the resting place of all good and honorable dwarves. This could only mean that Nyr Avi was not merely a nexus between worlds for the elven people, as he had been taught. It was more likely a waypoint for *all* people.

Following that logic, Mikallis supposed that the other doors were meant for other races. *But the missing door...*

Mikallis shook his head against the idea. *No. It cannot be. Aria would have no cause to be there.*

Five doors. The five dominant races of Greater Tahr? But what of the orcs? What of the trolls? Different as they were, surely they were human, possessing a soul. Were they all gone, and thus needed no door? No, they could not be. Half-orc families were known to live along the Sapphire coast. The trolls, while diminishing in number, still controlled much of the swampy region south of Mor. It was even rumored that full-blooded orcs still lived west of Eyreloch, though no one had verified this in generations, not since the way West had been closed by the Airies.

And why doors at all? If the members of each race had their own predetermined destination after their first life, why present a choice? Where but Stonarris, for example, would any dwarf choose to go?

Mikallis turned to the crystal door, again, for what may have been the hundredth time. *Beyond,* he thought. *Life after life, where one would find the answers to the unknowable questions and mysteries of all things.* The elves believed in the Beyond. The choice he expected he would someday make, perhaps this very day, would be between venturing Beyond and remaining behind to serve his people. Surely that was what was needed here... he must remain behind. But how? Through which door?

Perhaps the clues are not what I suppose them to be. Perhaps this is not the door to Stonarris. Perhaps that is not a door to the Eyre.

How could it be? If one could travel from death to the Eyre, where then were all the once-dead elves in Eyreloch? They certainly were not within the Elms, and if they were in the heart of Eyreloch, the Airies made no mention of them. And what of the boulder, and the iron gate?

And what of the sixth door? Mikallis resisted the urge to turn towards that empty space between doors. *She is there. I know it.*

He recalled the Father's voice:

"...she is lost to me, for now. To us. There is no door."

Mikallis shuddered.

"she must find her way back. When she does, if she does—"

If.

"—she will need you."

Mikallis set aside the question of Aria, of the sixth door... of where that door might lead, were it there. He felt certain that the answer lay not in where Aria was, in any case, but in where he must go to prepare for her return.

If this door leads to the Beyond, and this door to Stonarris, then this must lead to the Eyre. Where else? If so, then these...

He turned to inspect the boulder, then the gate.

...these must lead to lands meant for the gnomes and men, after their first life.

Mikallis believed it did not matter which was which. Neither could be his destination. Neither could Stonarris, nor the Beyond. That left only the wooden door, the knocker in the shape of an elm...

But why? We had all just come from the Eyre. Why return there?

"There are those who might teach you, but as they guide your path, so you must lead them."

The Father's clue could not mean the Eyre. Lady Lor had already given her life to teach what she could, and she bestowed no such gift upon Mikallis. Lady Lor? She would follow no one.

But she may have answers.

Or she may not.

Incomprehension became hot frustration.

"'Choose wisely,' you say! I cannot! No one could! If this is a test, it is a fool's test! Why hang the fate of the world on a riddle? This is madness!"

Mikallis chided himself for his impertinence, his irreverence.

This was a holy place, he knew. He should not bring forth anger here. Yet he could not help himself, even as he recalled the Father's words.

"...you must choose, young Mikallis."

"How? How do I choose!?"

Mikallis turned the problem over in his mind, again and again. Time passed, or did not, as the dead elf alternately paced, grumbled, and cursed. The more he agonized over his decision, the more impossible it seemed. Every clue was contradicted by the next, every logical conclusion laid waste by a plausible alternate idea. There were only so many clues. Five doors. Varying shapes. No inscriptions. Only the axe and the elm, symbols that may carry obvious meaning, or could as easily carry none. After all, how old were the Doors? Did they not predate the world? No, they could not, or how could they resemble familiar things, things shaped by the hands of humans? So, they came after... but when? And how? By the Father's hand? Or was he merely a gatekeeper? Was it even the First Father whom Mikallis met?

"You know how you have come here."

No.

"And you know my voice."

I do.

Father.

"Of a sort."

Another riddle. Was it of consequence, or just another

unknowable thing, irrelevant to his choice? Mikallis listened to the windless air, if it was in fact air within which he existed. He heard nothing. Less than nothing. Complete, total silence.

"Why!? Why be silent? If this choice matters so much, why say so little!?"

"I can tell you no more, only that you must have faith, and you must choose wisely."

"Faith! Faith in what, in riddles? In my ability to make a wild guess? In my superior intellect? Even Neral knew I am a fool!" *Every decision I make is folly, from the moment I inserted myself into Aria's quest... did I bring this about? Is she lost because of me?*

Mikallis discovered then that he could cry in this place, that his body, such as it was, could make tears, that his chest could heave and sob, that he could fall to his knees, though upon what he knelt, he did not know.

Guilt, shame, sorrow, fear... is this what death was? The bitter realization that one was helpless, flawed, and alone? That one's deeds in life could never be undone, one's failures never remedied?

He had failed Aria, failed his people, shamed himself, and even at the end, in his wild, headlong rush unto death, he accomplished little. The beast endured. Mikallis' last memory of life was the sound of its roar as darkness narrowed his vision for the last time. It still threatened. How could his friends have survived? They could not, not against such power.

Mikallis considered the missing sixth door.

No. She lives.

Somewhere, Aria needed him, or she would. When? As he dithered here in this timeless place, how much time passed elsewhere? How much time did he have? How much time did *she* have?

"Father, please! I cannot do this alone! Help me decide, I beg of you! Before it is too late, before time runs out!"

Time.

The thought rang in Mikallis' mind like a bell.

Time.

The hint of a hint worked its way through his mind, not quite taking shape, but drawing nearer.

Time.

He recalled his first thoughts when the Doors appeared...

He turned to his right, to the fifth door. There he saw a huge boulder, perfectly spherical, at least on the side that faced him. Thick, damp moss hung in clumps and strips from the stone. The scent emanating from the door was the first aroma he had noticed since his awakening; an old smell, ancient even. If Mikallis were to name it, he would call it the scent of time.

Time.

Mikallis stood, turning towards the fifth door. The old scent filled him, along with something else:

Faith.

Without hesitation, in complete absence of doubt, Mikallis placed a hand on the cool, damp stone.

X: FURY

CREECHING HOWLS of hunger and rage echoed through iron passages. The tunnel walls reverberated as if alive, thrumming in appalling, dissonant harmonies as they carried forth the sounds of approaching death. Lucan indulged no illusion on that point; what came was most certainly death itself.

But not mine. Not ours.

"Aria! Get beside me, we'll take the right tunnel!"

"We've got the left!" bellowed J'arn. "Shyla, Wolf, to me!" Lucan saw the dwarf instinctively reach for his axe.

He shouted a warning. "No blades, J'arn!"

"Arrgh! Fine!" J'arn's hand dropped, fist clenching at his side. A skittering, scratching sound overtook the echoing howls in volume, an awful sound that could only be claws on metal. The discordant noise came from everywhere; it was impossible to tell from which tunnel their enemies came. Lucan met Cindra's silvery gaze. The witch understood. She edged towards J'arn.

"Do as I do, J'arn! Just as I do!"

J'arn nodded at Cindra, unsure.

"It'll be all right. You too, Shyla! As I do!"

Shyla nodded. Wolf growled, baring teeth, crouching.

A hand grasped Lucan's own. *Aria.* He turned to the princess, suddenly aware that his own hands were clammy with sweat.

"Stay by my side," she said firmly. Lucan could not tell if she meant to ask his protection or offer her own. He decided it did not matter.

"This is not our end," Lucan vowed.

"No," she agreed, the two sharing a memory then, a glimpse of a dream they had shared so many times before.

Lucan stared into the dark tunnel before them. Only blackness... and noise... *So much noise!* He could barely think, until, suddenly, the howling just... stopped. The distant cacophony of scrabbling claws diminished as their enemies slowed their approach.

Wolf let out a whine. Lucan kept his attention fixated on the tunnel ahead, peering into blackness, straining, listening. The silence deepened. He could hear his own rattling breath. Someone behind him—Shyla, perhaps—let out a gasp. Aria turned. Another gasp.

Lucan whipped around to see what Aria saw. Past the others, down the tunnel... a sickly yellow glow, brightening. Lucan blinked, forcing himself to focus, and then he saw. Hundreds upon hundreds of pairs of lights, mustard-yellow, pulsating... almost blinking...

Blinking...

Eyes!

As if on command—no, surely on command—the eyes began to brighten. The howls returned. Lucan had no doubt... whatever controlled these beings had waited until he and his companions had counted their number before releasing them into battle. Now, they came, screeching unintelligible curses, clambering over one another in a roiling stampede. The companions stood rooted, frozen in fear. Only Cindra stepped forward, arms outstretched from within tattered robes. From where Lucan stood, he could not see her eyes, but the glow they emitted bathed the tunnel before her, washing their enemies in silvery light.

Lucan had no time to make out their forms before twin gouts of flame erupted from Cindra's hands. Shyla quickly added her own fire to the deluge, and a moment later J'arn did as well, though he and Shyla together emitted but a fraction of the conflagration that Cindra sent forth. Screams of pain replaced howls of rage as their enemies burned. Lucan had just raised his own hands to add to the torrent when Aria screamed behind him.

Lucan turned. Twice the number of eyes as before stared back at him. Three times. Aria ignited her own streams of fire. Lucan joined her. Red and orange light poured forth from the pair through the mouth of the tunnel before them, but unlike the left side, their flames did not roll along the walls and fill the breach. Here, the tunnel widened after only a few paces. Here, their combined power was no more effective at stemming the tide than a stone in a river.

The first few came through burning, smoking, stumbling, their forms still unrecognizable. The scent was vile, nauseating.

Aria called out. "Cindra! Help us!"

Lucan knew she could not. He bore down, sending more of his will into the magic, finding more power, sending more flame... it was not enough. He and Aria began slowly walking backwards, their retreat unintentional, their fear absolute.

With a deafening roar, louder than the already ear-splitting noises resounding around them, a black, lumbering beast came through the flames on four impossibly thin legs—no, *two* legs, and two arms!—each the length of the other, long, lanky, segmented things, hands ending not in fingers but single, blackened, dagger-like blades, feet a mess of claws with iron talons attached to razor-sharp shins... Lucan turned his flame into the abomination, into its emaciated torso, only then gaining the courage to gaze into its face.

Here Lucan saw what was perhaps once the skull of a man; that, or a hate-inspired mockery of what a man might be. Elongated facial bones gave only a hint of human cheeks. Thin, impossibly long teeth, sharpened to a point, longer on the bottom than the top, bulging from within a jaw too narrow to contain them. Smoky yellow light emanated from within the black skull, illuminating fissures between its skull bones, pouring out from misshapen eye sockets.

No flame would have effect on this creature, Lucan knew, this atrocity made wholly of solid iron and pure hatred. Cindra had warned about beasts that might bleed acid. This creature would not bleed at all. This was something else.

Aria must have recognized the same as she quickly changed tact, but her adjustment in strategy proved disastrous. With a cry she extinguished her flames, reared back, inhaled, and extended her hands forward again, this time sending a gust of wind into the long-skulled beast, clearly hoping to blow it backwards. All she managed to do was extinguish Lucan's own gouts of flame. The beast dug its rear claws and hand-daggers into the floor of the cavern, and thin as it was, the wind Aria sent forth could gain no purchase. Lucan felt certain the faceless aberration smirked at him then, mocking Aria's folly.

"Down!" yelled Cindra. Lucan and Aria dove to their bellies. The beast roared again, lunging for the pair as the gnome witch ran between them. With a heave and a cry Cindra launched herself at the horrid creature's midsection, somehow driving her own hand directly into the creature's iron chest. Its dagger-hands swung inwards, training to sever Cindra's head from her neck. Before they could make the arc, the light in the creature's eyes went out.

Lucan lay in petrified awe as the next wave of horrors came pouring through the tunnel. They crossed into the chamber, bathed in a strange red glow that now emanated from the witch. Now, Lucan saw, and what he saw deepened his paralysis.

Cindra turned as she and the creature fell into a heap, her silver eyes boring into Lucan's own. "Defend me, dammit!" Lucan sensed something awful there, a sort of lust... an ecstasy... her hand remained embedded in the iron beast's chest.

Aria reacted first, a ball of pure, concentrated flame flying from her hands over towards the... things. Time slowed as Lucan's mind struggled to process what had just happened, what was still happening. A score of six-legged creatures, some the size of rats, some the size of dogs, black as the blackest night but for eyes of yellow fire, racing forward, snapping, snarling...

... the ball of flame exploded overhead...

... faces... awful, soulless faces...

...the red light around Cindra brightened to white, he could see nothing but the glow...

...a concussion from above, pressing him harder onto the iron floor of the chamber...

...heat... ringing ears...

... a scream behind him... his name?...

"Lucan!"

A strong hand yanked Lucan up by the collar.

"We got to go, damn ye! This way!"

Lucan gathered his wits, enough at least to stumble after J'arn on gelatinous legs. The dwarf led Lucan and Aria down the left tunnel, now cleared of beasts but drenched in a revolting residue of bone fragments, bile, and boiled ichor for a dozen paces. A path down the center of the tunnel had been cleared by some spell, probably cast by Shyla. Wolf barked a warning from somewhere ahead.

An orb flew over Lucan's head, lighting the way forward. "Keep running, Shyla!" yelled Cindra. "Run 'til yeh can run no more, then go right!"

Lucan turned to see Cindra running behind them, slowing to fire off some spell at their pursuers. Whatever it was, it was working. The sounds of howls and snapping fangs became more distant as they ran.

Lucan ran, his lungs burning. He became aware again of how difficult it was to breathe here. The tunnel took an undulating path, straight for the most part but treacherous, blackened rocks and iron bulges of every shape and size jutting out here and there. The dim light of Cindra's orb cast odd, moving shadows, exaggerating the slope of the terrain in places, concealing dips and trenches in others. He kept to J'arn's heels as best he could, the dwarf far more sure-footed than he. Finally, J'arn slid to a stop as the passageway ended. To the right, a sloping tunnel led downward. The orb of light took the turn. J'arn followed. A cry from behind turned Lucan around. Aria tumbled to the ground.

"Aria!"

"Run, Lucan! I'm fine!" Aria took a step and stumbled again.

Cindra helped her to her feet with one hand, casting another orb of light with the other. A grimace of pain etched itself across Aria's face.

"Twisted her ankle!" said Cindra. "Carry her! Move!"

Lucan scooped Aria into his arms and raced to follow J'arn, Shyla and Wolf. He turned to the right as the tunnel ended, hearing Cindra's footsteps come to a halt behind him. He turned to see her gesturing, casting some spell.

"Just go!" Cindra commanded.

Lucan obeyed without argument.

The tunnel here was narrower, shorter, the ground flatter but no easier to traverse. The passage was solid, unblemished iron, its walls and ceiling red with rust, its floor trod smooth as glass. Repeatedly Lucan slipped and slid as he tried to keep up with J'arn.

Aria spoke through gritted teeth. "Use your magic, Luc!"

Lucan understood. With a thought, his feet left the ground. He began to float along the passage, following the orb, touching the walls and floor here and there to alter his trajectory. He absently noted that had he not been fleeing for his life, the sensation would have been wonderful. Soon he had nearly caught up to J'arn.

"Can you heal your ankle?"

"I'm trying," Aria said through clenched teeth. "I think I broke it."

J'arn slowed. Lucan caught him just as he reached Shyla and Wolf. The tunnel widened into a large chamber. It was hard to tell in the shadowy light, but several passages seemed to branch off in every direction.

Shyla spoke first, winded. "Where's my grand... uh, where's Lady Cindra?"

"Coming, I think," said Lucan, setting Aria down gingerly. "She stopped to cast a spell."

"*Keep yer voices down!*" whispered J'arn. He knelt to inspect Aria's ankle. Aria suppressed a cry as he examined the injury.

"Broken," J'arn said. "We gotta heal this and fast."

"I can do it," Aria said. "I'll need some help, though."

Lucan understood, and knew the others did as well. Lady Lor had bestowed them all with a comprehensive understanding of healing magic. She had also imparted something else: while they each possessed great power, its strength could only grow through use and experience. As such, while healing a broken ankle might someday require less than an afterthought, the process was still foreign to them all—all save Aria, who had trained for years under Pheonaris at the Grove. To do this now, quickly, would require a sharing of all their power.

"Just lay your hands on me," Aria said, "and relax. I will channel your strength."

Shyla knelt beside Aria, placing a hand on her thigh. J'arn grasped her shoulder. Aria looked up at Lucan. He thought he saw a pleading there in her frightened blue eyes, something more than a mere appeal to help heal her ankle. Lucan placed a hand on her cheek, gently.

The sensation was both jarring and pleasant, even sensual. As Aria drew from Lucan's power, so did he draw from hers, as was required. What she took from him—what he allowed her to take—was raw and simple, an unrefined energy without form or definition. What she returned to him, however, was more complex, more distinct. These were emotions. There was gratitude here, and respect, but also resentment, distrust, fear... and desire. More compound emotions, some convoluted, some unnamable, but all things Lucan well understood. He knew these things for what they were—the entirety of Aria's feelings for him. Such was the intimacy required in sharing magic. The feeling left Lucan breathless.

"Oh, Mawbottom! What are yeh doin'!?" Cindra's voice interrupted the spell.

"She's hurt, Lady Cindra, we were healing—"

"Yeh cannot do such magic here! It be a beacon!"

Wolf let out a low growl.

~THERE YOU ARE.~

The screeching, howling cries of their enemies returned. From everywhere.

Shyla jumped to her feet, her pink eyes wide with fear. J'arn again reached for his axe before stopping himself. He bent to help Aria stand. "Get up! We gotta fight!"

Aria took J'arn's arm. She stood and tested her ankle, crying out in pain. Lucan caught her as she fell.

"Get her back in the tunnel!" yelled Cindra. Lucan wasted no time, carrying Aria beyond the threshold of the tunnel from which they just emerged. Shyla and J'arn moved to follow them, Wolf snapping at the darkness behind them.

"No!" cried Cindra. "Yeh have to lead them away!"

"What? We ain't gonna leave—"

"Do as I say J'arn, or we all die!"

Cindra turned towards the tunnel, gesturing again as she had before.

"Stand back!"

Cindra's hands twisted and writhed as she cast. Lucan moved back, carrying Aria a few paces deeper into the tunnel. He set her down. He could feel the heat from Cindra's spell as the mouth of the tunnel began to glow crimson, then pink, then a bright, almost blinding white. The iron began to melt, hot metal oozing from the ceiling. Lucan struggled to see past Cindra as gouts of flame cast by Shyla and J'arn met a cascade of screeching devils. Cindra's spell manipulated the dropping metal, thickened it in long ropes which descended, slowly, all the way to the floor. Wolf growled and snapped. Torrents of flames flew now from Shyla and J'arn in opposite directions. His friends were surrounded.

Cindra screamed into the minds of the companions. ~Down! Now!~

Lucan and Aria dropped to the floor. The princess threw her body atop his as a frigid burst of bone-chilling wind washed over them. The gust accelerated, faster, impossibly fast, faster than any wind Lucan had ever experienced. The tips of his ears began to burn. He covered them with his hands. Within moments, his fingers hurt. Lucan knew nothing upright could withstand the freezing blow. Even lying flat, the unrelenting wind slid Lucan and Aria backwards across the iron floor. All the companions screamed and howled in pain and fear, Wolf loudest of all.

The deluge stopped. For half a breath, all was silent.

Lucan looked up through newly-cast iron bars, these now solid. Cindra turned to J'arn and Shyla. The air around the gnome witch shimmered with power as she commanded J'arn and Shyla.

"RUN!"

Cindra's hands dropped to her sides. Lucan could see they were caked in frost. She glanced back at him, answering the unasked question.

"Survive."

For just a moment, before she turned away, Lucan thought Cindra's shining, silver eyes had turned to gold.

Or perhaps yellow.

XI: HIGHMORLAND

HE DOOR TO THE CABIN opened enough for half a face to peer out. Silver-haired, a head shorter than Mila, a stout woman jammed a foot against the door. Mila inclined her head and folded her hands. The deferent gesture felt awkward—it had been a long while since Mila Felsin submitted to anyone—but she had no intention of alarming this woman.

The woman opened the door a bit more, enough to stick her head out.

"I am alone, I swear it."

"Hmph. Well, ya would wouldn't ya? Don't suppose you'd just wave your cutthroat friends over 'til I open the door proper."

"Emma, who're you talkin' to? Who's there?" A man's voice, elderly.

"Oh, just the king of Mor, Fillip. Come to make you a knight."

"All right."

The woman shook her head. "Lotta help he is, deaf old goat. Well, come on in, I suppose if you were gonna gut me, you would have already. Kick that snow off your boots, if you please."

Mila did so and followed the woman inside. Warm air and the sweet smell of stew greeted her like a long-forgotten friend; she could not recall the last time she ate.

"Well, close the door! And bar it, would you? Mind that hook, now, damned thing's hangin' by a nail. Oh, just let me..."

Mila stood aside as the woman fiddled with the rotten wooden bar. She didn't bother commenting on the uselessness of the ordeal; the shabby door looked like it could be kicked in by a gnome. The rest of the cabin, however, was sharp as a pin, immaculately clean and well-cared for. To the right of the door lay two small beds, each tightly made with matching quilts and embroidered pillows. Across the room from the door, a hotstone hung suspended within a small hearth. The chimney, made of light-colored rock, appeared as clean as if it were just mortared. To its left, against the wall, four rows of shelves lined the wall, these displaying plates, bowls, and every imaginable shape and size of pot or pan. From the bottom shelf, a variety of spoons and knives and other kitchen implements hung, each equidistant from the next. Mila marveled at the exquisite organization of it all as the woman looked on, her expression satisfied.

To Mila's left stood a long table with benches on each side, suitable to seat perhaps eight, though set with care for six. In its center stood a large covered pot, presumably of stew. On one side of the pot, a plate with bread; on the other, a quarter-wheel of hard cheese. These, too, were set perfectly equidistant from one another, as were the six lace doilies upon each of which lay a wooden plate, a wooden cup, and a single spoon. A balding, white-haired man sat hunched with his back to Mila, his face buried in a book. A wrinkled hand held a small candelabra to light the pages, which to Mila seemed unnecessary. Every few feet around the cabin, a lantern or candle was lit.

"I thank you, Madame. I—"

"Madame? Ha! Hear that, Fillip? I'm a madame!"

"Huh?" Fillip turned around in his chair. "Oh! Who are you!"

The man appeared terrified.

Mila leaned forward, speaking up. "My name is Mila, sir. It is a pleasure—"

"Easy, now! You don't have to yell, I ain't deaf!" His eyes lowered, taking in the shape of Mila.

Emma put a hand on Mila's shoulder, pulling her upright. "Sure, and he ain't blind, either." Emma shot a glance at Mila's bosom, then back into her eyes. "All the same, watch your robes there, *Miss Mila*."

"Oh! I'm sorry..." Mila looked down to see her robe was clasped at the neck beneath her cloak, but the plain hint was well received. "Again, thank you so much, Lady Emma. But... have I interrupted something? Do you expect company?"

"Company? In this mess? Ha!"

Mila smiled demurely, knowing the woman had been delighted to so dismiss her faultless housekeeping, but then glanced at the table.

"Ah. Never mind that", said Emma, "I just like it set, is all. Now come on, give that cloak here before you drip all over the house..."

The stew was delicious, the bread sweet and soft, the wine new, but delicious. Mila skillfully guided the conversation away from herself, not merely to avoid detailing the unpleasant circumstances that brought her to their home, but in genuine desire to fill her mind with thoughts of anything but her own life.

Her hostess was more than happy to lead the exchange, launching effortlessly into breathless narrative. Emma and Fillip Manchele, purveyors of fine candles, honey and honey-baked goods, had been living in Highmorland since they were wed one golden spring day by her uncle, fifty-and-two years before at the Lorday Festival. To hear Emma tell it, in the dreamy tones of a young lover, one might have believed the wedding was days past rather than decades. So handsome had Fillip been, so respectful to her father, grower of wheat, owner of the mill, brother to the prior of their small village on the north side of the Morline, Windfall, so named for the miracle of one bountiful apple harvest generations past. So proud was her mother—lovely woman, just *lovely*— spending the whole of winter sewing her blue dress, weaving the banners, painting the traditional green leaves on long, brown ribbons. So envious were the girls of Windfall, Emma landing the comeliest, if among the lowest born, man in all the farmlands. Not that it mattered, mind. They had no intention of staying long on the farm, did we Fillip? No, Fillip dreamed of bees... bees and honey, liquid gold, and the best place for bees was, of course, the floral pastures of Highmorland, and in any case his inheritance, or rather the lack of one, would have been of no consequence when compared to the wealth of her father. He owned the mill, you see. Did you know his brother was the prior? Devout man, that one. Loved Lor with all his heart. Shame about the highwaymen.

Fillip looked on quietly as Emma told the story of their early lives, how Fillip and she built their first cabin, their first hives, their small but scrappy business. That first winter, they had returned to her father's house, too poor to feed themselves. By their third winter together, they had built their own inn to house the merchants, human and elf alike, even the occasional dwarf, who traveled far and wide to buy quality Manchele honey.

Emma nearly began speaking of that next spring. Nearly, until Fillip and she shared a glance. The old man then looked down, returning to his book. Mila sensed the need to change the subject.

"Do you still manage the inn?" she asked.

"Oh, no child, at our age? No, the Manchele Manor has been gone for years now. What do we need with such things, anyways? We've got plenty of gold, don't you worry."

Fillip looked up. "Emma!"

"Oh, I wouldn't worry much about Miss Mila here. I suspect she's got her own problems. Problems gold won't fix, if I'm not mistaken."

The sorceress met Emma's knowing gaze. Emma seized an opportunity to press.

"Mila. Such a lovely name. What did you say your surname was?"

Mila blinked, turning her head away, towards the fire. Her breath caught in her throat. Time stood still as the young Incantor gazed into the fire, past it, towards something else.

"I did not say. But..."

A hand rested atop Mila's own. Fillip's hand. "Are you all right, dear?"

Mila forced a smile. "I... yes, thank you."

"You were saying, dear?" Emma urged. "Your name?"

"It is... Brennan. My name is Brennan."

And it was. Mila Felsin, once Freya Brennan, daughter of Shane and Amelia, had not thought of her true own name in as long as she could remember. Tears welled in her emerald eyes.

"Oh, dear, come now, come here." Emma embraced Mila before she could resist.

The woman's embrace was too much. Mila's shoulders heaved, but she could not draw breath. A wagon parked itself on her chest. Soon Emma's silver hair was soaked in tears as the horrors of Mila's life swept through her mind like a gale. It had been so long since someone cared to know her, to hold her...

Earl.

Silent sobs became faint cries. Mila returned Emma's embrace. The older woman rocked the young guest in her arms for a time, longer than strangers might, before Mila pulled away, wiping her face.

"I'm so sorry," Mila began. "I don't know—"

"You've lost something, dear." Emma's voice had lost its lilting timbre. The old woman shifted her glance to an empty place setting. "We understand."

Eventually the conversation returned to recent things. By unspoken agreement, neither the Mancheles nor Mila dug into one another's hidden aches. They discussed the infernal volcano, Fang; or rather, Fillip did. An omen, he promised, and a bad one. Worse things were to come, and soon. Did Mila not know about the fires? Lost ten hives to the last one, they did, not three cycles past. Barely got it out before the whole glade went up. Mila nodded politely but did not fail to notice Emma noticing her. She could not bring herself to lie to these people, but neither could she bring herself to say what she knew. She did not want to be Mila Felsin here, Incantor, sorceress, drug-peddler, killer, soon-to-be prey of the fearsome, now-curiously-silent Kalashagon. She wished to be a Brennan, for just a while longer.

"Help me clear the table, Mila."

Fillip stood gingerly, with the belabored movement of the elderly. Mila could practically feel the ache in his joints.

"Taking a walk."

Emma glanced towards one of two small windows in the room. Mila followed her gaze. Night had fallen.

Emma took a cloak from a hook behind the door, throwing it over her husband's shoulders. "Bring a lantern, dear."

"Bah."

Emma and Mila busied themselves quietly until Fillip had closed the door behind him.

Emma set down a plate and towel, eyeing Mila. Mila dipped a rag into a bucket and wiped a cup clean. She caught the hint but turned away, seeking something inane to say. A hand on Mila's shoulder turned her back around.

"Who are you?"

Mila swallowed.

"You don't want to know."

"If I didn't want to know, young lady, I wouldn't have asked."

"I know. But maybe you don't."

Emma held Mila's gaze. "And maybe I do."

Mila sighed, glancing towards the door. "How long do we have?"

"A few turns."

Mila shook her head. "Not long enough. Not nearly."

"The short version, then."

Mila moved to sit. Emma had none of it. "Oh no, you don't. Clean while you talk. Unless you'll be paying for supper?"

Mila nearly laughed. Emma sensed Mila was dangerous, of course. She was afraid. But she would not show her fear. *This is one strong woman.* The Incantor handed the cup to Emma and grabbed another from the table.

"I'm a sorceress."

"Sorceress? Incantor, you mean? From the tower?"

Mila shook her head. "That also, but... well, more."

"Lor help me. One of Sartean' D'Avers whelps, in my own home."

"I am *not* one of his whelps."

Emma stopped drying the cup for a moment, the briefest pause before reaching for the next.

"And in any case, you need not worry about Sartean D'Avers anymore."

Emma looked up, incredulous. "Oh, no? Killed him, did you?" She reached for a plate. "Hmph."

"I did."

Emma's hands began to shake.

"Please, do not be afraid. I will not—"

"Afraid? Young lady, this is my *home*. It will take more than a little girl to frighten me." Emma dropped the plate.

Mila bent to pick it up. She set it on the table and took Emma's trembling hands.

"Listen to me. I know fear. I've instilled plenty of it. But you don't have to fear me. I swear it. But... what hunts me..." Mila glanced towards the window, letting her voice trail off. Emma's hands tightened around her own.

"You were afraid when you arrived here."

Mila nodded.

"I heard something. Something big. Flying overhead yesterday. Then a bright light. From the bridge?"

Mila nodded again.

"The bridge is a long way from here. That light—"

"Sartean's doing," Mila said. "To lure the beast."

"The beast?"

Emma released Mila's hands. She reached behind her to feel for the bench. Mila helped her sit.

"It is called a dragon, I think. Its name... its name doesn't matter. But it slaughtered nearly all of Kehrlia. How long has it been since you heard news from Mor?"

"Oh, I don't know. A cycle, maybe?"

"I thought I saw fresh tracks. Horse tracks."

Emma shook her head. "Not from Mor. A friend, Chaliq. Looks after us. Lives nearby."

"Chaliq? Is that... orcish?"

"Half-orc. Though, he's maybe a sixteenth, at best. Ran through here a year ago, come up from the Sapphire. We took him in for a time. Taught him how to build a cabin, so he looks in on us. Never mind him, though. He hasn't been south of the bridge in a year."

"Then you've missed quite a bit. Halsen is dead. Mor is leaderless, and likely starving. It's going to get dangerous soon. Everywhere."

"Says the sorceress in my house, who killed Sartean D'Avers and is being chased by... by what again?"

"A dragon. Listen to me, Emma. If you hear it, hide. In fact, I would not go out during the day. I promise, you have never seen—"

Steps sounded on the porch.

"Not a word. I'll tell him tomorrow."

"I should leave. It's not safe—"

"Yes. You should. At dawn. I'll feed you breakfast, but—"

The door flew open. "Cold as a witch's arse out there!"

"Fillip! We have a guest!"

Fillip smiled, pretending not to hear.

"Where's the lantern? Did you leave it in the privy again?"

"Bah!" Fillip eyed Mila. "Gettin' old is a calamity, young lady. Dunno if it starts in the head or the bowels, but eventually, they both get clogged up."

"Fillip!"

Mila couldn't help but to laugh. "It's all right, Emma. I'll go get the lantern."

"Fury you will!" the man said. "Not if you like breathin'! Ain't safe in the privy for an hour at least."

"Fillip Manchele, you are vile!"

Fillip and Mila laughed again. "Don't fret, miss. I know my way back to the privy. Ain't all that dark yet."

"Take another lantern, Fillip."

Fillip either didn't hear his wife or again pretended not to. He stepped back out the door with a wink to Mila.

"Lovely," said Emma, rolling her eyes in mock exasperation. "The sight of a young girl, the cold night air... he'll be all hands tonight."

Mila smiled. "Well, at least you have two beds."

"Not tonight. You take mine; I'll sleep with Fillip. I wouldn't mind a wandering hand or two tonight, besides. Who knows how much longer we've got, way the world is going."

Mila nodded. "I know what you mean. But I can leave tonight, Emma. It's no trouble, I have magic to keep me warm."

Emma took a long measure of Mila before she spoke next.

"It's not that sort of warmth you need right now, dear. Stay. But just tonight."

Mila sighed. "All right. Just tonight."

The women stood and continued tidying up.

"So, this dragon. You said it has a name? You mean, like it's someone's pet?"

Mila thought for a moment. "Honestly, I don't know. But it's intelligent."

And terrible.

"Well, if it's chasing the woman who put down Sardine Cadaver, it might not be all that bright."

Mila said nothing.

"So, magic, eh?"

Mila nodded.

"Show me."

"I'm sorry?"

"Come on now, before Fillip comes back! Just something little. I find it so fascinating."

Mila smiled. "All right. Here."

Mila closed her eyes as she considered a spell. She gestured delicately towards the bucket of water, enchanting not only the bucket but also herself, just for a moment. It had been long since Mila took joy from such a small thing. Wisps of steam rose from the bucket.

"There. Now we can wash the pot properly."

Emma's jaw dropped. "That... wow. That was—"

A distant roar sounded.

~Mmm... little witch. How delightful. I smell you again.~

XII: THE TEMPLE OF KAL

HE CUT NEVER CAME. Nia was certain her life was at an end. the Daughters would bring her bodily to the altar. The Mother would slice out her still-beating heart. Her last moments would be spent in terror and agony. She would die forgotten, buried in an unmarked grave, if buried at all.

Clearly, the Daughters present in the altar room expected something similar. When the Mother stepped down from the dais, leaving the knife on the altar, their jaws dropped. Sharp glances were exchanged. Jealous, hate-filled scowls turned towards Nia.

"Never mind them," the Mother said softly, no doubt reading their expressions on Nia's face. She turned around briefly. "They will do as they are told. Won't you, my Daughters?"

"Yes, Mother," the six replied in chorus.

"See? Pliant. Obedient. Mindless. Unlike *you*."

Nia blinked. The Mother placed a hand on her shoulder, turning her away from the altar. "Walk with me."

Nia moved to fall in line behind her superior, but the Mother took her arm like a sister.

"I did not say 'follow me', Nia of the sea. I said 'walk with me'. We are equals, are we not?"

"I... I mean, I do not presume—"

"It would be my presumption to assume otherwise. You have never taken the Oath, and therefore you are not in my service. You are no different from any other citizen of Tahr. Your own creature, with your own will." The two rounded a corner. Nia could see the Mother was leading them to her personal chambers. "I would know your will. What drives Nia of the sea? What end does she seek? Please, go in." The mother held out a hand, beckoning the girl to enter the room.

Nia obeyed, trembling. She entered the small room, only twice the size of Nia's own but far better appointed. Lush red carpet covered the floor from wall to wall. Fine cabinets and display cases lined the walls, each rumored to contain items of immeasurable power. A four-poster bed of stained cedar, this draped in velvet blankets atop mattresses that rose to Nia's bosom, supported an ornate tester from which hung sheer black netting and thick, opaque woolen drapes. In the center of the room stood a darkly polished rectangular table with a carved wooden chair on each short side. In the center of the table sat another display case, small and unopened.

"Sit," the Mother commanded, the previous pretense of equality in her tone abandoned. Nia obeyed, taking the chair opposite the bed. The Mother sat opposite.

"Well?"

"Um, well what, Mother?"

"What end do you *seek*, Nia? Speak up, now, lest I reconsider my assessment of you."

Nia cleared her throat and thought for a moment. She would need to choose her words carefully.

"I can say more about what I do not seek, Mother. I—"

A subtle frown creased the corners of the Mother's eyes. "I already know what you do *not* seek."

Nia swallowed. "I suppose you do. Then, I will say this: I seek a better world."

The Mother arched a thin eyebrow. "A better world."

Nia nodded. "Yes. And I realize how naïve that must sound—"

"Naïve? That's quite the understatement. But go on."

Nia swallowed. "Very well. A world without poverty, without cruelty. A world where people are not born into servitude. Where they are free to make their own choices. Where—"

"Let me stop you right there. What you want is impossible."

Nia felt her bravery returning. "Why? Why is it impossible?"

"Because it is a dichotomy. The ultimate dichotomy, in fact. Freedom of choice is the singular cause of poverty and cruelty, Nia, or have you not yet learned as much? One man's choice is another's enslavement, as often as not. This has always been true."

"No, I mean, you're right, and I do understand that. But that's what I want to change. I want to make a world where such things are no longer allowed, where those who commit such evils are punished—"

"You would put an end to all bargaining, then?"

"No, of course not—"

"Or do you propose supervising such bargains, perhaps regulating them?"

"I am not referring to bargains, Mother. I am—"

"Of course you are. How else does one obtain power over another? A woman needs food for her child. A working peasant needs a breast for his babe, its mother lost at birth. A bargain is struck. A peasant wishes to own his own plot. A landowner needs her fields plowed. A bargain is struck. That landowner wishes safe roads on which to travel. A soldier has a family to feed. A king wishes to fill his coffers. Taxes are levied. A bargain is struck."

"Yes. I understand. But not all bargains are fair. Nor honest. In fact, most—"

"Most are anything but fair, Nia. On this we agree."

"So why not do something about it? Why not change things? As I said, make a better world?"

A sarcastic expression crossed the Mother's face. "With our power."

Nia nodded eagerly, knowing she was being mocked.

The Mother leaned forward. "Very well. Let us assume it can be done, never mind that such a thing would require changing the very nature of humanity. Who would lead such a revolution?"

Nia responded without hesitation. "We would."

"We?"

"Yes, we, the Daughters."

"And that is why you have come to the temple, Nia of the sea? So that you might one day convince the Mother to lead Tahr out of bondage?"

"Well, no, I mean, I didn't really have a plan, exactly—"

"Of course you did. You sought power, did you not?"

Nia thought for a moment. "Yes."

"How much power, Nia? Enough to persuade me to your cause? Or more?"

Nia remained silent.

"I asked you a question. More? Perhaps *all*?"

Nia looked down.

"No! Do not be ashamed! Look at me! That is why you have come, Nia! That is why you excelled at Kehrlia. That is why you killed your young lover, rather than allowing him to kill you. Do you think I do not know the truth of that day? You meddled in magic you could not yet control. It was a tragedy... but when all was said and done, you not only survived, but you turned the affair to your advantage. It is not murder that has drawn Kal's gaze to you. It is your strength of will! Despite all you have endured, here you sit, before the Mother of the Temple, in a room among the most powerful artifacts ever created, *possessing the will to defy even me.*"

Nia sat quietly, thinking. *She is right. That is why I came to the Temple. For the power to do these things. The power to end suffering. The power to punish those who enslave, who treat human beings like chattel. The power to prevent such practices from ever existing again. For all the power.*

"You need not agree aloud, Nia. I see it on your face. You wish to become Mother one day. And more. *And you shall.*"

Nia's eyes widened.

"But first, we must address a more immediate concern. The beast defeated the Master of Kehrlia. Most of the army has abandoned the city and gone south. Mor is leaderless."

The beast survived? Sartean is dead? "South? To the Sapphire?"

The Mother nodded. "I cannot imagine the people of the sea will fare well when they arrive."

Mother. Father. Miano, Pito, Ethie, Lani...

"They must be made to return," said the Mother. "Order must be restored. The beast still threatens. Mor needs its army."

Nia nodded. "What can I do?"

The Mother opened the display case. She withdrew two small rings, one silver, one gold, each set with a simple, mottled grey stone.

"Are you ready to wield true power, Nia? To shape this better world you wish to create?"

"I am, Mother."

"This is what you must do..."

~

Nia walked briskly, more to combat the cold of near-dawn than to avoid being seen; she possessed plenty enough magic to handle any would-be robbers or other dangerous denizens of Mor. *This is my chance,* she thought. *A chance to finally make a difference.*

It was good to be out of doors again, but better to be out of her usual temple garb. The Mother had assigned a Daughter to bring Nia a change of clothes—normal clothes; simple, comfortable, brushed leather boots, soft, grey leather leggings, an undershirt and tunic, and a fine grey woolen cloak. She could barely recall the last time she had worn clean garments, let alone comfortable ones. *If nothing else,* she thought, *the Temple has taught me humility.*

The walk to the Grand Barracks was not a long one. Two sentries stood before the entrance to the courtyard.

"State your business, ma'am."

"I am here to see the General. I bring a message from the Temple."

"The Temple? At this hour? Doubtful." said one.

"And you're no Daughter," said the other.

"I am. I swear it."

"Dressed like that? No matter. Give us the message and we'll deliver it."

The Mother had warned Nia not to use the silver ring until she was in Slater's presence—its range of effect was small, and it would not last long. Better, she had said, to use her magic to get near him. The implication was clear: subdue or slay any who stand in the way. Nia shrugged and brought the ring from her pocket. She removed the stone and placed it in her mouth as the two sentries looked on, confused expressions on their faces. She bit into the stone.

"What the... are you eating *rocks*, girl?"

A sweet liquid oozed from the center of the stone. Nia swallowed.

"I'll need to pass, boys."

The two men looked at one another, then back to Nia. For a moment, she was certain the magic did not work, until the first sentry spoke again.

"Right this way, ma'am. Can I walk you there?"

"No, let me! Here, follow me ma'am—"

"Shut your bread hole, Theel! I outrank you—"

"Stop!"

The sentries fell silent. Nia smiled.

"Stand on one foot."

The sentries immediately lifted a leg.

"Hop around."

The pair began hopping, the worst, most uncoordinated dance Nia had ever seen.

"Give each other a little kiss."

The men hopped towards one another, arms outstretched.

Nia laughed musically. "Ok, enough! You can stop now." The

men stood dumb.

Nia looked at the ring. *Well, how about that.* "Let's all go together. Come on now."

"Should we hop, ma'am?"

"No, that's all right. Just get us there quickly."

The men took off at a run. Nia shrugged and followed.

A turn later, the three stood before the command table as dawn broke. Slater arrived just on time, as the Mother said he would, cup of tea in hand.

"What's this?" he asked, eyeing the three.

Corporal Smit spoke first. "General, this lady—"

"That's fine, I'll take it from here," Nia said. The corporal fell silent. "General, I have been sent by the Mother of the Temple of Kal to enslave you with this."

Nia tossed the gold ring onto the table.

Slater eyed the ring without discernible expression. He looked to his corporal. "Smit, what in Fury is going on here?"

"Tell the General," Nia commanded. "Start from when we met."

Smit and Theel fell all over one another to please Nia, describing how she had approached them, chewed up a rock from her ring, and how they both suddenly realized how perfect she was, how beautiful, sensual, inviting...

"Skip to the part where I had you hopping around."

"I hopped real good, General! Better than Smit, at least!"

"Yeah, but you never let me kiss you! You would have swooned, I swear it!"

"No, *you* would have swooned! No way you kiss better than Jaysen Theel! Here, I'll show you—"

"That's enough, boys," said Nia. "Go back to your posts."

"Yes, ma'am!" Smit and Theel turned on their heels.

"Now wait one damned turn, I didn't dismiss—"

"They won't listen, General. I've spelled them. They're mad with love and will do anything I command. As you would have been, if I cracked my ring open in your presence."

"Fury I would have. What do you aim to do then, use this one to spell me the same way?"

"No, General. The Mother wanted me to use the first to enchant you, so I could tell you to wear the second. If you put it on, she said, you would be a slave to my will for as long as you wore it."

Slater eyed the ring again, this time more warily.

"Except I don't think you would have been my slave. You would have been hers. She claims she wanted to send you south, to reunite the army, but General, I think she might have commanded you to do far, far worse."

"Like what?"

Nia shook her head. "She is a servant of Kal. Of death. As are all the Daughters. You're a general. Not hard to figure the rest out."

"Sweet Lor. And you? Are you a Daughter?"

Nia took a breath. "I was."

Slater nodded, holding Nia's gaze. A long moment passed before he spoke again. "Why didn't you obey her? Why are you telling me this?"

Nia straightened. "Because I do not serve Kal."

~

"But how can you know?" the Daughter asked. "I mean, for sure?"

"Exactly," said another. "The girl is not one of us."

"She never has been," said another. "There's no telling what she—"

"QUIET!" commanded the Mother. "I swear, you all bicker like hens, and you're no brighter. She will never obey my command. Enslave another to her will? Nothing would appall her more. And she almost certainly sensed the truth... the ring would enchant Slater to me, not to her. No, she is no fool. She would not blindly believe what I told her."

The Daughters exchanged offended glances.

"Besides, it does not matter what she does. If she obeys me, Slater is mine. If she defies me, he will wage war with us." The Mother turned, leaving the altar room.

"Either way, Kal will be served."

XIII: THE MAW

ang swallowed the Twins in billows of smoke and ash, bathing the Maw in shadow. The barest handful of faint, lonely stars dotted the sky here and there, only those bright enough to pierce the pall that had come to blanket Tahr these past cycles. Beneath this gloomy canopy, Nishali kept dark vigil, her brown, red-rimmed eyes focused on the horizon, waiting. When the last splinter of Twinlight surrendered to Fang's hunger, the First Ranger of Thornwood gave the silent order.

~For our fallen. For Kade!~

They descended on the dwarven encampment in three Tenths, Nishali leading the first into its center, the meager light of sporadic campfires guiding their approach. No light from above or behind would reveal their approach. They would not be seen. She and her rangers glided over the ice and snow, propelling themselves magically. Such a feat came at a cost, but no crunch of winter footfalls would betray their stealth. They would not be heard.

When her Tenth neared the northernmost tents, she gave the second order.

~Down. Wait. Watch. Listen.~

On command, in total silence, the rangers floated themselves prone, settling upon drifts of snow and ash, coming to rest like so many feathers. Nishali listened. She had expected to hear...

something. Snoring dwarves. The crunch of nighttime patrols. Banter among the watch. She heard nothing.

~Lyan, report.~

After a short delay, the captain of the second Tenth, Lyan Swiftspring, issued her reply from across the encampment, from the west.

~Nothing, Nishali. Less than nothing. No movement.~

~Simmon, report.~

Simmon Heartwood, the oldest and most experienced ranger under her command, replied quickly.

~Same. Nothing.~

Where in Fury are they? Nishali wondered. She lifted her head towards the encampment. *Who is tending the fires?*

A bell rang.

Nishali sensed the pull of a crossbow trigger just before she heard its distinctive *snick*, but only just. She rolled to her left, narrowly avoiding the iron projectile that embedded itself in the ground where her own head had just lain. The bolt would have killed her instantly.

~We are detected! Find cover!~

For two members of her Tenth, Nishali's warning came too late. A hundred bolts flew through the air at her rangers. Only three found their mark, but they found it well. One through the neck of the ranger nearest Nishali, two more in the breast of another.

Nishali's mind raced. She ran to take cover behind a tent. She pulled her dagger, the only weapon she had brought along. Kalder and Macon, the two dwarves who had rescued the gnome woman, had begged Nishali to forgo a ranged attack. There would be no way to tell combatants from ordinary dwarves at range, he had argued. Errant arrows could kill innocents. Reluctantly, Nishali had agreed, and now two of her rangers were dead—at least two, for she could only feel the losses within her own Tenth.

Rage welled within the First Ranger as she issued her next order.

~Kill anything that holds a weapon! Meet me in the center of the camp!~

Inhale.

Nishali become one with her surroundings. Time slowed. She spun around from behind the tent just as a bolt whipped past. She turned, sensing the direction from which the bolt came. In three powerful strides, she was in the camp and upon the attacker, a dwarf reaching into a quiver for another bolt. Before her enemy could lift a foot to take a step backwards, Nishali struck like a cyclone. In one fluid, sweeping motion, the First Ranger spun, her dagger severing his windpipe on the first pass, embedding itself to the hilt in the ribs below his armpit on the second.

An alarm sounded in Nishali's mind. *Bolt!*

Nishali ducked low, the bolt striking the shoulder of the dead dwarf who had not yet fallen. She yanked her dagger free, easily, too easily—this dwarf wore no armor.

Exhale.

She considered the fact as she raced to the right, towards her next victim, a youngish female dwarf, the panicked woman also hurrying to reload. Nishali caught a glimpse of her face in the firelight as she drew near; there was naught but terror there. The dwarf's clumsy, trembling fingers dropped a bolt an instant before Nishali's dagger found its target.

Again, no armor.

Nishali turned left, towards the center of the camp, speeding between two tents when a dwarf jumped from behind one, screaming as he swung a warhammer wildly. The weapon was far too heavy for the dwarf; he lost his balance as Nishali easily dodged the blow and buried her dagger beneath her attacker's chin.

Absently, Nishali detected the heavy, pungent smell of pitch as she crept towards the center of the camp, cutting through the dwarves of Belgorne as she went. In total, eight dwarves died by her dagger before she approached what she assumed must be the command tent, it being far larger than the others. Distant screams were cut short, the sound of death coming nearer from the west and the east, her second and third Tenths quickly making their way to her position.

Too quickly. Too few screams.

Nishali threw back the flap of the tent to find it empty and dark, save one candle sitting atop a long table, burned nearly to the brass.

Dammit!

Nishali stormed out of the tent just as Lyan and Simmon approached, each bearing pensive looks.

Nishali struggled to ask the question. Lyan answered before she could find the words.

"Four, First Ranger. Please forgive me. We had no warning. The bolts came out of nowhere."

Nishali nodded and turned to Simmon.

"One," he said, through gritted teeth. "You?"

"Two," Nishali replied. "Injuries?"

The two shook their heads.

"Something is odd here, Nishali," began Simmon. "These dwarves—"

"This was an ambush," Nishali finished. "Dohr guessed we would come at night. We must have triggered some alarm."

"Yes, that, but, these..." Simmon gestured towards a dead dwarf, shaking his head in dismay.

"These were not regular soldiers," Lyan continued. "I killed four, and not one stood a chance."

"We are rangers of the Wood, Lyan," said Nishali.

"Yes. But dwarven soldiers are fierce. These—"

Simmon suddenly grabbed Lyan and Nishali, shoving them to the ground. "Get down!"

Nishali fell to the ground, her face smashed into the snow... and pitch.

Oh, dear Father...

~RUN!~

Nishali pulled Lyan and Simmon back to their feet just as the first flaming arrow struck the command tent. In the span of two breaths, it was fully engulfed in flame. Fire rained down upon the rangers, more than a few arrows striking elves, but most setting tents ablaze. The inferno spread quickly between tents, across the ground, up trees, racing the elves to the edges of the camp. Nishali ran as fast as her legs would carry her, her speed enhanced by all her elven magic, as did her rangers, each as fast as any horse at gallop, but they were not fast enough. Screams came from everywhere.

Thirty rangers left Jayne's Valley to avenge Kade Calayaan and his escort on Nishali's orders. Eight would return. Neither

Lyan nor Simmon would be among them.

~

Dawn broke like a snapping twig, its sudden, unwelcome light a vulgarity, an irreverent offense against the grieving elves. The eight trudged north in cold and silence. When they reached Jayne's Valley, Marchion, Kalder, and Macon stood waiting.

Nishali told of the battle, such as it was, as the three listened quietly. When she finished her tale, Sergeant Macon moved to speak, but a look from Sir Marchion stayed his tongue. Captain Kalder either did not catch the hint or ignored it.

"You say these were not soldiers. What does that mean?"

Nishali glared at the dwarf. "Does it matter? They are dead now, whatever they were."

"You're bloody right it matters!" said Macon. "Where were the soldiers, then? Where were the rest of the dwarves? Do you mean to tell me Dohr had them all just cut south like, like—"

"Like the craven bastards they are? Yes! I mean to tell you exactly that! Brave, heroic dwarves! Sending your weak against us to die in fire!"

Kalder took half a step forward. "Now, wait a turn there, Ranger—"

Nishali's dagger was at Kalder's throat before he could finish the thought. Nishali leaned in, whispering.

"Cowards. All of you. To a one. Deny it, so I can name you liar as I cut your throat."

Kalder swallowed. "Says the woman with a dagger to the neck of an unarmed friend."

"Friend? *Friend?* You are no friend, dwarf! Your king brutally defiled and beat a gnome woman, for no reason! Not a soldier, not a hunter... a mother! A wife! An innocent! And what did your people do? Nothing! Your spineless king was then approached with honor, under truce, given time to arrange his affairs before answering to this crime. What did your people do? They murdered seven elves! In cold blood! And now, when we come for him... his soldiers abandon their encampment. They send the weak to ambush us, to die in the place of soldiers, while they run south! The blood of cowards runs in your veins, Captain. Your people are my enemy! *You are my enemy!*" Nishali screamed. Her fingers flexed around the hilt of the dagger.

Sir Marchion stepped forward. A look from Nishali made clear that a second step would bloody her blade. The knight spoke gently. "Nishali Windwillow. You are better than this. The captain is our guest."

Tears welled in Nishali's eyes at the sound of her full name. The last to speak it had been Kade. The knight had reached some dying part of her, but the effect did not last. She could not let it. She began to shake with wrath, taking notice of the pulsing vein in the captain's neck. To his credit, he did not flinch, but the rhythm of his pulse belied his fear.

Marchion's voice filled Nishali's mind. *~Do not do this, First Ranger.~*

Nishali grimaced in disgust. *~Look at him. Look! See how his craven heart hammers as dozens of elven hearts are now still forever!~*

~He is no coward, Nishali. He came to us. He defied his king in the name of what is right.~

Nishali screamed, long and loud into Kalder's face. He shut his eyes against the cut that was coming, but it never did.

Nishali turned to Marchion as a crowd began to form. "They killed your people, knight! Our people! Twice, now! Elves of the Wood! Elves who have committed no evil, in deed nor thought! Fathers and mothers and brothers and sisters of good elves! Until they are avenged, I name you coward as well! Rangers, *on me!*"

Nishali stormed away. Her rangers followed.

XIV: THE LANGUID LADY

'D PREFER YOU REST another few days."

Vincent eyed the wizard. "I'm not tired, Gerald."

"I'd prefer *I* rest another few days."

"And delay a refreshing ride north?" Vincent stood to dress. His knees wobbled.

"Refreshing! Ha! Which part will leave me feeling so revitalized, I wonder? The fresh air? No, Tahr is choking in ash. The mild temperatures? It's cold as a witch's heart out there. Oh, I know, the freedom of the road! Except, wait, no, the roads aren't free. They're being patrolled by a flying pair of jaws born of the fires of Fury."

Eriks Lane entered the room, closing the door behind him when he saw Vincent struggling to pull a fresh shirt over his head. He slapped Gerald on the back. "Jaws that breathe their own fire, don't forget."

"Yes! Exactly!"

Vincent managed the shirt and tied his pants closed. "Good thing we have the most powerful wizard in Tahr protecting us."

"Protecting you? Vincent, I don't think you realize—"

Vincent glared at Gerald with his one good eye.

"Ah. Well. I suppose you do."

"The ride will do you good, Gerald." Vincent sat on the bed to pull on his boots. He made as if to bend over but winced in pain. Lane took a knee and helped Vincent shove a foot into a boot.

Gerald's protestations continued. "I hate the cold. I'm old, Vincent. Look at these wrinkled hands. Feeble, I tell you."

"But think of how much you love being on horseback," deadpanned Lane. He slid the other boot onto Vincent's foot.

"Oh, you're a riot, Lane."

A knock sounded at the door.

"Come in," said Vincent.

Kalindra entered, glancing briefly at Vincent. She averted her gaze, turning to Eriks Lane.

"Any luck?" she asked, her voice unsteady.

Lane shrugged. "I'm sorry, Kalindra."

"About what?" Vincent asked.

"It's nothing," said Kalindra. She and Lane exchanged a glance. An uncomfortable silence followed.

"What is this? Secrets? Am I still running this little clique of ours, or not?" Vincent asked, an edge to his voice.

"Sorry, Vincent," Lane began. "We're having a bit of trouble hiring a guard for the Lady."

Vincent nodded, thinking.

"Well, we would, given everything. How are your stores, Kalindra?"

Kalindra sighed. "Insufficient. But Maris did not want me to—"

Vincent interrupted her. "Lane, you'll be staying behind."

"What?" asked the others, in unison.

"We are the Merchants, are we not? What is our code?"

No one replied.

Vincent's good cheek began to redden. The edge in his voice sharpened. "I asked a question! *What is our code?*"

The three replied as one.

"Fidelity. Sacrifice. Justice. In all things, honor."

Vincent nodded. It had been a long while since he had heard anyone repeat the words of their code. The effect buoyed his spirits. "Thank you. Fidelity sets our course today. I trust no one to protect the Lady, and its ladies, more than you, Lane. Anyone else would try to rob them."

"They might try," Kalindra said. "We're no less lethal than you lot, as you well know."

"As I well know," Vincent agreed. "But this is not a time to test yourself. There's safety in numbers."

Kalindra did not relent. "But Vincent, your mission—"

"My mission is to reach out to the elves. A company of soldiers will make that no easier."

Lane shook his head. "Vincent—"

"He's right, as usual," Gerald said. "We'll be far safer without a company of horse than within one. The only threat I'm concerned about at this point is that damnable dragon, and your soldiers are of no use against it, Lane. Intending no offense."

"None taken."

Vincent continued where Gerald left off. "All you'd accomplish is making us far easier to spot. Pick your two best soldiers and send the rest back to Slater. But I'll ask you a favor, Eriks."

"Anything."

"As soon as we leave, go to Concorde. Release my staff from service. You know where the gold is; give them each a year's salary. Tell them I'll find them when I return, and they may then rejoin my household or not, as they prefer."

"Not all will want to leave," said Gerald. "Some have nowhere to go."

"Then they can stay. As long as they like. Pay them regardless. Gold may not be worth much these days, but it's all I have to give."

"Food," said Lane, the word a powerful note, not needing accompaniment.

Vincent nodded. "I know. And there's nothing I can do about that, not without the elves. I'll trust you to keep everyone alive, Lane. Kalindra, share your stores with Lane and his people as best you can. You'll need to establish rations—"

"I know what to do, Vincent."

Vincent nodded. "Of course you do. But I will ask something of you as well. A favor to me."

"I will take care of my sister. I promise."

Vincent took a deep breath. "And Chaneela. And yourself."

Kalindra nodded, meeting Vincent's gaze for a brief moment before again looking away.

"I'll take care of myself," Chaneela announced, entering the room. "It's you two who need looking after." She threw a cloak around Gerald's neck and handed him another, for Vincent. "Your bags are on horses."

"Thank you, my dear." Gerald leaned in for a kiss. She offered her cheek.

"Hmph. Save the kisses for when you come back."

"We will come back, Chaneela."

"I know that, you old fool! I said *when*, not if!"

"When indeed," Vincent said. He gave his friends a long look. "That'll be it then. Keep an ear to the ground for the others."

No one replied, each knowing in their hearts that had the other Merchants survived the past cycle, they would all be in this room.

Lane offered Vincent an arm, who took it and stood. The soldier offered his friend a drink of wine from a skin.

"Eyes to the sky, Vincent."

Vincent swallowed, handing the wine back. "Eye, you mean."

Lane offered a half-smile, uncomfortable. The room fell silent.

Vincent shook his head. "If you people haven't come up with some good one-eyed-man jokes before I return, I'm going to have to find new friends."

Lane took a long pull from the skin. For several breaths, no one spoke.

"You'll need help," Chaneela said, finally.

"I'm sorry?"

"Finding friends. Finding *anything* with one eye is bound to be a chore."

A spray of red wine flew from Lane's mouth, showering Vincent's fresh white shirt.

Vincent shot a glance at Chaneela before falling into laughter. "It's official. If anything happens to me on the road, I'm leaving the crew in your charge."

"Hmph. As if it isn't already," said Chaneela.

~

The air was colder than even Gerald had predicted, and just as choking. A harsh wind accelerated between buildings, buffeting the pair in sheets of ash as they rode the streets of Mor. Vincent tried to suppress a cough, the act still painful despite how quickly he had healed. The acidic taste and caustic quality of the air was clearly impossible to ignore, however, and he was hacking before they had made more than a few blocks.

"Sir! A bit of food, yes?"

The ash-covered boy appeared benign, but Vincent knew his look. Or, rather, the Merchant did. If they stopped, they'd be set upon by a dozen thieves or more.

"Fresh out, kid. Move along."

The boy jogged along beside the riders. "Aw, come on, just a nibble. Look how fat those bags are!"

Vincent pulled down his hood. The boy came to a sliding stop, gaping. Vincent slowed his horse for effect. "Yes. Fat with the meat of streeters! I said move along!"

"Aaaaahhh! I'm sorry!" The boy ran like he had been set afire.

Vincent pulled his horse back to Gerald's side.

"That was effective," Gerald quipped.

Vincent began to laugh, but his laugh became a cough, then a fit, bending him over the saddle horn.

"Might want to reconsider this, Vincent."

Vincent wiped his mouth. Specks of red dotted his hand.

"And let you put your feet up at the Lady while the world collapses around us? You'd like that, wouldn't you?"

"I'd like it just fine, thank you."

Vincent coughed again. "I'm not meeting my end like that. And neither are you."

"Instead you'll meet it coughing up a lung on the side of the road. An inspired plan."

"Stop harassing me and cast me a spell or something."

"I can dull your pain, but I'll dull your senses, as well. The way you're sitting in that saddle, I'm not so sure that's a good idea."

"It's a new horse, that's all," Vincent lied.

"It's that, yes. But this air is no good for burned lungs."

"Just cast the spell, Gerald."

"*Just cast the spell, Gerald*'," the wizard mocked. "If I had a scale for every time you told me that—"

Vincent pulled his horse to a stop. "You'd still be hungry. Now hurry it up."

"Fine. Stay still."

A wave of euphoria washed over Vincent. His vision swam for a moment while he acclimatized to the spell.

"Better?"

Vincent took a deep breath. "Much. Tell me, why don't you just walk around casting this on yourself all the time? It feels wonderful."

Gerald urged his horse forward. "Who says I don't?"

"Very funny."

"Wasn't joking. How do you think I get around like I do, at my age?"

"I thought you were just particularly virile."

"I am, thank you. But my knees are a disaster."

"Well, then you should be glad to be off them for a few days."

"Hips aren't much better." Gerald's tone changed. "Eyes up. Moat bridge ahead."

"You ever wonder why they built a moat inside the walls? Seems pretty dumb to me."

"The walls went up after, Vincent."

"Well, they should have put the walls up first. Dug the moat after."

Gerald cocked his head. "Centuries after. We've discussed this before."

"Or I guess it doesn't matter what order they built them, does it? Ha! They could have dug another moat *outside* the walls."

"Certainly," Gerald jibed. "And used the water from the first one."

"Exactly!"

Gerald smiled, and Vincent saw it. Vincent understood—he was making little sense. Everything felt... fluffy. Like a dream of clouds. He decided it would be best to ride in silence and enjoy the lack of pain for a while.

They crossed the ridiculous inner moat and passed the gates unchallenged. There was no one to man them, Vincent knew. A few would-be thieves advanced here and there, but something about the riding pair made clear that there were easier targets to be had. Vincent considered how often that was the case when he rode with Gerald, deciding that the wizard must have regularly employed some magic to dissuade malefactors.

What a wonder, to possess such power, Vincent thought, not for the first time. No sooner did he have the thought, however, than did he question the morality of its use. Gerald's power was, largely, mundane magic, the sort of thing one could learn at Kehrlia, given patience and talent. Certainly, he was exceptionally gifted with its use. Vincent's very life, however, was proof that the wizard dipped his brush in darker paints. Vincent had pushed the thought from his mind repeatedly since the day Gerald brought him back, and he decided to do so again. He recalled the line of a poem his mother often recited when he was a boy:

A step will mar the road once placed;

No deed of man can be erased.

Vincent had little time to ponder the matter in any case. They came upon what was once the Morline Bridge near to midday.

"Sweet Lor, what happened here?" Vincent asked rhetorically. The answer was obvious: the dragon.

A heavy blanket of snow and ash shrouded the worst of the carnage, but frozen limbs and white faces still lay exposed here and there. The Morline ran like sludge, all ash and ice, breaking against and over protruding blocks of stone that were once the great bridge.

The two stood on horseback silently for a turn until Gerald spoke.

"No one came for them."

"Who would?" Vincent asked. "Bleeding tower lackeys. They loved only power. They won't be missed."

Gerald cast Vincent an icy glance.

"I'm sorry. That was—"

"You do not know, Vincent. You cannot know. To discover you have command of the elements, to whatever small degree, is to feel... it is as if you might someday gain the keys to all doors. More. Like you can reshape the very world. No one is immune to the lure of such power. No one. These..." Gerald looked around. "These were children once. Children who discovered they could manipulate the very fabric of existence. Children who were broken, remade in Sartean D'Avers image, and set against one another as he dangled the next key." Gerald turned again to face Vincent. "Kehrlia was once glorious, my friend, as were its works. As were its wizards."

"I am sorry. Truly. I spoke unkindly. Kehrlia can be glorious again. You can make it so."

"Me? Please. I can do no such thing."

"You defied him, Gerald. You left Kehrlia. You resisted the wicked uses of your craft."

Gerald glanced towards Vincent's chest. Vincent could swear he felt the wizard's eyes trace the scar. "Did I?"

Vincent did not reply. He did not need to.

Gerald dismounted his horse. "Wait here."

Vincent waited and watched as Gerald made for the riverbank. He began to gesture wildly before a large chunk of stone from the bridge. A turn passed, then another. Vincent began to think Gerald had lost his mind when the stone suddenly shattered into a thousand pieces, each the shape and size of a standard wooden plank.

"Walk the horses down! Hurry!"

Vincent heard Gerald chanting as he neared, watched as his gesticulations became more exaggerated. The planks of stone began to shift position, locking into place... Gerald was making a bridge! By the time Vincent arrived with the horses, the task was complete.

"Get them across. Can't hold it long. And be careful... it will be slippery."

Vincent wasted no time. The horses shied at first, but he managed to walk them atop the stone. They crossed quickly. When they all reached the northern bank, Gerald followed at a jog.

When Gerald reached the bank, Vincent expected him to drop the spell and the stones would fall into the river. Instead, he turned. His casting intensified.

Vincent watched in awe as words began to etch themselves onto the stones. *Names.* Beneath each name, the symbol of the Tower of Kehrlia appeared as well, as if chiseled by the most expert mason. One by one, the stones flew upwards and away, dozens, in all directions, some to positions close by, some a hundred paces away or more. When the last stone found a position beside the bridge, Gerald raised his hands high above his head, turned his palms downwards, and brought them down with a primal cry. The wizard fell to his knees.

The gravestones set themselves deep into the ground, each at the place where its respective Incantor of Kehrlia fell. Turns passed in silence. Vincent watched as tears began to freeze on his friend's cheeks.

Vincent said nothing. After a time, he placed a hand on Gerald's shoulder. The wizard nodded and stood.

The two friends mounted their horses and rode north.

XV: FURY

**Y**OU HAVE TO let me, Aria."

"No. They'll come back."

"And they'll leave again. They can't get in."

Aria shook her head, forgetting Lucan could not see her. "I cannot die like that. Not here. Not to those things."

"Which is why I have to heal you. We do not die here, Aria. You know that."

Aria took a shaking, labored breath. "I know what I saw in a dream. No more."

"It was real. It *will* be real."

"How can you know?"

Lucan did not respond for a long moment.

"I know."

Aria shifted position, the hard, cold floor of the iron tunnel paining her. She inhaled sharply. Moving hurt more.

"I'm doing it. Help me or don't."

"Lucan, don't—"

Aria felt the warmth of Lucan's hand on her knee, the sensation somehow of more consequence than the healing that followed. She placed her hand atop his, and the two shared their magic.

Her ankle throbbed with each beat of her heart, with each beat of Lucan's, the pain all but overwhelming. As their hearts fell into time, Aria knew what each beat revealed to the street hustler from Mor. The notion frightened her nearly as much as the creatures their magic would call. Nearly.

Again, I sense nothing from him. Nothing at all.

Aria had shared her magic with countless others over the years. The procedure was common among those of her Order, and always, each time, without single exception, the act was one of total vulnerability, a communion of mutual exposure, the unrestrained display of one's innermost feelings. Yet what she felt from Lucan... power, yes, and intent... he wanted very much to heal her, as was necessary for such magic to be effective, but the heart of the man remained guarded, hidden away, as if behind a locked door. The magic should not work without his honesty; her years training at the Grove taught this; years spent, chiefly, in learning to open oneself to such things. Its absence incited suspicion in Aria, a feeling to which Lucan must now be privy.

"You hide from me."

The distant sound of scraping claws sent a chill down Aria's spine.

"No," said Lucan softly. "Never that."

The magic Lucan sent deepened then, widened, hastened... more power than Aria had ever felt, save that which she was given by Lady Lor. More even than what she had shared with Pheonaris. Yet it was an empty sort of power, bereft of emotion... *No. Not empty. Not hollow. Singular?*

A single droplet of sweat—

Not sweat, it is too cool here.

—splashed against Aria's shin.

Pure?

"Then why—"

"Please do not ask me, Aria. Never ask me."

The howls returned. Lucan's power doubled. The sensation was an ecstasy.

"Oh, Lucan..." Aria reached for his face. He pulled away. Her ankle was healed.

"We need to fight again," Lucan said, his tone cool.

"Fire?" Aria asked, her head still spinning as she reached for her magic.

"We'll see." Lucan lit an orb. It hovered above them, deep violet in hue. "Can you stand?"

Aria nodded. "Maybe we should move back. So they don't see us."

"They know we're here. We need to see them."

Aria shuddered. "In case something new comes."

"In case something new comes."

The mewling, screeching horde drew nearer.

"You have to tell me something, Lucan. Make me understand."

Lucan remained silent.

"You are different since the Eyre."

"Yes." He replied quickly.

Louder. Closer. Aria gathered her magic.

"Since you were with Lady Kal."

At this Lucan turned, eyeing Aria briefly. Over his shoulder, specks of yellow light through the iron bars pulled her gaze forward.

"Same as before!" she yelled. "Fire, now!"

The minions of Fury threw themselves with hateful abandon

at the bars of Lady Cindra's iron prison, screaming, yowling, baying in desperation as Aria and Lucan bathed them in sorcerous fire. They broke against the flames like a river dammed, wasting themselves into smoldering pools of ichor and bone. Still, they came. Clawed arms reached through gaps in the crude bars, scorched upon contact with the now-glowing metal. Still, they came. A pool of viscous, acidic, blackened liquid boiled flesh from bone as they scrambled for purchase. Glowing eyes were extinguished, darkened by death. Still, they came.

"Aria! The bars!"

Aria saw. In the center, the glowing bars began to sag inwards. Near the floor, acid began to dissolve the iron. It would take time, but eventually, the bars would fail.

"They won't hold! We have to move back!" Aria yelled.

"Back? To where?"

Aria ceased her flaming deluge. "The other tunnel!"

"Cindra blocked it off!"

"Just move, dammit!" Aria grabbed Lucan by the sleeve, pulling him behind her. The two began running up the tunnel. Lucan lit another orb, sending it forward.

Aria's heart hammered. Terror took hold as the situation became clear. "We have to get out, Luc! When they realize the bars are failing, they'll send everything they have!"

~EVERYTHING, LIESPEAKER? YOU ARE A FOOL. WE ARE UNCOUNTABLE. YOUR SECOND DEATH COMES SOON.~

Second death?

"We are not dead!"

~YOU ARE IN MY DOMAIN. NONE COME HERE BUT THROUGH DEATH.~

Lucan and Aria came to a sliding stop before another set of bars, these too shaped by Cindra to block their previous escape. Aria moved to speak, but Lucan put a hand over her mouth.

"Listen to me," he whispered, barely loud enough to hear. "It's fear they track. Love. Your heart. You must not feel in this place! You must only choose!"

"Choose? Choose what?"

"Your next action, no more."

"How can you know this?"

"I just know!" Lucan hissed. "Now think with me. What would Cindra do?"

Aria was familiar with the process of centering herself, though doing so in the fresh air was far easier. A deep breath and a quiet thought were all she would need, but here, it was all she could do to keep breathing at all. Her thoughts were a chaotic tangle.

"Use your will, Aria. As the Lady taught us."

My will. Yes. Aria understood. *Sorcery. I am a sorcerer. My magic is a product of my will. If I will it, it will be.*

"Concentrate," Lucan whispered.

Concentrate. My will. Gah, I cannot! My mind is in disorder! Disorder.

A thought formed. The screeches and howls of their foes began to diminish. A chill ran down Aria's spine.

"Luc. He said 'we'."

"What?"

" 'We'. He said, '*We* are uncountable.'"

"Why is that significant?"

"I don't know."

"Yes, you do. You sense something."

"I do. It's right there..."

"Think. Trust your mind to do its job. *Will* it to. You know something. What do you know?"

Aria shook her head. "This magic, Luc. It's so foreign to me."

"Listen to me. I think I understand this. You have to let go. All the way. Unlearn what you think you know. Whatever your elven power, this is greater. Use it. Use your will to clear your mind."

Aria forced a deep breath.

"'We'," Lucan pressed. "He said 'We'. Why does that mean something to you?"

"Well, it just doesn't make sense. He is not..." Aria glanced down the tunnel, "one of these."

Lucan frowned. "He isn't? What is he, then?"

Aria eyed Lucan. "You do not know?"

Lucan shook his head.

"He is the Hand of Disorder. Or, well, at least... he should be..."

"I don't know what that means."

Aria continued. "Fury is *his* domain, but he would never deign to put himself in parity with these creatures. He does not see himself as mortal, let alone something akin to these mindless beasts. It makes no sense."

"Hmm. Unless you're wrong."

"I'm not wrong, Lucan. I know who he is. I might be one of only a few alive who do."

"How? How do you know that? Explain."

Aria paused before responding. "I cannot."

"You mean you will not."

"Call it what you like. The knowledge is a duty of my station. I will not betray an oath."

"Your station?"

"As Princess of Thornwood. Have you forgotten that already?"

"I suppose I had. Seems like a minor thing, considering."

"Minor?"

"We're in Fury, Aria. *Fury*. Devils and all. The place adults made up to scare us into behaving."

"Fury is no fiction, Lucan."

"Well, that's all it ever has been to me. Look, you—"

"Lucan, a part of my knowledge is rooted in faith. There are things I've been taught. I... I do not understand them all, but they are things I know to be true, and I cannot make you believe."

Lucan stared into the darkness for a long moment.

"Very well."

"Very well, what?"

"Very well, I'll trust what you say and not question you. But my faith is in *you*, Aria, not whatever gods—"

"Listen."

Lucan listened.

"They've gone. You were right. But how? How can you know anything about this place when you never even believed it existed?"

Lucan shrugged. "A guess. Maybe an instinct, I don't know. It just... it seems like the beasts can sense feeling. Makes sense, doesn't it? Probably nothing but rage down here. Anything different must stand out."

Aria nodded, agreeing. "The more frightened we were, the worse things got."

"That, and..." Lucan hesitated.

"When you healed me."

Lucan nodded, clearly anxious to move past Aria's meaning. "Cindra said it was a beacon, but she couldn't have meant magic. Not simple magic, at least. It's taking magic just to breathe. If that was what drew them, we'd be dead already."

"Assuming we're not."

"We're not."

"Are you sure?"

Lucan nodded. "I'm sure. I keep telling you. This is not the end. In any case, we'll not want to end up that way. What do we do?"

Aria sighed, unwilling to challenge Lucan's belief again. She thought for a moment. "I think we start with deciding what we *can* do."

Lucan smirked, a ridiculous, haughty, inappropriate expression, given their circumstances. "We're sorcerers. Easier to list what we can't do."

Arrogant fool.

I love him.

A cackling shriek echoed through the tunnels.

"Dammit!" Aria said. "That was me. Sorry. Come on, I have an idea." Aria pulled Lucan back from the bars and led him back down the tunnel.

"Where are we going?"

"We have to figure out where the walls are weak. Burn through. Find another tunnel. Put a hand on the wall, like me. See what you can feel."

"I feel cold iron. And rust."

"I thought we were sorcerers," Aria replied, trying her own

smirk. "We can't see through a bit of metal?"

"Ah, now *that's* an idea. Better hurry, though. They'll be back soon."

"Well, if you can manage to be quiet for a turn..."

Lucan smiled at Aria and turned to his side of the tunnel.

Aria had no idea what she was doing, but she felt like it could be done. *Just a matter of will.* Try as she might however, no amount of will allowed her to see anything but the darkness in front of her.

Lucan fared no better. "Nothing," he said.

"Me neither."

"Maybe we're doing it wrong."

"Clearly."

"No," Lucan said. "I mean, I have quite a bit of experience with metal. Iron, in particular. Iron *locks*, specifically."

"I'm not sure I want to know this."

"You don't. But there are four ways to open an iron lock without a key. You pick it, you get a big, strong, long iron bar and pry it, you bash the Fury out of it with a hammer, or, in winter, you freeze it."

"Freeze it?"

"Yep. A thimble of hot water in the keyhole and let Brother Winter do his work. The water expands as it freezes, and if you're lucky, the lock will snap right open."

"But we don't have a door."

"Sure we do. We just don't know where it is." Lucan took Aria's hand in his own and moved it to the wall. "There. Feel that little crack? Who knows how deep it goes?"

"That's not much of a crack."

"Freeze some water inside it, it might be bigger than you think."

Aria was skeptical. "Assuming you're right, we don't have any water."

"There's water everywhere. Even in this awful air. There has to be; Cindra's hands were caked in frost after her last spell. We just have to, I don't know, pull it out, get it into the cracks, and freeze it."

"I don't know, Lucan—"

"Watch."

Lucan closed his eyes and held his hands out before him, cupped together. Aria could see he was concentrating, gathering his will. His brow furrowed as he strained to do... something. A few moments later, Lucan opened his hands.

"See!"

A thimbleful of water, perhaps two, rested in Lucan's hands.

"Go ahead," he said. Aria brought his hands to her lips and drank. Salty, but good. She had been so afraid for so long that she forgot how thirsty she was.

"Clever, but we'll need a whole lot more than that."

Lucan sighed. "That wasn't very easy. Maybe if you help—"

The sound of an explosion, from somewhere, rumbled through the tunnels. *The others.* Flakes of loosened rust fell down on the pair from above. A memory from Lady Lor's life flashed in her mind... Airies singing, shaping a great tree...

"I have a better idea."

Aria placed both hands on the wall. She sent a deep, powerful, tone into the iron, its frequency too low to hear. More rust fell from the walls and ceiling. The tunnel began to vibrate. She let her mind's eye follow the waves of sound into the walls, across the floors, through empty caverns... when she finally gained control of the spell, she began to sense where the iron and stone of Fury was... and was not.

"It's working! Help me!"

Lucan placed a hand on Aria's shoulder and fed her his own power. The range of their sonic vision increased, wider and further. Aria could see a vein of empty space running from just beyond the cavern where they had last been with the others, far deeper into the ground, left, right, then up, then a long, long drop...

Lucan gasped. "Oh, wow... I can see it!"

"Memorize it! That's our way out!"

"I don't think that will get us out, Ar—"

~YOU SEEK ME, LIESPEAKER? COME, THEN. PLAY WITH ME.~

Aria stepped back from the wall, cutting the flow of magic. Her voice bore an edge of determination. "We have to get through those bars."

"*Through* the bars? Are you out of your mind? That's where they're coming from!"

Aria pulled Lucan close and kissed him. Their lips met violently, too quickly for Aria to know whether Lucan might have kissed her back, but she did not care. The kiss was not for him. "You said it yourself, Luc. This is not the end. I trust you."

Aria turned and ran down the tunnel, not entirely sure if she meant what she had just said, but she knew this much: if they were to make their way through these tunnels, they would first need to abandon all fear.

XVI: HIGHMORLAND

HAT WAS that?" Emma asked, jumping to her feet. Mila rushed to the door.

"Which way is the privy?"

"Around the cabin to the right," said Emma, her voice quaking. "Behind the barn. Was that—"

"I'll be right back."

Mila stepped out into the cold night to find the light of the Twins mostly obscured by Fang's belching discharge, adequate only to cast the snowy landscape in hues of darkest violet. She listened for a moment, hearing nothing, the forest utterly devoid of sound, even her own next crunching steps muted and hushed. She stepped off the porch to the right, falling into a knee-high drift of snow and ash. *Dammit.* She thought to blast the drift away with a spell, but Kalashagon had already sensed her; more magic, she assumed, would only help guide him. A barn lay before her. Mila clambered forward, high-stepping through the deep snow. After a few clumsy steps her feet found the worn path to the privy. Rays of light from what must have been Fillip's lantern flickered on the far side of the dark building.

"Fillip! Can you hear me?"

A gust of icy air buffeted the sorceress. Another. The third nearly knocked her from her feet.

The weight of the dragon came crashing down on the barn. Mila had no time to cry out before Fillip's own screams shredded the silence of the night. They lasted but a breath. The mournful wail from inside the cabin lasted far longer.

The door to the cabin flew open, slamming against the building. Mila turned to see snow cascade from the roof as Emma spilled out onto the porch. The woman rounded the corner of the cabin, still wailing, loud and long, her sharp keening heavy with will and resolve, as if the force of her cries might undo what had just been done. Behind her, Mila could hear Kalashagon tearing through the beams and walls of the barn, thrashing violently, no doubt clearing a path towards her, but she could bear neither to look nor act. Her eyes and heart sought only Emma. The light was insufficient for the sorceress to see the expression on the old woman's face, but it did not matter. In her mind's eye, she saw the mask of horror etched there as if it were brightest noonday.

Mila stood motionless as the thrashing stopped and Emma pushed past her on the path. She did not immediately turn, her eyes still fixed in the direction of the cabin, seeing nothing, dazed by the dawning of one ineffable truth: all goodness, if there ever had been such a thing, had truly gone from the world.

A booming step turned her head reflexively. Twenty paces separated her and the mighty jaws of Kalashagon, and between them, the still-hollering widow of Fillip Manchele, former innmaster and purveyor of fine candles, honey, and honey-baked goods cursed the beast to Fury.

Mila readied a spell to protect the woman, to pull her back to safety, but the dragon was far too fast. Kalashagon lunged forward and snatched the woman from her feet as a bird might snatch a fish from water, tossing his head back, mercifully swallowing her whole.

When the dragon brought his head down again, Mila saw a hint of orange light begin to glow at the back of his throat. The thick, wafting scent of sulfur nearly gagged her. Her emerald eyes began to emit a glow of their own; she knew what came next and did not delay.

The casting came naturally, instinctively, cascades and sheets of snow flowing in from all directions, concentrated shards of ice flowing out of the sorceress as if she were a living blizzard. All the frozen might of her magic, however, melted upon clashing with Kalashagon's river of flame. She circled left; the dragon circled right. With a roar, Kalashagon's deluge of fire doubled in power; with a cry of rage, Mila met its intensity. The battle raged for a full turn, longer, but Mila had no illusions after the scene at the bridge. Kalashagon toyed with her. She would need more power. Far more.

My gems.

She had not tried the spell since Kehrlia. She had never tried it without the stored power of a gem. It would either work, or she would not live long enough to know it failed.

With a flourish and in a blink, Mila vanished, appearing again in the cabin. *Whew.* She could see the glow of dragonfire through the window as she quickly tied her cloak around her neck. When the light went out, Kalashagon roared.

~You hide from me, witch? We have not yet begun to play!~

She withdrew two gems from her pocket. Any would do but the largest, the diamond, which she would keep in reserve, for now, hoping beyond hope that she would not need it. She chose her two rubies and quickly probed them, pleased to discover both filled to bursting with concentrated magic. *Perfect.* In another blink, Mila appeared behind the dragon, just off his right hind leg, where his missing right eye would prevent him from glimpsing her. She took the gems in each fist and thrust her hands forward with a loathsome scream.

"You're damned right we haven't!"

An explosion of boiling steam caught the dragon wholly off guard, blasting him into a roll to his left. As he struggled to gain his footing, Mila vanished again, appearing directly behind him. Another blast. Blink, to the right. Another. Blink. Another.

The gems were nearly empty, but Mila had done what was needed. Clouds of steam surrounded the confused and battered Kalashagon, and a simple spell froze the droplets of water in place. She could not see beyond the thick clouds... and so neither could the dragon. She dropped the rubies in the snow along with a third gem from her pocket—one of two remaining sapphires—and, using the last of the stored power in the rubies, she blinked away again, this time hundreds of yards to the north.

Mila's heart hammered as she ducked behind a tree, waiting in silence for some sign that Kalashagon had chosen a direction. Her last spell came wholly from the rubies; there would be no residue of magic, she hoped, clinging to her when she reappeared. If she could only just keep herself hidden, for just a while—

~Again, you hide. So unworthy of a witch of your power.~

Now the game would begin.

~Is that so? Well then, come punish me, mighty dragon.~

Mila waited in silence. She was rewarded by a roar moments later. He had found the sapphire.

~Clever girl.~

~Don't you think? You won't find me now, beast.~

And he would not, at least not by tracing her magic, or so she hoped. The sapphire in her pocket would quietly convey her thoughts to the other she had left behind. It, in turn, would amplify those thoughts a hundredfold, making it near impossible to determine her location. Its magic would, hopefully, drown out any inadvertent signals she herself sent. At least as long as the magic held.

~I should shatter your little trinket, witch. Crush it between my fangs and come find you.~

Mila conveyed a mirthless laugh through the gem.

~Be my guest.~

She should have said nothing. She should have allowed the dragon to try—the explosion would be heard for miles—but her hatred for the beast got the better of her. *Let's see how he likes being mocked.*

~Very well. I will play this game with you, witch. For now. It is a good game.~

~I am no witch.~

~Still you deny it? Poor little witch. Why do you resist your nature? Why deny the truth of what you are?~

~You do not define what I am, devil.~

~Devil? Please. No devil in Fury can match my potency. No hundred devils. But what you say is true. I do not define you. Your actions do, Mila Felsin. Or would you prefer Freya? No, it does not suit you, does it?~

~You have no right to use that name! How do you know me?! Speak true!~

~I always speak true, little witch. Lies are the refuge of the weak. Why might I lie? None can defeat me. I require no guile nor

deception to protect me. It is the one promise I will make you: in the hours you have left alive, you shall hear no lie from me.~

~A promise? You speak like a great liar, dragon. I have known many.~

~Believe what you will. You know nothing of me. But I know a great deal about you. All there is. My master has taught me. Told me of your secrets, he has.~

Mila fumed at the thought of this beast knowing anything at all about her. No one did! No one alive! *Save Earl*, she reminded herself. But even he knew so very, very little. She would not, however, give Kalashagon the satisfaction of realizing how much his familiarity offended her.

~Your master, you say. So, you are but a slave, then?~

A slight pause before the dragon replied told her all she needed to know on the subject.

~I am far more than a slave, witch.~

~But a slave nonetheless. Who is your master, slave?~

~Do you truly not know? Why do you ask foolish questions? Come now. You will bore me of this game.~

Mila did know. This was a beast of Fury, from the Hand of Disorder's own realm.

~Fine. Then tell me this: why are you here? Why chase me, of all the people in Tahr?~

~Another boring question. One you should be able to answer without my help.~

~Very well. A more interesting one, then. Why the rest?~
Silence.

~Why these two, this old man, this old woman. They have done you no harm!~

~*I must eat, witch. I am not unlike you in this.*~

~*You said you would not lie to me.*~

~*I do not!*~

Mila sensed the dragon's rage at the accusation. This, too, told her much.

~*I saw the carnage you left on the road. You didn't eat a tenth of the people you killed.*~

~*I said that I must eat. I did not say it is my only reason for killing your kind. I did not lie to you.*~

Again... the insistence at his own honesty. Why? Does this beast actually possess some code of honor? Surely not.

~*Very well. You did not lie. But you did not tell the whole truth.*~

~*Nor must I, witch.*~

~*No. But what is the harm in telling me? As you say, none can defeat you. You need not deceive. Tell me why you kill as you do.*~

~*You seek to manipulate me. I am no fool.*~

A pause.

~*But I will tell you, because it is as you say. I need not bother to deceive. I kill your kind, Mila Felsin, because you are evil.*~

Mila sat in silence, thoroughly baffled by the dragon's preposterous reply.

~*You can't be serious.*~

~*Do not again question my words, witch, or when I kill you I will spend days at the task!*~

Mila had never sensed such wrath, not in all her life. Not even her own.

~*Forgive me,*~ she said, immediately ashamed to be

apologizing to the beast, but she knew then with certainty that he spoke to her the truth, as he believed it, and to accuse him of falsehood in this game was, somehow, bad form.

~It does not matter if I forgive you. You will be dead soon, witch.~

Mila continued. *~You must understand my perspective. You are born, what, of the fires of Fury? Willing slave to the master of the very prison to which all evil beings are sent upon death? You rise from the mouth of Fang and wreak death and havoc on the world. How can——~*

~And what of you, witch? What have you done? How many have died for your ambition, for your meaningless campaign of revenge?~

~Those are my sins. You would not understand——~

~Your sins? They are the sins of humanity, repeated over and over throughout the ages, without end. I understand perfectly, witch. I have seen the flow of souls into Fury. I have counted the horrors your kind commit. For a thousand years I have sampled the taint of humanity. I know its flavor. I tasted it on these two, these whose innocence you foolishly proclaim. It is you who do not understand!~

Mila made no reply for several turns as she huddled in the cold beneath a pine. She could not argue for humanity. Certainly not for her own. Who was innocent, truly? Her parents? She could not say. What crimes might they have committed? What harms might they have been responsible for? Darrin, the man who took her in, the man who might have become a father, only to seek to defile her when she came of age? No. Her peers at Kehrlia? The very embodiment of selfish ambition. Who, then? Who had she ever met, in all her life, who she could name innocent and true?

An image of Earl flashed in Mila's mind.

Some. Some are.

~There are good people in this world.~

~Show me one, so that I might taste them and tell you if you speak true.~

Bastard. Why does he hate us all so? Why does his hatred seem so... so personal?

~There is more.~

~Why must there be more? Are the truths I have told you insufficient?~

~They are. Even if what you say is true——~

~It is.~

~Fine. Assuming that, why do you care? All-powerful as you are, why trouble yourself with the morality of humanity?~

~I do as my master commands me. It is why I am here.~

~No. There is more.~

~Why? Why must there be more? Do not presume to know me, witch! I grow tired of this game!~

Mila barely had time to sense the change in the air before the dragon crashed down through the pines. She was not surprised he had found her. She was ready.

~Now you die, witch.~

Mila stood, holding the fist-sized diamond before her.

"Then we both die!"

XVII: THE GRAND BARRACKS

’M GOING TO NEED you to stay here, miss...?”

“Nia.”

General Slater regarded the woman. “Just Nia.”

Nia nodded. “Or Nia of the sea, if you prefer.”

“Thought as much.”

Nia frowned. “Why?”

“Your accent. East or west?”

“East,” Nia replied. “Far as the crags.”

Slater’s eyes widened. “The crags? Damn. Rough country.”

Nia shrugged.

“Fishmonger’s daughter, then?”

Nia was already tiring of standing and answering questions, but she understood.

“My father was a bait man.”

Slater nodded slowly. The implication was clear: she was the daughter of a seaslave.

“Was?”

Nia sighed. “I’m not sure anymore.”

“Under whom?”

Nia shrugged. “No idea. Some waterlord.”

Slater waited. Nia took a breath, steadying herself.

“Kehrlia took me when I was eight, maybe. After that—”

Slater interrupted, relenting a bit. “Your father should be well off then, miss Nia. As should your... mother?”

Nia nodded. "And four siblings."

"I'll guess you were the oldest."

"I was. I am."

Slater chewed a lip for a moment. "They'll be well off," he repeated eventually. "Whatever might have been true about Kehrlia, the bastards weren't cheap."

Weren't. The word stunned Nia, and Slater saw it.

"You don't know."

Nia did her best to hide her shock. She failed.

"What *do* you know?"

Nia chose her next words carefully. "I suppose not much. I've been in fasting."

Slater frowned. "I thought you said you didn't serve Kal."

Nia's expression hardened. "I don't. But neither can I conjure food from thin air."

"Hmph. Funny you bring that up."

"I'm sorry?"

"Later. Before I say more, how do I know this isn't all just some elaborate swindle?"

Nia offered a thin smile. "I guess you don't."

"I guess I don't. Sit." Slater motioned towards a chair and waved to a soldier. "Sergeant, some breakfast for our guest."

The man replied crisply. "Right away, sir. Anything for you?"

"Just more tea. Maybe an egg."

Nia watched as the soldier quickly moved to follow the order. "Well disciplined," she commented.

Slater frowned. "Unlike you, clearly."

"Excuse me?"

"My staff follow orders. You say you were ordered here to

carry out a mission. You didn't. Why should I trust a woman who betrays her orders?"

Nia glanced downwards, then back to the general.

"Well?"

"All right. You shouldn't. But I'm not asking you to, General. You can do what you like with what I've told you. My reasons are my own." Nia shifted in her chair. "I appreciate the offer of breakfast, but—"

"But you'll sit there and eat it. As I said, I'm going to need you to stay here."

Nia's lips thinned. "You cannot hold me here, sir."

"This is my barracks, miss. I most certainly—"

"You misunderstand. You *can* not. I graduated Kehrlia at the top of my class. If what you say is true and the Incantors are no more, there's no one in this building that can keep me from leaving."

Slater sat back, crossing his arms. The two glared at one another for an uncomfortably long time.

"That's the problem with you lot," he began. "You think you're above regular folk. Just because—"

"No, I did not mean—"

"I'm not finished. Just because you can do a thing does not mean you have the right to. You spell my men. You come here into my barracks with this... thing. You throw it down here like I should be grateful you didn't use it to enslave me. Young lady, I'm a *general.* I've earned my seat at this table through a lifetime of dedication to Mor. And you sit here like you belong here. Why? Because you can? That's no reason. I lead an *army.* What do you think I could do with it, if I saw fit to misuse it?"

Nia was taken aback by the tirade, but she answered the rhetorical question.

"Anything you wanted, I suppose."

"*Any damned thing I wanted.* That's exactly right. Especially now. And you know what? It's about damned time I do. Halsen dies, Sartean wants the throne. Sartean dies, now the Daughters want it. You spell weavers are a blight."

"Now, wait a turn, General, I came in here—"

"Yeah, you came here to warn me. Maybe. Well, let's find out. You want to help me? Then you sit there, you eat your breakfast, and you answer my questions. After that, you go where in Fury I ask you to go, and you help where I tell you we need it. Otherwise, you can slink your hungry arse back to Mother, and I'll see you soon enough. I might not have the men here in the barracks to stop you from leaving, but you can bet your last scale I've got the men to take the Temple."

Nia sat deflated. Not since her first year at Kehrlia had she been spoken to in such a manner by anyone but a more senior Incantor, or later, by more senior Daughters. In her world, for so many years, power dictated authority. Magical power, specifically. She could burn this man to ash, snap his bones like twigs. She knew it, and he knew it. Yet there he sat, glowering at her, waiting for her to act without a shred of fear.

"Well?" he pressed.

Nia straightened. "Do you mean to?" she asked.

"Do I mean to what?"

"To take the Temple?"

Slater hesitated, nostrils flaring. "Is everything you told me today true? I swear to Lor, if you're lying—"

"It's true, General. Every word."

The general's eyes held Nia's fast as the sergeant returned with two plates, one with a single boiled egg, the other near overflowing with fried eggs, sausage, and fresh bread. He held her gaze as the sergeant poured the tea. He did not blink when asked if there would be anything else. The sergeant moved on, and Slater nodded. "Then yes, Nia of the sea. I intend to take the Temple. In fact I have little choice."

Nia returned the nod. "Then let's have breakfast."

Slater narrowed his eyes.

Nia smiled. "By your leave, of course."

The two ate a long breakfast, longer than Nia would have had it. She was starving, but she stopped to answer Slater's questions as he asked them. Soldiers came and went, Slater issued various orders, few of which she understood. When she had satisfied him with answers, he brought her up to speed on much that had happened in Mor in recent days, the first battle with the dragon at Kehrlia, the second at the Morline. There was a plan, Slater said, to address the food scarcity in Mor, but it was magical in nature, and he admitted understanding little of it. Now that Kehrlia had fallen, the help of the elves would be crucial, he said. Nia nodded, agreeing that whatever the plan, elven magic would certainly be useful.

"It's a damned shame your lot want to use this chaos for their own ends," he said. "They could be a lot of help."

Nia shook her head. "You really don't understand the Daughters, do you?"

"I suppose not."

"They're fanatics, General."

"I gather that much."

"I'm not sure you do, or at least you don't understand what they're fanatical about. They worship Kal. The god of death. With all sincerity, most of them. To them, there's nothing more divine than a good famine. Or a dragon. Or chaos itself. They believe their power stems from the degree to which they serve him—"

"Does it?"

Nia hesitated.

"Don't beat around it. Are the gods real? Do you know, one way or the other?"

Nia recalled a spell she had once seen, cast by the Mother, just after another Daughter had gone missing. The Daughter was out of favor. She was never seen again. But the power of that spell... and then the amulet, the sheer weight of the thing...

"I cannot say. Not for certain. But I suspect they are."

Slater nodded. His manner remained sure, though his complexion paled.

"I've seen things, General. Even participated in them. There's power out there that's beyond what I can explain."

"Well, that's not saying much. I can't explain a bit of what you snake charmers do."

"But you know it's real."

Slater nodded. "Yeah. I guess I do."

Nia recognized the expression on Slater's face. She had felt it on her own once, years before, when she came to realize there truly was more to life, and to magic, than what she had learned at Kehrlia. Far more. The recognition was sobering, as it bore repercussions about one's own mortality, one's standing in the world, how one's life might be measured on Lor's ethereal scales, and what might come after. The idea of it all chilled her even then, and as uncomfortable as Slater seemed, she supposed he still had little appreciation of just how much power the gods—if they existed—might wield. The thought queued another.

"You say the Incantors are gone. All of them?"

"Far as I know."

Nia shook her head. "I just... it's so hard to believe. The power it would take to kill so many. Have your men counted bodies?"

"Some. Near to a hundred at last count, though plenty were just... well, partial remains."

"That's not enough. There should be twice that number."

"I'm sure there are a few house wizards—"

"No," Nia said. "Not just house wizards. The call went out before Sartean made his move. Most would have returned to Kehrlia. Any within Mor, certainly. There are a few unsanctioned wizards here and there, but only a few. Hmm..."

"What are you getting at?"

Nia shrugged. "There should be more. Lots more. Several dozen, at least."

"Maybe the dragon ate them."

Nia nodded. "Maybe. But maybe not. Do you have a room I can use? Preferably on the top floor?"

Slater frowned. "I do. Why?"

"Well, there's a spell I learned at the Temple—"

"I don't know—"

Nia held up a hand. "It's not dangerous. I promise. But it takes a bit of time to prepare, and I'll need absolute quiet."

"What sort of spell?"

"The sort of spell that will tell me if there are any Incantors within a hundred miles."

"All right. But why?"

"If you're going to go after the Mother, you're going to need all the help you can get."

"From Sartean's pups? You must be joking. No, thank you. The last thing we need is more magic mucking things up."

"Exactly. Which is why you need to know if there are more magicians out there before you act. I'm not suggesting you need to recruit them, but at the very least, if I'm right, you had best make sure they don't side with the Mother, or you'll be slaughtered."

"Hmph. But you think I should recruit them."

Nia smiled. "At least for the farming operation you mentioned. Certainly, that would be wise, would it not?"

"Hmph."

"How about if I first see if there's any 'them' to recruit?"

Slater nodded, standing. "Fine. But if you blow up my barracks—"

Nia stood as well. "Then none of this will matter, and we'll soon know the answer to that question you asked earlier."

Slater threw a napkin over the gold ring and shoved it into a pocket, shuddering. "You're a morbid bunch, you know that?"

"You have no idea."

The pair made their way to a stairwell. On the second landing, Slater turned to Nia.

"How long did you have to complete your task today?"

"If I'm not back by nightfall, they'll assume I failed."

"And how long does this spell take?"

"A few hours, if I want it to work."

Slater stood back, gesturing for Nia to pass. "Top of the stairs.

First door on the left. I've got work to do."

Nia nodded and started back up the stairs. A hand grasped her arm just above the elbow. She turned.

"I'm trusting my gut with you, Nia. I have a son your age. Near where you grew up, as I understand it. I'd like to see him again."

Nia placed a hand over Slater's. The unexpected warmth of his hand, its leathery texture, his kind eyes...

"I'd like to see my family again, too."

Slater gave her arm a fatherly squeeze. "Then get to work."

XVIII: THE MAW

AK AND ARGL would not shut up. They had begun arguing when Lux and Oort secured Thinsel to the sled. The topic then had been the tunnels: how would they be dropped? What if they collapsed? Who would be in charge of such a job? They continued squabbling as they built a fire for lunch, a task such a company would ordinarily skip in favor of a walking meal, or perhaps a brief snack and a rest. But Thinsel could eat nothing but broth, and the thought of feeding her cold soup had never even crossed Oort's mind. The topic had barely deviated throughout the morning and early afternoon, Rak insistent that the engineers of G'naath had surely planned for such circumstances, Argl convinced that too many generations had passed since such plans, if they existed at all, were originally laid. They quarreled through the afternoon and into evening as they helped Lux raise tents at the base of the icy hill they would need to ascend at first light, Rak then bent on persuading a skeptical Argl, and perhaps himself, that the gnomes would not succumb to starvation before winter's end. They were still arguing when Oort fell asleep beside his wife, his fingers intertwined with hers as the newly minted king whispered words of love and encouragement to his queen, she occasionally awake but ever silent, still too injured to speak. Oort woke to hear them bickering at dawn, awakened by a squeeze from Thinsel, the two speaking then in more hushed tones as Lux gathered wood. Had

enough of G'naath accepted Oort's authority? Could the backbiting, gossipy lot of them be brought to heel without the political power of the Elders? Could violence be avoided? The topic changed quickly when Oort emerged from the tent, a new debate begun as they broke camp and ascended the hill.

Oort understood. More, he was grateful. Rak had disobeyed his initial order to depart for G'naath days before, as had Argl, and had they not, his own trek would have been a lonely one, if not a violent one. Their relentless yipping served as a useful diversion; perhaps, Oort considered, Rak and Argl understood that their roles on this journey were, chiefly, to prevent the Wolfslayer from shoving Lux from the top of a cliff if the dwarf dared speak.

Lux, for his part, clearly understood his role as well, and while Oort despised acknowledging as much, even to himself, he was grateful to the dwarf. His rage had not diminished, not by a finger, but the fairest part of his heart knew such anger was misdirected at Lux. The dwarf had taken Oort's worst, yet here he was, lugging Thinsel across the Maw, not for recognition, not for gold, not for any reward but that which came from within when one's sense of duty was being fulfilled.

Oort's position in the procession was third, behind Lux and Thinsel. As they marched, he spent as much time gazing into his wife's bruised and battered face as he did on the path ahead. She slept mostly, a sedative draught given them by the elves easing her pain and hastening her healing, but when her grey eyes were open, they were locked with Oort's, and he was loath to look away. He had come so close to losing her, *so close*, and he counted every moment in which he could measure life in her eyes as sacred.

The climb was far less difficult than what Oort had imagined,

Lux demonstrating impressive skill in selecting their path to the top of the rise. The snowy tops of trees which had draped their camp in shadows at dawn were now well beneath them, and here the sun and the glare were blinding, at least to the gnomes whose eyes had rarely been exposed to more than the auburn flames of candles and torches.

The wind picked up when they crested the rise. Oort had grown steadily more accustomed to the cold but had not yet learned to enjoy it, if such a thing could be enjoyed. The climes of the tunnels were constant; a bit of labor kept one warm enough, and even in the peak of summer one could sleep with a blanket or not as they preferred. Here atop the hill, the air again became a cruel, biting thing, and Oort was about to call a halt to better wrap his wife when Lux stopped of his own accord.

"Smoke ahead," Lux said, not turning. His voice struck Oort as no less cold than the air, and just as brittle. A new chill took hold within Oort as understanding dawned.

Oort squinted to see what Lux saw. "How far?" he asked, his own eyes inadequate to the task.

"Not very. An hour's walk, maybe less."

"We'll go around."

Lux turned, meeting Oort's eyes for the first time since they had left Jayne's Valley. "I don't think we can. Not without losing a day, maybe more."

Oort looked down at his wife, hoping to find guidance in her expression. She slept.

"I know these dwarves," Lux said. "They'll not harm ye."

"So yeh say. Forgive me if I don't take yer word."

"What's going on?" asked Argl, he and Rak catching up to the sled.

"Smoke ahead," Oort repeated. "Dwarves."

"I told yeh!" Rak said to Argl. "No way we make it to G'naath without—"

"Don't the two of yeh start," Oort said, startled upon hearing his own tone, noticing for the first time that an air of royal authority had begun to take hold. "We canna lose a day," he said to Lux, this said with gentler manner.

Lux nodded. "Let me speak to 'em. Hatchet needs to know what Dohr's done, and when he finds out, this whole mess might get straightened out."

"Just like that? A starving army heads back down the hill and puts the world right?"

"I'd bet on just that."

Oort shook his head. "Yer a fool. Or a liar."

Lux gnawed his tongue and took a breath. He took a step around the sled towards Oort. Rak and Argl reached for weapons, but a look from Oort stayed their hands. Lux closed the distance between himself and the Wolfslayer, not quickly but with purpose. He stopped just short of stepping on Oort's boots and looked down at the gnome. What Oort saw there might not have exactly been anger but was no doubt a near cousin. Oort did not budge.

"A fool I may be, but a liar I ain't."

If it truly came to it, Oort could not fight Lux, and he knew it. Even with Argl and Rak's help, a weapon drawn would end with grievous injury or worse, and likely not to Lux. Yet Oort was not afraid, and not because he did not fear death, but because he trusted the dwarf.

Oort nodded. "No, I suppose yer not."

Lux returned the nod. "I'd sooner die than lead ye to harm, King Oort. Twice for Lady Thinsel. I'm a Scout, and I don't expect ye to know what that means, but it means more than ye know, and ye don't get named such by speakin' lies an' breakin' oaths. Whatever that might mean, whatever poor honor I might carry in my whole heart, it ain't but a sliver of what Hatchet carries in a finger. I swear to ye, if it be in his power, he'll put an end to Dohr's reign when he hears what's been done."

Oort knew without question that Lux believed what he said, but Oort did not. Could not.

"If yer wrong, maybe your Hatchet goes north. Maybe he gets to the gates afore we can drop the tunnels."

"And if I'm right, ye won't need to drop the tunnels at all."

Oort leveled his gaze at Lux. "I'll be droppin' the tunnels. I said I would, and I will. If yeh hope to change my mind, it'll take more than words, and I hope things between you and me don't come to that."

Lux held Oort's eyes for a breath. The gnome knew the dwarf was sizing him up, no doubt marking the same differences in tone and demeanor Oort was beginning to notice in himself. "Aye," Lux said finally, taking a step back. "Then ye'll drop the tunnels. But might be we can keep what's left of Thornwood and Belgorne from paintin' the Maw red. And there ain't all that much left of either. Enough innocent people have died, Wolfslayer."

Lux did not need to say that they died by the actions of gnomes. The weight of that truth hung heavily in Oort's heart. He wanted to tell himself it did not matter, that those who had committed such atrocities were dead and gone, but the argument fell flat as a slab of shale. It had been gnomes to bring this cataclysm, setting in motion events whose reverberations still rung across Tahr, relentless waves of death and destruction; no matter how Oort might wish to lay the blame squarely upon the Elders, the truth of such things was never square. The Elders had been named by the gnomes of G'naath. Perhaps no one knew of the dark magics in which they meddled. Perhaps no one knew the horrors they planned. But all of G'naath knew of their pettiness and contemptible character, and none demanded better. G'naath had been content to be led by a miserable, power-hungry cabal of wretches, and if blame were to be laid, it fell at the feet of all gnomes.

"Ain't got much choice here, do we?" Oort asked, though not quite asking.

"We double back or talk to Hatchet," Lux said. "And if we double back, we might run into 'im anyways."

Oort glanced to Rak and Argl. Both nodded.

"All right," Oort said. "We'll find a place to tuck in. Two hours?"

"Call it three," Lux said.

"Three, then. And if ye don't come back?"

"Then come get me, if ye please, 'cause it means I broke a leg."

Oort stared at Lux.

"Or not," Lux added soberly. "As ye prefer."

Oort reached for the reins to the sled. "Don't break a leg."

~

The four gnomes were warming themselves around a small fire when Lux returned in the company of two armed, grizzled-looking dwarves. Rak and Argl looked up, the pair obviously too cold to bother reaching for weapons. Oort stood. He felt Thinsel's hand on his calf as the red-bearded one spoke.

"Oort Greykin?"

Oort nodded. The black-bearded dwarf moved to the other's side. They each took a knee.

"An honor, Wolfslayer," said the first. "The general asks that ye join him beyond the next ridge."

Oort looked to Lux, who did not speak.

"Ye'll come to no ill in our company, King Greykin," said black beard. "On me honor."

Oort nodded but did not reply. He looked again to Lux.

"Was just as I said, Sire." Lux, too, took a knee.

A squeeze of his calf decided the matter. Oort turned to Rak and Argl.

"Take up the sled," he ordered.

Lux rushed forward before the two could rise and took the reins.

"That'd be my job."

THE DAYS OF ASH AND FURY

PART EIGHT

XIX: ELSEWHERE

EAMS OF GOLDEN LIGHT shone through a thin canopy of maple and oak. Leaves the color of washed carrots and overripe tomatoes danced to the tune of a breeze, casting restless shadows across a clearing of pickle-green, wide-bladed grasses, these yielding in waves to gentle currents of cool air. An unmistakable scent of autumn rode the wind, almost sweet, not-quite-musty, redolent of windfallen apples and freshly harvested wheat, the exquisite yet subtle fragrance that visited each year, only once, to thank the summer for its sunshine, the trees for their shade, and the land for its bounty.

Where am I?

Mikallis stood, a squish of mud and grass between his toes alerting him to his nakedness. He turned quickly, modesty in mind, but saw no one. What he did see defied logic.

Far in the distance, the silhouette of a mountain range serrated the horizon. Mikallis thought he recognized the tallest of the peaks towering at the far left of the range, but no, it could not be. The sun shone above his left shoulder. The cool wind came from behind. The mild air... it had been winter, before.

Where am *I?*

The trees would tell.

Mikallis turned and walked towards the edge of the clearing, the sun now to his right, each step tentative, high grass making it difficult to see where he stepped. He approached the trunk of a young maple... nothing, on either side. He walked deeper into the forest, the grasses replaced here by a blend of roots, clovers, and fallen leaves. A great, gnarly oak stood proudly beneath its crimson crown. On the side facing him, nothing. On the other...

Odd.

The Knights of Thornwood spent a year in tutelage with the Rangers before earning their brooch, and that year had taught the lesson: *one tree may lie, but a forest speaks only truth.* After inspecting a dozen trees of varying size and species, the truth was told in moss, and that truth was this: it was morning. The sun climbed in the east, the forest was north of the clearing, and the mountain range to the southwest was not supposed to exist.

What *should* have existed was not there. The stone boulder, the door he had gone through, was nowhere to be found. This Mikallis could accept. He had returned to the world of the living, and such a thing was nothing if not magic. Where magic plays, Barris had once taught him, logic slumbers. *But this...* Mikallis imagined a map in his mind, imagined the mountain ranges he knew. The range to the southwest could be neither the upper nor lower jaw of the Maw; if it were, the clouds of ash and soot from Fang would be visible, somewhere. They were not. He could not be within a hundred miles of the Maw, he decided; the air was too sweet, the ground too pristine.

The weather... Mikallis might have imagined such warmth far to the south, nearer to the Sapphire, but there was no sea between his position and the mountain range, and there was no mountain range between Thornwood and the Sapphire Sea.

A gust of wind rustled the trees, loosing a cascade of leaves from above.

It was, most certainly, autumn.

Mikallis struggled against the most obvious idea as he wandered the forest looking for signs of human life, but he kept returning to it. There could be only two explanations: the first he ruled out, that he was dreaming; no dream had ever been so vivid. The second and most obvious he could not shake, that he had come to a place far, far from the lands he knew, and he had arrived there at least two cycles earlier than he had left. It could not be later; time pressed upon his friends, and Aria needed him; the Father would not send him forward.

But back! The thought filled Mikallis with hope. If he had been sent backwards in time, if such a thing were even possible, he could warn Aria, change the events that led her to... to wherever she might be. More, he could warn Barris and the queen! He could save his people from the collapse of the Citadel, save the dwarves of Belgorne...

... if I can find my way home.

A great sense of purpose filled the captain then, and with it the weight of duty. He stopped his wandering, realizing that he had walked well into the forest; the clearing was no longer visible. He would need to choose a direction. Not south; whatever range lay at the western edge of that horizon, it was not one he recognized, and would not lead him home. Not north; if he did not recognize what lay south, home could not be north. East or west, then. But which?

A rustling sound to his left interrupted the thought, the noise a dozen paces off. He turned, peering into the shadows, listening.

Nothing. But there had been something.

Perhaps it is a sign, Mikallis decided. *West it is.* He began to walk.

He kept the moss to his left and walked carefully, but not overly so. Time was his enemy. Wherever he was, home was far off, and there was no telling just how far. He would need boots, shoes of some kind. Clothing. He was not cold, but he could tell he would be once night fell. His elven magic could keep him warm, could help him keep his feet, but to sustain such magic for long would take its toll, a fact he discovered astride Triumph on the road from Thornwood.

How long ago was that? he wondered. *A cycle? Even that long? Feels like a lifetime ago.*

Mikallis laughed at himself. *It was! You died!*

His mood was high. Not even the memory of his death could darken his disposition. He had a purpose now. A mission! He could make amends for his reckless declaration at the Council. He could take back the harsh words he had exchanged with Aria. He could prevent those events from ever—

Again, a rustling. Now, a dozen paces behind. Mikallis froze, not frightened, but wary. Again, he listened. Again, nothing. He turned—

"Hve nü?"

Had Mikallis been wearing boots, he would have jumped out of them. A fat, bald elf stood before him in long, brown woolen robes, leaning on an oaken staff. His flesh was as smooth as Mikallis' own, but his eyes reminded the captain of Goodfather Neral.

"I... hello. You startled—"

"Hve nü?" the fat elf repeated, fingers tightening around the staff. "Vy nü haih?"

Mikallis recognized the language as Old Elven. *Who are you? Why have you come?* He tried a response.

"Em Mikallis, öhr... öhr Rattüs bus. Hva nü nahm?" *I am Mikallis, son of Stinky wood. What do you eat?*

The elf cocked his head, furrowing his brow. Mikallis frowned in return. He assumed he had misspoken and tried again.

"Em Mikallis, öhr Rat..."

The elf reddened as Mikallis labored over the pronunciation, but not in anger. By the time Mikallis repeated *Stinky wood* for the third time, he could take it no longer. He laughed long and loud and hard, holding his belly as he bent forward, leaning on his staff. It was Mikallis' turn to redden.

"Shem!" the elf called, waving to someone who approached behind Mikallis—another elf, also bald, also fat, dressed identically but female. "Hlaj er min! Mikallis, öhr Rattüs bus!"

"Rattüs bus?" the woman replied. "Öhr? Ha!" The woman fell into laughter as well.

"Hva *nü* nahm?" the first asked between howls. "Rattüs bus?"

"All right, very funny. Do you speak the common tongue or not?"

"Oh, yes, yes," said the male. "But *you* do not speak the Alvi!" The elf's accent was foreign to Mikallis; he had never heard its like. Before he could say as much, the male reached forward, fast as a striking viper, and tugged on Mikallis' left ear. "From where you get this?"

Mikallis slapped the elf's hand away. "From my mother, I assume. Now, what's so funny? What did I say?"

"Was she stinky?" the woman asked. The two again fell to

laughter.

"Not so far as I recall," Mikallis deadpanned. "I meant to say that I am Mikallis of Thornwood, and I asked your name in return."

The laughing elves grew silent and exchanged a glance.

"Thornwood? No," said the male.

"Surely no," agreed the woman.

"Surely yes," Mikallis insisted.

The female stepped forward, looking Mikallis up and down. "Then you come very long way without clothes, Mikallis."

"Very long," the male agreed. "You should no be here."

"Which is where, exactly?"

The woman frowned. "You not know?"

"I do not."

The two traded another glance.

"We believe you no," said the male.

Mikallis would suffer no more. "Sir, I care not whether you believe me. Much depends on my return to Thornwood, and I do not know the way. Will you aid me or no?"

"No." The woman replied before the male could.

"No?"

"No," she repeated.

"And why not?"

"Because you speak lies," said the male. "You will come, speak to Ronun."

Mikallis seethed but kept his tongue civil. "Who is Ronun?"

"Ronun is Ronun. Come." The female grasped Mikallis' arm above the elbow. He yanked it away. The male raised his staff.

"I will come! You need not handle me."

"Then come," said the male, pointing north. Mikallis nodded and began to walk.

The march north was near to the pace Mikallis had set going west. The day had not grown colder, yet his nakedness began to trouble him. His captors avoided the clearings they passed, keeping to the shadows of the forest; the canopy thickened, and the forest grew cooler. Eventually the trees did thin, but by then the shadows had lengthened and the warmth of the day began to fade. Mikallis could tell they were going uphill, though the incline was subtle, and knew they had been walking steadily north, but beyond that much, he saw nothing he recognized. They stopped only once, at what must have been suppertime. The elves shared a meal of nuts and dried fruit with him, but they did not speak, not to each other nor to Mikallis, and neither did Mikallis attempt to engage them. He could see little point in doing so; they would not believe what he had to say, and they would not say anything that might help him. He considered making a stand more than once; he could, perhaps, snatch a staff from one or the other and fight his way free, but to what end? He would need help, and clearly these elves were part of some remote sect; if he offended them, he could not expect help later from their friends, nor this Ronun, and there was no telling when he might come across others who might assist him. This logic was not, however, what decided the matter. It came down to faith. He knew, in the deepest part of himself, that the door he had chosen was the right one, and thus he was exactly where—and *when*—he was supposed to be.

The "where" became more confusing when the three emerged from the trees at dusk. This was no remote tribe. They passed the first cabins, these as well-built as any elven home of Thornwood, dozens of elves in their own brown robes milling about. Pens of goats, swine, and black, flightless birds Mikallis did not recognize filled the spaces between homes. A pair of elves busied themselves lighting lanterns hung on poles which lined a narrow street paved in grey stones. Wide eyes began to fall on Mikallis as his captors took this path, murmurs and pointed fingers marking his passing. Soon he noticed a procession of gawkers forming behind him as he walked, each step taking him deeper into the more densely populated city.

A city!

The narrow stone path opened into a square as grandiose and immaculate as any village square in Thornwood, save perhaps the market that once stood at the foot of the now-destroyed Citadel. Lush, tended gardens lined the perimeter. Vendors closing up stalls for the evening stopped their work and stared at Mikallis, but none dared come too near. Perhaps his captors were revered in some way? Not necessarily, he decided: two known locals escorting a naked foreigner could only be a prisoner walk, in this or any other city.

On the opposite side of the square, Mikallis could not help but stop. The light had dimmed considerably, so he could not be sure of what he saw, but before him towered a steep cliff face, as tall as a score of elves, taller, and from its very face, or so it appeared, was carved what he could only describe as one half of a castle. A prod from behind got him moving again, and as he neared the immense structure, his first impression was confirmed: this was indeed a castle, and it was indeed carved from the solid grey mountain behind it.

As the three ascended the first of three flights of stone stairs,

Mikallis gave voice to his marvel.

"How..."

"Walk," said the female.

Mikallis walked, his neck craned, his jaw hanging open.

His captors spoke in clipped tones to sentries posted at the entrance. One took off at a jog, ahead, into the castle. The other replied, pointing inwards and to the left, no doubt explaining where Mikallis should be taken. Another prod from behind got him moving again as he wondered at the enormity of the grand foyer. Light was sparse, and he could make out little detail, but the echo of the jogging sentry's boots on stone resonated as they might in the Citadel of Thornwood—no, he decided, listening to the echoes. This structure was larger by no less than half.

Mikallis was shuffled into a room to the left, empty but for a stone table and four wooden stools. "Wait," said the male, neither taking a seat nor offering one. Standing still for the first time in hours, Mikallis then realized how weary he was, his aching feet covered in mud past the ankles, his knees beginning to quake as his muscles tightened. And now, standing on hard stone with the sun gone down, he was cold to the bone.

He would not ask for comforts, he decided, believing that his strength of resolve somehow mattered here. He had been named a liar, and in Mikallis' experience, liars complained and pleaded when they were made uncomfortable. Those who were honest and honorable accepted their fate without protest. Perhaps his captors would see this, perhaps not, but he could withstand far worse and resolved to do so with dignity, at least as much as one could muster while standing naked before strangers.

Fortunately, that problem was soon resolved. The woman

returned with a thick grey robe and a pair of fresh sandals. She tossed them at his feet.

"Thank you," he said, meaning it.

"Dress. You see Ronun now."

Mikallis did as he was bid. As he knelt to lace his sandals the sentry returned and nodded towards his captors, who turned to Mikallis. Another prod was unnecessary; he stood and followed the guard as expected.

Mikallis counted his steps and noted the turns as he was led down a series of hallways. If he found himself in trouble, recalling the way out could make all the difference. Or not, he admitted. He was alone here. Friendless. He had been marched naked to this place. No one in this city would give him succor. Even if he could escape, even if he could evade detection while doing so, he did not even know where to run. Yet, he counted his steps, for Barris would have him do so.

Mikallis reached a count of one hundred forty-seven steps when he rounded the last corner, the hallway not opening into a grand throneroom as he expected but rather a humble office, not unlike the one in which his queen spent many an afternoon teaching him to read. This one was even more modest, in fact; no dark exotic woods nor handmade chairs, only a rough wooden table with a bench on either side, suitable to seat no more than ten. Old tomes lined wooden shelves along the walls. The room smelled of ancient inks and leathers. A single lantern sat upon the table.

"Wait," said his male captor, pointing to a spot on the floor. Mikallis obeyed, eyeing the bench but remaining on his feet. The sentry and his captors left him there, stepping back out into the hall. They whispered among themselves for a turn until slow, deliberate footsteps drew near in the hallway. Mikallis steeled himself, preparing mentally for the confrontation to come. The steps grew closer, a short conversation ensued, and Mikallis soon found himself facing an elderly elf, he also bald but far thinner, also attired in brown wool.

"You must be tired, Mikallis of Thornwood. Sit, if you will."

The elf's gentle voice shattered any defense Mikallis might have put up. His was a fatherly tone, mild and kind, familiar, bearing no accent. It might well have been Neral speaking.

"Thank you, Good—" Mikallis nearly said "Goodfather"— "good sir." Mikallis sat, immediately regretting that he had not waited for the elderly elf to sit first.

"You may call me Goodfather, if you like. It is not unlike the title given me by my people." The elf rounded the table and took his own seat.

"Ronun," Mikallis said.

The elf nodded. "It means 'king' to some, 'father' to others. In truth, it only means that I am old."

"I will call you Ronun then, if you please. The name Goodfather is dear to me, reserved for another."

Ronun nodded with a knowing expression.

"You will have questions of me," Mikallis said.

Ronun shook his head. "No, I do not. Shem and Kallar told me all I would know."

"They think me a liar."

Ronun nodded. "They do."

"And you?"

"And I what?"

"Do you think me a liar?"

The elf pursed his lips and looked down for a moment, then back up to Mikallis. The tone of his next words, still gentle, still kind, did not pair with his sharp declaration.

"If you are not from Thornwood, then you are a liar. If you are from Thornwood, then you are a liar. Thus, I do not have questions for you, Mikallis, for I do not expect true answers."

Mikallis fumed. "You impugn me, sir. And I have done you no—"

"From your point of view, perhaps. But your anger is misplaced. And vain, I might add. Indignation will not avail you, and thus it is of no value. Set it aside and ask me what you will."

Mikallis took a breath, no less indignant but seeing the wisdom in setting his pique aside.

"There is much I would ask, if you will allow me."

Ronun nodded, saying nothing.

"I suppose I will start with the obvious. Where am I?"

"Where do you think you are?"

Mikallis shook his head. "Nowhere I have ever heard of. I know the land and how to read it... but I am lost, as lost as I have ever been. Everything is... out of its place."

"I see."

Mikallis knew he was expected to continue. "When I... when I awoke—"

"You were sleeping?"

Mikallis immediately regretted his choice of words. He had proven his captors' accusations true in barely more than a turn.

"No, but I do not think you will believe me if I tell you the truth."

A look of disappointment crossed Ronun's face. "Then why speak at all? Look around you. I have plenty of tales in this room to entertain me."

Mikallis nodded. "I am sorry. Will you forgive me, and allow me to begin again?"

"My pardon will bring no truth to your words, but continue, if you wish."

Mikallis told all, barely taking a breath for an hour, sparing only inconsequential details, beginning at the Council at Thornwood, ending when he arrived in... wherever he was. Ronun listened intently, never speaking, never frowning, never giving a clue as to whether or not he believed a single word of Mikallis' narrative. When the captain completed his account, finally, Ronun spoke.

"Your tale is well spun, Mikallis."

"It is true, Ronun. Every word, at least as well as I can relate it."

"I believe that you believe so, though how you could, I do not understand. But it is impossible."

Mikallis slammed a fist on the table. "How can you say that? Which part do you not believe? And why?"

"I did not say that I do not believe you. Only that your tale is impossible. Truly, completely impossible."

Mikallis waited.

Ronun waited as well. A silent turn passed before the old elf shrugged. "Very well. You speak of Ya Di."

Mikallis nodded. "As it was explained to me by Barris, in the poem—"

"I am quite familiar with the verse. To your credit, you recited it nearly perfectly, though you missed much if its meaning. But Ya Di is not upon us."

"It will be! This winter! Listen to what I am telling you, I have to get back to—"

Ronun stood, turning to the shelves behind him. Mikallis stopped speaking, waiting politely as the elf perused the wall of leather-bound tomes. A turn passed, and another, but Mikallis remained silent.

"Ah. There. Would you care to reach that for me? It is just a bit too high."

Mikallis stood and did as he was asked. The egg-white volume was a thin one, comparatively. Many were as wide as Mikallis' hand; this one was no wider than two fingers. He handed the book to Ronun and the two sat again at the table. Ronun began thumbing through the book, his movements delicate, taking care not to damage the binding nor its faded vellum pages. He settled on a page and turned the volume sideways.

"Do you read Alvi?" he asked Mikallis.

"Poorly," Mikallis replied.

Ronun shook his head. "A shame. Then let me tell you what it says. Here, you see these lines?"

Mikallis nodded.

"This is the first verse of the Oath of Ya Di. You recognize the cadence at least, yes?"

Mikallis nodded.

"This next verse..." Ronun turned the book to face himself again. "I will not read it to you, as it is not for me to do so. But I will tell you one part, so that you might understand. In the third stanza, it says that Ya Di will come when the Twins become one. Do you understand this?"

"I think so. When the Twins appear to merge in the night sky."

"Just so. Understand, the verses of Ya Di are not strictly prophecy. You know this, yes?"

Mikallis shook his head. "I thought that is exactly what they were."

"No, young captain. The Oath is, in part, merely a calendar. A special one, to be sure, a magical one with extraordinary detail, but a calendar nonetheless. This section about the Twins tells us one thing and one thing only: the year in which Ya Di will come."

"Exactly!" Mikallis said. "Have you seen the night sky? The Twins grow nearer at their zenith each cycle. This is why I cannot delay! By winter's end, at the very latest—"

"Mikallis, you are mistaken. The Twins have barely shared the night sky in two seasons. Kal will not eclipse Lor for another fifty-one years. Yes, this will happen in winter, but many, many years from now."

Mikallis felt his mouth go dry. "No. That cannot be."

"Fang has not erupted. Stand upon the battlements with me at dawn. Look to the southwest. You will see for—"

"To the southwest? No, I saw the range, that is not—"

"Ninety-three miles to the southwest lies Fang. Almost due south, in fact. I assure you; it has not stirred in an age. Do the elves of Thornwood still keep to the royal almanac?"

Mikallis felt his breath catch. "We do."

"And the Evanti family still rules?"

"Yes."

"And what year is it, to your mind?"

To my *mind?* "Come, now! It is the year nine hundred and fourteen!"

Ronun shook his head. Mikallis felt lightheaded. He knew what came next. He knew it in his bones.

"If your tale is true, young captain, the Father has sent you much further into the past than a single season. By the Evanti almanac, today began the tenth cycle in the year eight hundred and sixty-three. So, you see, your tale *cannot* be true. If it were, you would not have yet even been born."

XIX: ELSEWHERE

XX: FURY

AVES OF DEVILS swept the four through the tunnels like a gale. The battle raged on without respite for what felt to Shyla like days, the unending dark yielding no reference by which to mark the passage of time. Each turn they took, each new tunnel they chose to escape a pursuing horde only brought them to face another.

There were those that swarmed, great, black masses of surging rage and claw. There were the longskulls, iron beasts which only Cindra could destroy, these given a wide berth by the hordes. There were others, unnamable things, some headless, some all jaws and teeth, all inventions of depravity. Cindra, J'arn and Shyla had long known they were being herded, but the knowledge made no difference. They fought, for they could do no more, protecting one another, protecting the defenseless Wolf, he whose bravery was not in doubt but whose own fangs and claws could open only superficial wounds in their enemies... wounds which leaked a vile residue. Shyla tasted the acidic ichor through her Bond. The foul liquid burned her companion like liquid fire, and she felt Wolf's pain as if it were her own. The exhausted gnome had nearly fallen to the horde trying to heal him. She had succeeded, pouring all that she was into the spell, but only just, two longskulls converging on them from either side as Cindra and J'arn fought with all that they were.

That might have been an hour ago. Or a day.

The bones in Shyla's hands felt molten. Jets of flame had been pouring from her fingers for as long as she could remember. Her mouth was a desert. The heat of flaming torrents had long evaporated all sweat from her pores. She had so far avoided injury, but soon it would not matter. Soon she would collapse. As they rounded another corner, Shyla fighting enemies from the rear, her flame faltered.

"Fight, Shyla!"

The warning from J'arn was not the first. Shyla redoubled her efforts. The result was far from impressive. She was flagging, and they all knew it. Cindra pushed her aside.

"Help J'arn!"

Shyla met her grandmother's eyes for only an instant. What she saw there was no less terrifying than the horde.

Each time Cindra had slain a longskull, her power had grown. There could be no doubt of this. But Shyla could not help but feel that each kill had taken a bit of Lady Cindra's soul, replacing it with some darker force. It was a ritual each time, Shyla knew. She did not merely kill these enemies. She devoured their lives, such as they were, their power, their very being. The mustard-yellow glint in her grandmother's eyes left no question: that which she consumed was beginning to consume her.

Shyla nearly tripped over Wolf as they made the corner. A frightened whine warned of some new terror. Cindra kept the horde from behind at bay, but when Shyla raised her eyes to peer into the darkness, she knew they would advance no further.

Here lay a cavern no less than five hundred paces wide, twice as long, its ceiling too high to make out. A tall, rusted iron peak rose from the center of the cavity, a winding path curling up its exterior. The spike—a tower, Shyla decided— was as wide as the Morline at its base, taller than what Shyla could estimate. Thousands upon thousands of shimmering yellow eyes, like so many hateful stars, lined the walls of the cavern on all sides, peering out from tunnels that led to the iron hollow, these too soaring high into the dark. Hundreds more pairs of eyes looked down upon them from the iron tower.

This was an army.

A blast from behind turned Shyla's head as Cindra obliterated a throng of devils. When she turned again to the cavern, the glinting stars had become a roiling sea, and the waves descended. A new orb of light from Cindra illuminated the fate before them.

At least I won't die in the dark.

Shyla knew. She would die here, and soon. She was not afraid; fear served as an alarm, warning one to fight or flee, and neither tactic would avail them now. She was *angry*. Angry that the world could be so vile as to allow such a place to exist. Angry that she would come to know such joys as her friend Wolf, such beauty as that which she enjoyed in Eyreloch, such friendship as she had experienced with her companions, with Trellia, even with Mikallis... and with J'arn... such love as that she had seen in her grandmother's eyes, before, only to have these stolen from her by these mindless, hateful monsters. She blinked away a single outraged tear, perhaps the last drop of fluid her dehydrated body could produce.

I shoulda stayed inside. I'm sorry, Mama.

As the scrambling, baying host worked its way around J'arn's flames—her brave prince, fighting to the end—Shyla did not bother raising a hand. She faced the tower of iron, balled her fists, and screamed, demanding an answer to the only question that mattered.

"Why!?"

As Shyla's final lament rang across the cavern, the hordes came to a sliding halt, heeding the silent command of their master.

~WHY? YOU DARE ASK WHY?~

The voice still resonated from within her mind, but she could now sense its source: the tower.

J'arn dropped his hands, turning to Shyla.

"Ye need not answer." J'arn tried to spit at the ground. Nothing came out. "He ain't but a dev—"

J'arn's words were cut short. He clawed as his throat. His heels came off the ground.

Something within Shyla cracked. *"You let 'im go!"* Shyla screamed, raging, sorcerous power amplifying her command, cowing the front line of beasts. "Come face me yerself, coward!"

J'arn's face began to purple. Thick veins bulged on his forehead.

~ANSWER, LITTLE WITCH. DO YOU TRULY NOT UNDERSTAND?~

"I don't understand none o' this! I ain't never hurt yeh!" Shyla's pink eyes began to shine, a new sort of power welling within her. "Ain't J'arn, neither! *Let 'im go!*"

J'arn fell to his knees, gasping, released by whatever force had been choking the life from him.

~AND WHAT OF YOU, PRINCE-THAT-WAS? ARE YOU AS IGNORANT AS THE LITTLE WITCH? WHAT DO THEY SAY IN

BELGORNE? WHAT LIES ARE PASSED DOWN THE
SILVERSTONE LINE?~

J'arn came to his feet, coughing.

"I know ye were evil in life!" J'arn coughed again. "An' ye be
evil in death! Liars, killers, and thieves, to a one! An' cowards,
looks like! Come out an' face—"

~AND YOU, MY FAITHFUL SERVANT? TELL YOUR
GRANDDAUGHTER THAT WHICH YOU MUST NOW KNOW.~

A hush fell before Cindra answered. "I'll not be yer servant,
fiend!"

The hesitation in Lady Cindra's voice was unmistakable. Shyla
turned.

~Grandmama?~

Cindra's smoky, yellowed eyes met Shyla's for half a heartbeat
before she looked away.

Shyla's heart shattered.

~OH, BUT YOU ALREADY ARE. LONG AGO YOU CALLED
TO ME.~

"Once only!" Cindra yelled. "And I gave yeh nothin'!"

~NO. BUT YOU TOOK WHAT I GAVE YOU, DID YOU NOT?
LOOK AT YOUR GRANDMOTHER, LITTLE WITCH. SEE HER
BEFORE YOU, A CENTURY OLD YET YOUNG AS A MAIDEN.
AND SUCH POWER! POWER CLAIMED IN BLOOD! YOU WILL
BE SECOND AMONG MY SLAVES, CINDRA SANDSHINGLE.
SECOND ONLY TO MY GREATEST CREATION. YOU HAVE MET
KALASHAGON, LITTLE WITCH, HAVE YOU NOT? AS HAVE
YOU, PRINCE-THAT-WAS. HAVE YOU EVER SEEN HIS LIKE?~

"An abomination!" J'arn hollered. "Born o' filth and bile!"

~MMM. AN ABOMINATION, YES. I DO NOT DENY IT. BUT BORN OF LIES, PRINCE THAT WAS. BORN OF THE LIES OF HUMANITY.~

Shyla turned from her grandmother and towards the iron tower. "Yeh speak in riddles, coward!"

~I DO NOT! YOU HEAR ONLY RIDDLES BECAUSE YOU KNOW ONLY LIES! YOU WILL DIE YOUR SECOND DEATH THIS DAY, LITTLE WITCH, BUT FIRST YOU SHALL KNOW THE TRUTH! NOT FROM ME, BUT FROM SHE THAT KNOWS! BEHOLD! I GIVE YOU THE PRINCESS OF LIES!~

The sea of devils between Shyla and the tower began to part. Two hundred paces separated Shyla from the base of the tower, the only light coming from the eyes of the horde and Cindra's orb. Her G'naari eyes could make out only shadows, but she did not need eyes to know who emerged; Lady Lor's gift had opened a conduit among the champions of Tahr.

J'arn spoke first. "No! It cannot be."

Shyla placed a trembling hand on his shoulder, which he grasped. Lady Cindra stepped forward to take position beside Shyla, but Wolf nudged his way between them, edging Cindra aside. He stood low, panting, his fangs bared, drooping ears as perked as they had ever been, black tail curling between his legs. His head swiveled at every sound in the great chamber. Shyla reached up to place a hand on the scruff of his neck. He let out a huff.

A turn passed. Wolf growled, a deep, rumbling snarl as a squad of demons came into view, a new sort of enemy they had not seen before. Heads like goats with long, twisting, bone-white horns sprouting from the sides of their heads... bodies the same blacker-than-black hue of the dragon, scaled but slick, vaguely human in shape. Each brandished long, wicked scythes, handles and blades as black as the demons which wielded them. As they closed to within fifty paces, the leading rank parted to display two shackled prisoners.

Lucan not-Thorne and Princess Aria Evanti had been poorly used. Lucan walked hunched, his face purple and swollen. Aria bled from a dozen wounds; wounds Shyla could see were not taken in battle.

"We'll free 'em," Shyla whispered. Wolf growled his assent. "On my signal."

"Shyla, we canna—"

Shyla scowled at her grandmother, pink eyes gleaming.

~FAR ENOUGH.~

The demon guard came to a halt.

~SPEAK, DAUGHTER OF LIES.~

Aria looked down but said nothing. Lucan fell to a knee, gripped by some unseen pain.

~SPEAK!~

Aria screamed. "Release him!"

~YOU DO NOT COMMAND ME!~

"Then I beg you! *Please*, release him and I will speak!"

Through her Bond, Shyla felt an anguish take hold within Wolf. His animalistic mind was simple, primitive, but far from dense, and he knew what he saw. He could not abide Lucan's suffering. He cared for Lucan. Knew him to be a friend. He knew he could do nothing. He knew Aria could do nothing. He was tired. Pained. Afraid. He longed for home, though he did not know the way. These and a hundred other desolations were given voice as

Wolf emitted a long, doleful, rising howl. The harrowing tone found a pitch which resonated within the hollow iron cavern, setting a harmonic note alive to resound throughout the tunnels, amplifying down one tunnel, returning through others, here an octave higher, there an octave lower, the tones fusing into one continuous, heart-rending chord.

J'arn's pain before had cracked a dam within Shyla. Wolf's howl now released a river. She sent a thought to her friends.

~Cover yer ears.~

Shyla Greykin, daughter of Oort and Thinsel, indolent outcast-of-G'naath-turned-sorceress, opened a font within herself, and lent her Wolf her power.

Wolf understood. He howled again, louder this time and with intent, quickly finding the resonant pitch to which Shyla added not merely the force of sorcerous magic, but the power of her very heart, the power of her pity, the power of her righteous fury at the discovery that the world she once so longed to glimpse was naught but a cesspool of death and horror.

The effect was terrible. As the note grew in volume, the host of scaled and iron horrors sought to flee, but there was nowhere to go. They ran in circles, flailing, moaning. All of Fury thrummed. The demons surrounding Aria and Lucan fell to all fours, wailing in pain. Further into the cavern, nearer to the tower where the power of Wolf's howl was most intense, yellow lights went out, minions of Fury reduced to quavering piles of death. Shyla could see J'arn screaming something, but she did not hear. Half a turn went by before she realized she could hear nothing at all.

Wolf's howl had deafened the companions, but the voice of the Hand came from within.

~ENOUGH!~

Shyla bore down, preparing to intensify her efforts. She tightened her grasp on Wolf's fur—but sensed him trembling. Shyla probed his mind, seeking to calm him. He responded to her, not in words; such was not the way they communicated, but in loyalty, and in love. He would help Shyla. Always. For all the days and nights and days. He was her Wolf. He was good. He would do as Shyla says. But he was afraid.

Shyla cut her flow of magic. Wolf whined and turned, bending to lick Shyla's outstretched hand.

Shyla replied silently to the Hand.

~Why should I not end yeh, devil? End yeh and all yer wretched lot!~

A low, rumbling laugh sounded within the companion's minds.

~YOU CANNOT END US, WITCH. WE HAVE NO END. SUCH IS OUR CURSE. BUT... I WILL YEILD THIS DAY.~

~Then release Aria and Lucan! Yeh canna—

~NO! THE DAUGHTER OF LIES IS MINE! YOU MAY HAVE THE IMPOSTOR; HE IS OF NO USE TO ME. BUT THE ELF I WILL NOT SURRENDER!~

J'arn asked the question. *~Impostor? What's he sayin', Luc?~*

Lucan responded to Shyla. *~It doesn't matter.~* He turned to the princess. *~I won't leave you, Aria.~*

Shyla could see Aria turn, reaching shackled hands to Lucan's face.

~You must. Go. I will return to you. This is not our end.~

~*Ain't nobody leavin nobody!*~ J'arn's words, though silent, conveyed his great desperation. ~*We came together, we leave together!*~

~*No.*~ Lady Cindra's declaration carried a finality to it.

Shyla turned, appalled.

Cindra continued. ~*This is Aria's debt to pay. We will accept your bargain, Darkest One. For today.*~

~*What? Grandmama, no!—*~

~*VERY WELL, SLAVE. YOU HAVE ONE DAY.*~

Shyla screamed aloud in protest as the horde withdrew.

No one heard.

XXI: THE NORTHERN ROAD

arris sent desperate word along the Winds. Pheonaris would hear or would not. She would come in time or would not. The waters of the Spring would serve, or they would not. If the waters were good and sentient as he and his people believed, they could not allow his friend to die, this majestic, devoted servant of Thornwood, of Tahr, of goodness itself. But these times were dark. All was corrupted. Why not the Spring? It mattered little. The Mistress of the Grove would come, she who loved Phantom nearly as much as Barris, but he could not imagine what magic might bring her quickly enough.

The night had been cold. Cold enough, Barris had hoped, to slow any infection that might insinuate itself into Phantom's wounds. An inspection of the sutures Barris had sewn the day before revealed no superficial taint, but Barris had seen the dark purple hue in many a horse's gums. He had felt the thumping heart, seen the shivering. The fever had struck quickly and from within. Barris' own heart pinched in frustration and sorrow. He could do nothing. He would have run for help, but Mor was too far, and no cure could be found there in any case. The Grove was even farther; a flat-out sprint, even enhanced by all Barris' magic, would take two days at least, and a day riding back at full gallop. Phantom had a day, no more. Perhaps less.

Barris spoke to his friend through panicked tears. Quietly, in a voice ill-suited to melody, he sang songs of love, of battle, of great deeds and valor, cradling the great beast's black head in his lap, stroking his mane. Lucidity came and went; Phantom thrashed now and again. When he did not thrash, he moaned, an awful, unfitting sound to come from so great a beast. His great soulful brown eye met Barris' gaze when the knight used his name, and the Bond between elf and stallion carried currents of fear and affection between the two dear companions.

The day wore on like a march. Barris left Phantom's side only long enough to tend the fire. By afternoon, Phantom would not take water. By dusk his breath came in gasps. His body began to cool. As night fell, the Bond grew quiet. The First Knight of Thornwood could sense only his own sorrow.

Barris cried out as his arms tightened around his dearest friend's head.

"What is my sin!?"

The forest gave no answer. Nor did the Father.

"What terrible crime, what grave offense that you should punish not me, but those who have loved me? Tell me!"

Silence.

A river of tears cascaded down the knight's tortured face. "TELL ME! Oh Father, please tell me! I will repent! I swear it!"

"Hello?"

The voice came from nearby. Barris lifted his head. Hooves crunched through snow a dozen paces west, from the road. The knight sent a tendril of himself outwards, sensing. Two riders. From these he detected no wicked intent.

"Here!" Barris cried. "Here! Please, come here!"

Feet struck the ground, the pair dismounting. Hushed voices shared words he could not make out; words, no doubt, of caution. Boots approached.

"I am alone! Do not be afraid! I am Barris, First Knight—"

"First Knight of Thornwood," a male voice continued. The two men came nearer, one older, one hooded but younger. They stepped to within the glow of the fire. "I recognize you," said the hooded man.

"Please, you must help me. My horse... he will not drink."

"The great Phantom. Nasty wounds. Here, let me." The older man moved to kneel before the horse.

Barris held up a hand. "Tell me your name."

The strangers eyed one another. The hooded man spoke.

"This is Gerald Longstock. I am Vincent Thomison. We are from Mor, and you can—"

"Thomison? I saw your trial. I... I saw you die."

"Didn't take," said Gerald, not quite flippant. "Will he thrash out?"

Barris shook his head. "Not since this afternoon."

Gerald lay his hands on the great stallion, inspecting his wounds. After a turn he stood.

"He is dying, friend."

"He cannot die. He *cannot*! He is Phantom of Thornwood, do you not understand?!" Barris cried like a boy, all pretense at bravery abandoned. "Do you carry any herbs? Anything? Please, I will give you all I have, and more—"

"I have some magic, First Knight. I might be able to ease his suffering, but—"

"You can do more than that," said Vincent.

Gerald turned. The two men shared a silent exchange.

"What do you mean?" pleaded Barris. "What more? You... you are an Incantor?"

Gerald turned back towards Barris. "Nearly. As good as."

"And you can heal? Then heal him, please! My magic... I was never good at these things. I will give you anything, on my honor as a knight—"

"It is your honor I would not impeach, friend. My magic... the magic I can use to heal him... you may not approve."

Barris blinked. Recognition dawned. He had heard of such magic. Phantom's breath began to rattle.

"No. Another way. There must be another way."

Gerald sighed. "None that I can provide. As I said, I can give him comfort, but—"

"From where?" Barris interrupted. "From where would you take this power? There is no one for miles."

Barris watched as Gerald looked around, at the ground, above and into the canopy of trees. The man was taking an inventory, like a librarian of so many books. Barris wiped tears from his eyes.

"There may be enough," said Gerald. "I cannot say for sure."

Barris swallowed. He tried his Bond again. Nothing. He nodded.

"Take it from me."

The man called Gerald frowned. "Sir, that... that could kill you."

And so I will repent, for whatever great sin I carry in my heart.

"Then I will die. Do it. Take it from me."

Gerald shook his head. "I... I'm sorry. I cannot do that, Sir. I will not."

"*Do it!* Please, do you not understand? This is my penance! He has given his life to me! All these many years! I will give it back! It is mine to give!"

Gerald took a step back.

"Please. I beg of you. Please." Barris pleaded. "You must." Barris stroked his friend's muzzle. "It is mine to give," he repeated pitifully.

"Gerald," said Thomison. Gerald turned.

Thomison addressed Barris. "Would you give us a moment, sir?"

Barris nodded weakly.

~

Vincent put an arm around Gerald and led him away from the fire.

"You've done this before," said Vincent.

"Not like this. Never like this. I've pinched a bit, here and there, from many. No one *died*, Vincent. I've never taken it all from one source."

"Then take only what you need to. If it comes down to it, cut the spell. Spare the knight's life."

Gerald shook his head. "This isn't like mixing some street cure. I choose the sources and open the channels. If I do it, I do it with the intent to get the job done, and once the veil is ripped..."

Vincent nodded. "It's out of your hands."

"For the most part, yes."

"Your best guess. Will it kill him?"

Gerald shrugged. "Possibly. Elves are a sturdy lot, but the horse is far gone. Awful infection."

Vincent nodded.

"It's a horse, Vincent. A great horse, but its life is not to be traded for the First Knight of Thornwood."

Vincent took a moment to reply. "You're right, of course. But we can't just do *nothing*."

"You heard him. He doesn't want the sort of help I can give."

"So he says."

Gerald shook his head again. "You know the elves as well as I do. Say what you like about the pointy-eared folk, but they *do* value life."

"True," Vincent agreed, taking another moment to think. He could hear the knight speaking to his horse. He could not make out the words, but the tone of grief was unambiguous. "Poor bastard. We have to help him."

Gerald sighed. "I just told you, he doesn't want—"

"I get it. He doesn't want to take life. Not from the squirrels or the birds or the little baby bunnies. That doesn't mean we can't *give* it."

"I don't follow."

Vincent shrugged. "Take half from me."

"Please. Take half of *what* from you? You're half-dead already."

"Maybe, but only half." Vincent threw Gerald a wink. The wizard was not amused.

"You want to go the rest of the way? This isn't kid stuff. It's not worth it. Not for a horse."

"What about for the First Knight of Thornwood?"

"For the First Knight's *horse*, you mean."

"Think about it, Gerald. Why are we here?"

Gerald rolled his eyes. "If you're going to launch into some existential sermon—"

"No, I mean *here*." Vincent lifted his arms, indicating their setting. "We're here to beseech the help of the elves. What better way?"

Gerald shook his head. "Dunno. Can't think of a worse one, though."

"I can. How about a man with half a face riding to the Grove, begging for Thornwood's help after letting Sir Barris' horse die on the side of the road?"

"Oh, to Fury with that," Gerald said. "You didn't wound that horse."

"You know I'm right."

"I know you're delirious. I'm not doing it, anyways. Think of something else."

Vincent took a step forward, lowering his voice. Gerald looked down.

"Oh, no you don't. Look at me."

Gerald stood still.

"*Look* at me Longstock. Come on."

Gerald looked up, irritation warping his features.

"I'm a ghost. Worse. I'm a *ghoul*. If we're going to win Thornwood over, my charisma isn't going to cut it."

Gerald huffed. "You are one ugly bastard. I'll give you that."

"Good. It's settled, then."

"Fury it is. Vincent, you could *die*."

"Ho, hum. That'd be what, three times now?"

"Not funny."

"Didn't mean it to be. Listen. No—just shut up and listen. You stole this life for me. But it's *mine* now. You don't get to decide—"

"Oh, piss off! You piss *right* off with that. You don't get to keep throwing your life over a cliff for me to hoist it back up. This noble-Merchant-martyr routine is getting a bit stale."

Vincent took a step back.

Gerald bowed his head. "I'm sorry. That was cruel."

"No, you're right."

"Don't do that. I said I was sorry. Don't make me feel—"

"I'm serious. You're right. It *is* getting a bit stale. All of this bellyaching is so much horse dung. Here's where we are, you and me. We've got a bloody job to do. We need the elves. This gets it done, or at least gets us a long way down the path. Yeah, there's a risk. And there's risk in doing nothing. And you know what else? *I don't wanna see that horse die.* Not if I can save it. That's *Phantom*, for Lor's sake. This isn't about my wish for death."

"Now *that's* horse dung. Everything you do is to get back to Anie."

Had Vincent swung for any other man, he'd have never seen the strike coming. As it was, Gerald was his friend, and so Vincent dropped his shoulder. The wizard turned his head just enough to avoid being knocked flat.

Gerald took a seat on the ground, his head in his hands. An awkward silence fell. Vincent knew his friend regretted bringing up Anie; no apology was necessary. Nor would Gerald begrudge him the punch. In a few turns, all would be forgotten.

He has a point, though, Vincent admitted silently. As they often did in such times, his thoughts turned to his late wife.

What would she do? What would she have me do? This night, to Vincent's mind, the question did not require much imagination. Had she not told him, in that place between places, just days before?

Above all, you must love Tahr, my brave, sweet man. For without your love, she will be lost forever.

Tahr. *What is Tahr?* Vincent let his mind dance around the question. *Is it this ashen land on which I stand? No. Dirt is dirt. Is it its people? Perish the thought.* In all his years as The Merchant, Vincent had learned one thing, if anything: perhaps most people were born neither good nor evil, but a single evil act could taint a victim's soul every bit as quickly and thoroughly as the infection that ravaged the knight's poor dying horse, and that taint was catching. Kindness was a salve, goodness not so much a cure but a medicine that might keep the world alive long enough that one could be found. And what would be this cure? Would he, Vincent Thomison, he the walking abomination, he the sewn-together embodiment of Gerald's dark magic, be the one to find it? Surely not. He might succeed in uniting the kingdoms, but it was doubtful. Too much distrust existed among the races. *Now*, as death bore down on them from the very sky above? *Now* they would put aside their fears, their prejudices, their differences? At *his* urging? No. Only the most extraordinary deed could possibly bridge such a divide.

Upon your deeds, all things rely.

A hand fell on Vincent's shoulder. The wizard had stood at some point during Vincent's reverie.

"What about Maris?" Gerald asked, his tone gentler than his previous comment.

Vincent sighed and shook his head. "I tried to love again, Gerald. I did. For one quick breath, I did. I still do. There, I said it. I love her. But you'll notice she wasn't waiting at the door when we left."

"Maris will come around."

She loves you, and you must love her in return.

A wistful smile crossed Vincent's mangled lips. "Yes. She probably will. Fool of a girl, she will. And she'll be cursed with a ghoul for a husband."

"Vincent—"

"Ah, come on, Gerald. She deserves better." *This is how I must love her. Ah, dear Anie. Death has made you wise.*

Gerald looked down.

"And Tahr deserves better, for that matter."

"*Tahr?* Tahr doesn't deserve a damned thing. Least of all your death. Mor could do a lot worse than to see you on the throne."

"To Fury with the throne."

"You keep saying that."

"This is bigger than Mor. Mor will be fine. Or it won't. If it's to stand a chance, we need the elves."

"Fine, but—"

Vincent turned to face his friend. "Gerald, this is my choice."

Gerald took a step back, finally raising a hand to rub his jaw.

"Did you need to hit me so *hard*?"

"I didn't. You're just old and feeble."

Gerald ignored the goad. "Look, I understand. We have to help him. And you're right, it could mean something in the end. But this is *risky*, Vincent. If we do this, I won't be able to help you if it starts going sideways. It'll take everything I have just to get the magic going."

"I understand."

"Uh huh. Understand this, too: if you die, I won't be able to bring you back. I won't have anything left after the spell. Not for a day, at least. Maybe longer."

"Then don't let me die, old friend." Vincent threw an arm around Gerald's shoulder, turning him back to Barris' camp.

"Hmph. I ought to. Just to spite you."

"You'd miss me."

Gerald did not reply, which was reply enough.

~

Barris listened as Gerald quickly explained. When he finished, the knight turned to Vincent. "Why are you doing this for me?"

Vincent shrugged. "Got a soft spot for horses."

Barris eyed the man. "No doubt. But that is not why."

"No," Vincent said. "Sir Barris, if we get through this, I'm going to need your help."

"I imagined this much. But you will know that I have my own burdens to carry, sir. My own duties, which I cannot abandon."

"I'm sure you do. I don't suppose those duties have anything to do with keeping Tahr out of the abyss?"

Barris thought for a moment, selecting his words carefully. "You are closer to the mark than you know."

Phantom kicked weakly. Time was short.

"We're on the same side, you and I," said Vincent. "Let's just get this done. If it works, we can talk about what happens next."

Barris shook his head. "These are dark magics. I... I am unsure." And he was.

"Magic is magic, elf," Gerald said. "But we can debate that later. We're out of time."

Barris turned to Phantom, then back to Gerald, nodding. The knight locked eyes with Vincent.

"I can make you no promise but this: if it is in my power, and what you ask of me is good and right, I will repay this debt. Ni oash'e en."

Vincent nodded. "Not sure what that last part meant, but good enough for me. Get to work, Gerald."

XXII: THE MAW

IKALUS DRONED ON. NOVA listened politely, if absently.

"...and then he says, 'That's the lesson, why I don't cry twice.' Pretty much, at least. I mighta mixed up some words. But that's smart, huh?"

"Seems wise enough to me," the dwarven scout replied. "Not always so easy, though."

Nikalus nodded. "Yeah. 'Specially when it still hurts."

Nova turned over on her cot to face the young stable hand from Mor. "Does it? Still hurt, I mean?"

"Nah, not so much anymore." Nikalus tossed his leg up onto his cot. He knocked on the cast of bark the elven healer Cloudia had shaped for him. "Wish I could leave this stupid tent, though."

"Lot happenin' out there," Nova warned.

"Exactly! I heard that Nishali lady this morning. She's mad."

Nova had heard as well. "She lost someone close."

"She oughta be sad, then."

Nova thought of Dohr and reddened, ashamed that her own king would dishonor Belgorne so. She could find no fault with Nishali's rage. "Maybe she's like Barris," Nova said. "Don't want to cry twice."

"More like she's gettin' ready to kill that jerk King Do... oh. I'm sorry. I didn't mean—"

"Sure ye did. And he's a jerk, no mistake."

Nikalus regarded Nova with intent. She sensed his question before he asked it.

"Are ya gonna help Nishali?"

"That ain't your business, kid."

"Aw, come on. You can tell me. Ain't like I got someone to tell anyways."

"Why can't ye just let me sleep an' quit chewin' me ears off? If I were an elf, nobody'd know anymore."

Nikalus laughed. "Come on. Tell me."

Nova knew the boy would not relent, but she had not yet made up her mind on the matter. She decided there would be no harm in saying as much.

"Haven't decided yet."

"I think you oughta," said Nikalus quickly, his response at the ready. "I think you oughta get a new king."

Nova laughed. "Just like that, huh?"

"Yep."

"Like who?"

Nikalus shrugged. "I dunno. I don't know many dwarves. You know any good ones?"

Nova eyed the boy.

"Aw, Fury. I'm sorry. I didn't mean it like—"

"Stop apologizing all the time. It's annoying."

"Oh. I'm sor... uh."

Nova smiled. "Say what ye mean, kid. Pretty words can't hide an ugly truth."

"Huh," Nikalus said. "That's smart."

"I thought so, too. Me cap used to say it."

"Is he dead?"

Nova recalled the last time she had seen Captain Latimer Flint. *The Hammer.* She wondered what had become of his niece, the barmaid Kari.

"Well, is he?"

"Dead? Hope not. Don't know for sure."

"Well, maybe he can be king."

Nova laughed. "He'd be a damned good one, sure as stone. Wouldn't want the job, though."

"Why not? Who wouldn't wanna be king?"

Nova sat up, resigning herself to conversation. She reached to a table that sat between the two cots, retrieving the water skin Cloudia had left for them. She took a long pull, frowning. *Fury, but I'd kill for some ale.*

"Here's the truth of it. Anybody who wants to be king would make a poor excuse for one."

Nikalus cocked his head. "That makes no sense."

"Sure it does. Think on it."

Nikalus screwed up his face. Nova remained silent as the boy puzzled it over. A flash of understanding widened his eyes.

"'Cause they want all that power?"

Nova nodded. "Yep. That's the big part of it. But it also means they're too dumb to know it's a dung-stinkin' job."

"A dung-stinkin' job? Come on! You get to be in charge of everything! You get to eat what you want, go where you want, sleep when you want—"

Nova laughed. "Sure hope we don't end up with a King Nikalus anytime soon."

Nikalus shot her a look.

"Don't get cross. Think on it. A king has to figure out how to make the whole world run. At least his part of the world. All day, every day, one trouble after the next. Maybe ye can eat what ye want, but I doubt ye get to sleep much, and ye muck something up, maybe people die. Muck up too much, maybe it's yer own head ends up in a noose."

Nikalus looked up, thinking. "Huh. Maybe that's what happened to your King Dohr. Maybe he just mucked up too much."

Nova shook her head. "Wish I could say that were it. No, Dohr flat out *wanted* to be king. Shoulda been his brother."

"Prince J'arn?"

"Aye."

"I heard he ran off."

"And how'd ye come by that?"

"I ain't daft. I listen. I know *some* things. But—"

"Well, ye heard wrong. J'arn's no coward."

"Well, then why can't he be king?"

Nova shrugged. "Don't know where he is."

"So, he *did* run off."

Nova scowled. "Now ye *are* bein' daft."

"Am not. Everybody knew *something* bad was happening, didn't they? Fury, even *I* knew—"

"Watch that tongue."

Nikalus sighed. "Fine. But I did. And he's a prince! He shoulda stayed to help."

Nova shook her head. "Ye have it wrong. He went to go *find* help."

"From who?"

Nova felt silly as she said it.

"The elves."

"Hmph. Well, he mucked *that* one up. Don't look like the elves like you very much."

Nova eyed the boy again. "Ye're kind of a pain in the arse, ye know that?"

"Hey! *You* said I should say what I mean."

The scout rolled her eyes. "Aye, s'pose I did."

Nikalus leaned back on his cot, arms behind his head. Nova could not help but appreciate how self-assured the boy was; prouder now, certainly, having bested an adult in debate.

"So, what're ya gonna do?" Nikalus asked again.

"Already said. Haven't made up me mind."

"I think you should help Nishali."

"Heard ye the first time."

Nikalus sat up again. "But think about it! You *have* to get a new king! Or the elves and dwarves are gonna go to war!"

Nova sighed. "There's something else Cap used to say."

"What's that?"

"Ain't nothin' simple. If it sounds that way, clean the..." Nova censored the vulgar expression, "well, open your ears."

"My ears aren't closed."

"Aye, they are. Now lemme open 'em for ye. I'm a dwarf, right?"

"Well, yeah."

"And ye think I oughta what, kill King Dohr?"

"He's a *bad* king, though."

"He is. But he's our king. King of Belgorne. You think Halsen was a good king?"

"Fury—I mean, *fires*, no."

"Well, then why didn't ye kill 'im?"

"Me? I'm just a kid!"

"What about your pa, or your ma?"

Nikalus took a moment to reply. "I ain't got no ma. No pa, either. Not really. Well, sorta."

"All right, then what about the soldiers in Mor? Why didn't they just kill 'im?"

"*Fur*—I mean... *fires*, I dunno! Maybe they didn't wanna fight the other soldiers!"

Nova nodded. "Now your forge is hot. And why didn't they wanna fight the other soldiers? You think they were cowards?"

Nikalus frowned. "Some, maybe."

"Some, but not all."

The boy met Nova's eyes. "I don't think you're a coward."

"Good. 'Cause I ain't."

"But... I mean, you're not really sick anymore, are you?"

"Not all that much, no."

"And you're not—"

"Never mind that. Why didn't they wanna fight the other soldiers?"

A look of understanding crossed the boy's face. "They didn't wanna kill their friends."

Nova nodded. "Ain't nothin' simple."

Nikalus sat quietly, looking at Nova. Looking her *over*, she decided.

"You're smart," he said eventually. "Maybe you oughta be queen."

Nova smiled a quizzical smile, taken aback by the boy's open admiration. "Well, that's a kind thing to say, Nikalus. I thank ye. But not even with an axe to me throat." She tapped the side of her head, winking. "See, too smart for the job." She glanced towards the flap of the tent. "Hush, now. Somebody's comin'."

~

"It is not good, Janna."

"Tell me something I do not know."

The ranger looked around. No one was near, but the night did little to hide elves from one another. They would not be able to speak long.

"I should not be telling you *anything*."

The knight stepped closer, her voice lowered.

"These are not ordinary times, Dell."

A long pause hung between the two, heavy as the knight's frosty breath.

"Out with it. What are the rangers up to?"

"We have been fletching arrows all day," Dell said, the implication clear.

"Father help us. When will you break camp?"

"Before dawn, surely," said Dell. "Just after middlenight, if I were to guess."

"So soon? She must wait until tomorrow, at least! If you leave now, you will arrive in daylight—"

"We are not moving on Dohr. Not yet."

"What? Then where?"

Another pause.

"North."

A look of momentary confusion crossed Janna's features, the expression replaced quickly by one of shock.

"Is she out of her mind? You haven't the numbers!"

"Keep your voice down! That is her position exactly, and I do not disagree. If we do not deal a blow to Hatchet's forces first, he could come up behind us at any time, and as few as we are, we could not stand. To be sure, if he returns and finds us engaged with Dohr's forces, he will not stop to ask why."

"Dohr has no forces. They're all north with Hatchet!"

"He had forces enough to kill three Tenths of rangers. You did not see, Janna. It was..." Dell's voice trailed off. "At least we will have surprise on our side."

"Oh, Dell. You will all die. This is foolhardy."

"Call it what you will, but we cannot bear to do nothing. We have lost dear friends, elves we have lived and trained with for decades. If we delay, we stand to lose more. There are no good options. This is the wisest course."

"The wisest course is to await our queen's direction, and act as one."

"Please, Janna. I would not argue with you. Not tonight."

The two held one another for a time. A sneeze from a nearby tent brought their farewell to an end.

"I must go."

"Dell... I must tell Marchion."

"You cannot! Dammit, Janna, I told you this in confidence!"

"I know. And I am sorry. But this brooch came with vows."

"And what of our vows?"

Janna leaned in, offering a long, soft kiss. "They shall last forever. Go. I can give you an hour, perhaps two. My conscience will allow no more."

Dell's gaze fell, only for a moment. "Such is your duty. All will be as it must be."

"As it must be," Janna agreed. "I love you, Dell Brightwater."

"And I love you. Return to me."

~

"Dammit Nikalus!" whispered Nova. "Could ye not be quiet for a turn!"

"I'm sorry!" said Nikalus, wiping his nose. "I didn't mean to sneeze, ya know!"

"Doesn't matter. I heard enough." Nova went to her knees, reaching under the cot for her boots. Nikalus sat up, anxious.

"What're ya gonna do?" The boy's voice trembled.

Nova laced up her boots and looked at Nikalus. "What would ye have me do?" she asked, her question not wholly rhetorical.

Nikalus frowned. "I... I dunno, miss Nova. I'm scared."

Nova leaned over and hugged the boy. He hugged her back fiercely.

"Me, too, kid. Me, too."

Ain't nothin' simple.

XXIII: DÓMUR ARUNDIR

A.Y. Evanti, 863, The Tenth Cycle

T IS NOT MY place, Mikallis," said Ronun, closing the book.

"Whose place is it, then?" Mikallis pleaded. His heart was in full panic, but his wits were intact enough to know the answers he needed lay in the verses Ronun withheld. "Are you not the elder of these people? Please, Ronun! I do not understand."

The elderly elf offered a sympathetic nod. "I can see that you do not. But that is not my doing, and I am not beholden to answer you."

"To whom, then? Whom do you serve, that would prevent you from aiding me?"

"Prevent me? None prevent me. I serve my people only, and above all, the truth."

"It is only the truth that I ask of you, no more! And I do not ask for myself!"

Ronun eyed Mikallis, his expression darkening. "It is such lies that have brought us to this moment in time. Of course you ask for yourself. Perhaps not *only* yourself, but a half truth is a full lie. Do you not understand this?"

Mikallis buried his head in his hands, concealing tears of frustration that began to form in his eyes. "I suppose I do not. Not as you do." Mikallis looked up. "But I mean you no harm. I wish to help my people. If you know things that will help me—"

"I know much that might help you. But I cannot tell it all to you in an evening, and whether I tell you anything at all will depend entirely on you." Ronun stood. "Your sight has been veiled by lies, young elf, and if the tale you tell is true, even death did not free you from them. But you will have time to learn. Decades, at least, should you survive here in Dómur."

Mikallis stood as well. The name Ronun spoke felt familiar, but his location was now the least of his worries.

"Decades? I will not stay here! I cannot!"

"You will, Mikallis Elmshadow. You must, and I am no more pleased about it than you. But you cannot leave. The threads of time are fragile."

Strong hands grasped Mikallis from behind. He pulled and twisted but could not free himself from the two sentries.

I will not stay here.

Mikallis centered himself and inhaled.

"NO!" Ronun's voice was a storm. Mikallis bent to its power.

"Hear me well! There is but one law you may not offend here, and but one penalty for its offense! *You shall use no magic in Dómur Arundir!"*

Mikallis blinked. In the space between two heartbeats he came to understand not only where in the wide world he was, but to whom he spoke.

This is the king of the Stone Elves.

~

Footsteps echoed, startling Mikallis awake. A film of dried salt caked his face, gumming his eyes closed. He rubbed them open, not because he wished to wake, not because he cared to whom the footsteps belonged, but because his sorrow and desperation demanded attention. He had wept for hours in the cold cell before exhaustion won out over anguish, but a few hours' fitful sleep shifted the balance back in favor of his grief.

Why do I grieve? he asked himself again, continuing the argument that plagued his heart and mind the night before. *The one I love has not yet even been born.* How *can I grieve? I have not yet been born!*

The door to his stone cell opened. The smell of fresh bread wafted in as murky, dusty light flooded the room. Mikallis blinked, the silhouette of an elf gradually coming into focus.

"You will eat, Mikallis of Thornwood, and then we will speak. I will answer questions you have, or I will not, and we shall not speak again until you discover the truth."

"The truth?" choked Mikallis, his throat raw from the night's weeping. "What truth—"

"Eat first," said Ronun. "Consider your questions carefully. Time will reveal that which truly matters, but I will offer what mundane answers I may. Or not."

The silhouette withdrew, replaced by two more. Mikallis stood.

"Follow," said a shadow.

Mikallis followed.

Two female sentries, thinner than those he had met the day before, each bearing half staves of oak, garbed also in brown robes but which fell only to the knee, led him through the castle to a vast dining hall. Four long wooden community tables lay parallel beside one another, each set for a hundred at least, with benches on either side. Sunlight filtered in through high glass windows, these clear and clean, illuminating rays of dust and reflecting dully off grey stone walls. A dozen elves shuffled to and fro with plates and pitchers, bowls and cups, platters decked with huge gourds and fresh breads, others with cheeses and boiled eggs, but aside from those serving, the hall stood empty.

The sentries stopped before the end of the nearest table. One motioned for Mikallis to sit. He did, and a plate was set before him. A cup was filled with steaming water; leaves floated to the top. Mikallis sat still with his hands in his lap, waiting for his captor's permission to eat. After a turn, a long turn whose purpose Mikallis understood to be a test, they eyed one another and nodded to Mikallis.

"Please eat quickly," said one. "The bell awaits you."

Mikallis did not understand the part about the bell, but he did not need to be told to eat quickly. He was famished. He stuffed himself with eggs, cheese, and bread, sipping just enough tea to lubricate his mouth for the next bite. He cleaned his plate quickly and moved on to a bowl of chopped fruit. The breakfast as a whole was humble but good, the tea bitter but strong, the bread fresh, the fruit fresh enough, and he reminded himself to be grateful despite his frustration. *You are a stranger here. They have housed and fed you. That is enough.*

"Thank you," he said to the sentries.

One leaned over Mikallis and poured him more tea. "You may bring this," she said. "Come."

When Mikallis stood, he saw several elves had been standing off behind him, watching him eat. They turned away, and one signaled to another far across the hall. The second turned and pulled violently on a long thick rope which Mikallis had not noticed before. A bell sounded, its low, powerful ring setting Mikallis' teeth on edge. A breath passed before the next ring, another before the next. Seven full rings sounded as Mikallis was led up a long, winding flight of stairs, the last a bit quieter than the first. By the time they reached the top, his legs ached, and he realized what the sentry had meant: the bell announced the morning meal, and it had been held in abeyance for him to complete his own breakfast. He could not decide if this was an honor or an affront.

He was led through a doorway onto an open parapet walk and around to its right, to the shaded side of a wide keep, and then left to the center of a narrower battlement, where Ronun stood gazing to the south and west. Mikallis deliberately did not turn to see himself; much like when he first arrived in Nyr Avi, he pretended that to not see a thing could deny its truth. The sentries came to a halt as he walked to meet Ronun, who kept his own gaze on the horizon as he greeted Mikallis.

"It is a fine day," Ronun said, closing his eyes and taking a deep breath of autumn air. When he exhaled, he turned to Mikallis. "You will not think so, I fear, and for that you have my sympathy."

Mikallis had forgotten how soothing Ronun's voice was. He took the elf's sympathy to be genuine, and in respect of its sincerity, he turned and closed his own eyes, filling his lungs with the same sweet air, trying to not only steady his nerves but to see Ronun's perspective.

"It is a fine day, Sire," Mikallis agreed. "Here at least."

"Sire? No, you need not call me 'Sire'. Ronun will do. Though I see you have reasoned much out."

"Some," Mikallis allowed.

Ronun nodded. "A fine day," he repeated, "but, I think you meant, '*now*, at least,' did you not? Your heart is not in the now, and so the beauty of the day will not sing to you as it does within me. Would you hear my viewpoint, for a moment?"

Mikallis nodded.

"Ya Di comes. Let us assume that before your arrival yesterday, this was already known to me. Not merely the truth that it comes, but the year, the day, even the hour. How might I view this morning then, given such knowledge?"

Mikallis considered his answer, sensing again that he was being tested.

"I cannot say," Mikallis said finally.

"No? Why?"

"Because I do not know you. You may see it as a gift, perhaps. Or it may fill you with remorse for that which may not always be. It may remind you of one lost, or one near. I simply cannot say."

Ronun nodded, looking back out over the battlement.

"This is a measured answer, Mikallis. Wise, perhaps, in the way one of Thornwood might weigh wisdom, but dishonest."

"Ronun, I did not mean—"

"Again, I will remind you that indignation will avail you nothing," Ronun said mildly. "But I will not chide you further. What would you ask of me?"

Mikallis took a swallow of his tea and finally allowed himself to look to the horizon. The day was not as clear as the one before, but he could still make out a hint of what must be Fang, many, many miles to the southwest. No great bellows of smoke emitted from its mouth; a fact which Mikallis found ironically disconcerting. He had been considering what his first question might be throughout breakfast, but the answers to every question he might ask were self-evident. Why may he not leave? Because he did not belong in his own world, not yet, and to arrive now could change the course of things to come, and perhaps not for the better. What would happen if he were to try? The Stone Elves would stop him, perhaps even kill him, to preserve the order of things. How do they expect to keep him here? They need not even make an effort. To leave might alter the events that led to his own birth. To Aria's birth. He would do as he must to keep Aria safe.

"There is one thing I would ask," Mikallis said finally. "Why have you outlawed magic?"

Ronun's eyebrows raised. "Of all the things you might ask me, you ask this first?"

Mikallis nodded.

"Tell me why you think it is outlawed here."

Mikallis knew the histories well enough. "There are two reasons I have heard. One, that at the Splintering, your people decided the cost of using magic was too high, that to sacrifice years of life in exchange for conveniences was an offense to life."

"And the other?"

"That you had suffered some great grief at the hands of death, and thus named it an enemy. To use magic would be to hasten death, and so you abandoned your gifts to spite death itself."

Ronin nodded. "I see. So you have been taught. But what do you *think*?"

Mikallis met Ronun's eyes, narrowing his own in thought. "Before last night, I thought it was the first, and perhaps a bit of the second, but only a bit."

"Why?"

"The sort of elves who would value life so highly would not indulge such a thing as spite, at least not overly so."

"Interesting observation. But you feel differently now? We seem more spiteful, now that you have met a few of us?"

Mikallis shook his head. "Not at all. I think neither are your reasons."

"Please, elaborate."

Mikallis shrugged. "I cannot. I only know that to punish one with death for using magic is inconsistent with both reasons."

Ronun offered an impressed nod. "That is true. And wise."

"Then why?" Mikallis pressed. "Why penalize an elf for the use of their gifts? I can see why you might disdain magic's use, but to sentence one to die... a stranger even, one who may not share your views? I cannot fathom this."

"I see that you cannot."

Mikallis waited. Ronun said nothing.

"Well?"

"I will not answer you. Not today, at least."

"Why not? What difference could it make?"

"Perhaps all the difference. Perhaps none. But in any case, you would not understand today, and so are not worthy of the answer. What else would you ask me?"

Mikallis fumed but did his best to hide his anger.

"Only this then, I suppose. What is to become of me here?"

Ronun nodded kindly. "That, young elf, I will answer. You will be kept largely away from my people, so that you might not overly damage the threads of time that hold Dómur Arundir together.

You will be given a generous plot of land, upon which you may farm and hunt, and you will observe three very important rules. First, you shall not use magic, not even to save your own life, not even to save another. The penalty for this will be your death. Do you understand this rule?"

Mikallis' jaw clenched. "I do."

"Second, you will not leave the boundaries of your land, for any reason, not even to save your own life, not even to save another. Do you understand?"

The loneliness of the idea was crushing, but Mikallis understood. "I do."

"Third, you will be visited each cycle by a sentry. He or she will make a great sacrifice to ensure your well-being and provide you fair opportunity to trade. You will tell this elf nothing of the future which you believe comes. You will hint at no prophecy, and you will ask no question that might beleaguer this elf with undue curiosity. Do you understand?"

Mikallis nodded. "I do."

"These things are horrors," Ronun said candidly. "Your loneliness will be profound. But such imperatives are necessary. Do you understand why?"

Mikallis nodded. "I do. I would not cause grief to your people, Ronun. I will keep to these rules."

Ronun smiled warmly. "If you do, I will visit you come next autumn, and you may ask your question again then."

"Will you answer?"

Ronun shrugged. "Perhaps. Perhaps not. But I will give you a question to ponder in the seasons between now and then."

"What question?"

"Only this: What is the truth?"

Mikallis frowned. "A riddle."

"Of a sort," said Ronun.

"I have never been good with riddles."

The old elf lay an arm across Mikallis' shoulders and led him back across the battlement to the rounded walls of the keep. The two sentries took charge of him. Ronun met Mikallis' eyes one last time before turning away.

"A riddle is but a veiled truth, Mikallis of Thornwood."

XXIV: MOR

IA SAT CROSS-LEGGED and naked within the circle, palms blistered and caked in blood. She had drawn the concentric rings, named the four points, and painted the positions of the Twins. She had used magic to cauterize her cuts, hastening the clotting process, the agony of this terrible but necessary. There was nothing more to do but wait; when the bleeding fully stopped, she could begin the spell.

She listened as she waited. Slater had spoken truthfully when he said he had work to do; the sounds of called orders, stamping horses, and marching boots from outside the barracks could only be an army preparing for battle. She was far less sure whether his prior declaration would ring true: that he had enough soldiers to take the Temple. Perhaps if they had the element of surprise on their side. Perhaps if they simply intended to burn it to the ground in the dark of night. If the Mother was prepared, however...

The Daughters were the most gifted casters in all of Tahr, and they wasted no effort at perfecting mundane magics. Bone and blood were their business, the magics one employed when taking or preserving life, and the Daughters of Kal had no interest in preservation. They numbered fewer than three score, but any one of them—Ordained or Unordained—could slay a company of foot soldiers in open battle. Why they had not taken Mor before this day was no mystery; Kehrlia had stood as a counterweight to their power, and the wretched Mother of Kal and her equally wretched son bore no love for one another. The uneasy truce between the tenants of Sartean's tower and those of the Temple existed only by the restraint of the Mother; had she stepped a toe over the line, her estranged son would have no doubt snipped it off, and the war between the great powers of Mor would have laid the city to waste. Such a result would have been in no way disdainful to the Mother, but it was said Kal cared little for the politics of cities and kingdoms; it was the world he was after, and should the Temple have fallen to Kehrlia before his domain was established, Kal would not have been pleased. Now, however, the great tower sat empty, and the son was not only dead but indebted to Kal, for whatever that might mean, and Nia felt sure it meant *something*. To the Mother's eyes, the time of the Temple's ascent was at hand... no, she would not be caught flatfooted, and neither would she be arrogant enough to presume Nia had followed her orders without question. The Temple would be prepared, and Nia of the sea feared neither Slater nor all the soldiers of Mor could stop its ascension.

Not without help.

Nia examined her hands to be sure her wounds had clotted over. She then examined every finger of her flesh, as best she could. The danger of casting within the circle was profound when attempted alone; if she missed even the smallest cut or scrape, if any vein or pathway to her lifeblood remained open, the ravenous magic would penetrate her body and consume her from within. The purpose of the awful penalty, or so she had been taught, was to demand patient meditation on the power of Kal within the circle. To hurry, to cast before a sufficient amount of time had been spent on one's knees waiting for the cuts to clot over, would be to embezzle Kal's power without proper recompense. Kal gave nothing freely. Typically, five Daughters would cast such a spell; one in the center, the others stationed at the four points of the compass, examining the supplicant's body for blemishes. When one was found, it was burnt and sealed by the Daughters outside the circle, this second morbid and painful practice meant to signify one's reverence for Kal, to signify that the god of death was deserving of not only total submission, but perfect supplication.

Nia had no intention of dying this day, terribly or otherwise, and thus she took her time. Nia had never seen a Daughter consumed by such a spell, but there were Ordained daughters who had, or at least claimed as much, and by all accounts, it was a terrible way to die. Nia found these accounts difficult to swallow whole, for ultimately, one had to *truly* believe Kal existed to accept such tales as fact. Nia had not equivocated when Slater asked her whether the gods were real; she suspected they were, and had said as much, but in truth she could not say. She could not, however, deny the way casting within a Kalian circle amplified one's power, for she had seen it with her own eyes. It was not too far a leap to accept the rest, and so she spent the better part an hour within the circle running her hands over her body. To one outside the circle, she might appear to be experiencing an ecstasy; in reality, there was only fear.

It was time. Nia stood.

No words were required to incant the spell; she must only focus her mind on the question and open herself to the answer. The question was asked, and the answer came swiftly: the Incantors who fell to Kalashagon were not the last of Kehrlia.

Miles to the north and west, how many she could not tell for certain, more than two score Incantors still lived. Why they lived was a mystery; why had they not joined Sartean in his great battle? Waves of power rolled over Nia's body, prying violently to gain entrance, but she had prepared herself adequately. She dared a second question, and the answer came just as swiftly as the first: these had abandoned their allegiance to Sartean, somewhere in the farmlands, some days before, and now they wandered leaderless.

A heat rose in Nia's palms. The power would soon overwhelm her, penetrating her newly closed wounds. She sensed she had but a breath, maybe two, before the spell would begin to consume her. She jumped quickly to her right, out of the circle. She fell to her knees. The blood with which she had painted the floor evaporated with a *hiss*, wisps of smoke rising from the pattern, blue, ethereal tendrils which reached towards her like ghostly fingers. She recoiled, scrambling on all fours to the far side of the room. A chorus of haunted whispers rose to an angry pitch. The heat in her palms became scorching. Nia cried out in fear and shut her eyes against what came next.

In the span of a breath, the pain and whispers were gone. Nia opened her eyes. A sizzling black residue lay where the Kalian circle had been drawn. It was over. Nia shuddered and looked down. A single droplet of blood wept from the wound on her right hand.

Fury, that was close.

~

"Have you seen Slater?"

The captain shook her head, not bothering to look up from the map of Mor laid before her on the command table. "Not for an hour."

"I need to speak with him."

The captain did not reply.

Nia pressed. "It's urgent."

The captain looked up. "And who in Fury are... hey, you all right? Your hands..."

"I'm fine. Please, I have to see him. Where would he have gone?"

The captain frowned. "You're that Daughter come by earlier."

"I am."

The captain nodded and stood. "He said to keep an eye out for you. He's in the square."

"Thank you." Nia turned away.

"Wait. Your hands."

"They'll be—"

"Shut up and sit down. Slater's occupied right now. You'll deal with me. *Theel!* Get your sorry arse over here."

Nia recognized the man as one she had spelled earlier.

"You!" Theel spat. "I should run you through—"

"Close your trap and get this woman two bandages."

"But Cap—"

"Move!"

Theel ran off, not before shooting an angry scowl at Nia.

"Captain Varyl," she said to Nia, offering a hand but pulling it back when she glanced again at the red messes at the end of Nia's arms. "We don't leave wounds untreated under my command."

Nia nodded, not bothering to say she could manage without help. Slater's admonition from earlier still rang; if she were to prove herself an ally to his army, she would need to demonstrate her acceptance of the hierarchy.

"Thank you. I—"

"Don't thank me. Just help. Gonna be one hairy spat, taking the Temple. What should we expect?"

Nia thought for a moment. "Well, that depends on whether they know you're coming."

"Assume they know."

Nia nodded. "I would. I'm no military mind, but I know how the Mother thinks. She won't risk herself, but she won't have the Daughters hole up, either. Our magic is far more effective in open ground."

Varyl nodded. "My thoughts exactly. We need to catch them in the Temple."

Nia shook her head. "You won't. They'll be all over Mor by now, or they will soon."

"Dammit!" Capatin Varyl crumpled up a hand-drawn map and slammed a fist on the table. "So what do we do?"

"I've been thinking about that. She sent me to enslave Slater, but she'll know by now that didn't happen. So, she'll be expecting an attack. If I were to guess, she'll be casting fortifications around the Temple to protect herself. She'll have Daughters stationed everywhere, waiting for your troops to take to the streets."

Theel arrived with bandages. He thrust them out before Nia.

"Wrap her hands, Theel. And not a word."

Nia looked to the man. "I'm sorry about earlier—"

"Forget him," ordered Varyl. "Eyes on me. What do we do? What's her weakness?"

Nia shook her head. "She doesn't have one, and that's no exaggeration. She has access to power I can't even begin to imagine, some of it stored in artifacts over the course of centuries. You can't assault the Temple the way things are, Captain. Not without help. Did the general tell you what I was doing upstairs?"

Varyl nodded. "Any luck?"

"As a matter of fact, quite a bit. There are a few dozen rogue Incantors northwest of Mor who might be persuaded to join your cause."

"How far northwest?"

Nia closed her eyes, trying to recall the feel of the location spell. She had never amplified such a spell from a circle before and so had no reference to gauge distance. "Hard to tell. Felt like a day's ride, maybe. Maybe two, but I can't say for certain. But—and here's the good news—they renounced Sartean before the end. They might be the sort to help. Ow!"

Theel yanked to tighten a bandage, a mean smile on his lips.

"Anything else, Cap?" he said, rising.

"Get a message to Bricks, and quick. I want a fresh squad of horse saddled and out front an hour ago."

"Captain, I'm not much of a rider."

"Then you're in for a couple miserable days," said Varyl. "Unless you have a quicker way to get to these Incantors?"

Nia thought for a moment. "I might. But you won't like it."

"I don't like one dung-dripping bit of any of this. But what do you have in mind?"

~

"She's not coming back," said the Daughter, refilling the Mother's wine glass.

"Aren't you perceptive?" The Mother rolled her eyes and took the glass.

"What, then? You have a plan, of course," said another.

"Of course," the Mother agreed. "And the six of you will be instrumental. You will be pleased to know I have not trained you in vain, ladies. Tonight, you will be given a great honor, though perhaps you might not all see it thusly."

"If it serves Kal," said one, "it is our joy."

"I'm *so* glad you think so." The Mother stood. The Daughters moved to stand as well, but a raised hand kept them seated. "Jaila," said the Mother to the Daughter seated nearest, she the youngest of the six, "how many does it take to perfect a circle?"

Jaila cocked her head, the question blindingly simple. "Four, Mother, and a supplicant."

The Mother reached up and removed her earrings, stones round and white as pearls set in silver. They were not pearls.

"And there are six of you. Two of you, I am sorry to say, will be redundant. But you will be given the honor of serving Kal nonetheless."

She cast the bone earrings onto the table and sauntered from the dining hall.

"When I return, we will know which of you deserve the honor of serving in my circle," she said, turning back when she reached the door, "and which of you will serve Kal," she glanced at the earrings, "in other ways."

The heavy oaken door closed behind the Mother without a touch. She had made it barely three steps when the screaming began.

XXV: FURY

HEN THE RINGING stopped, Cindra spoke. "Yeh canna let me sleep," she said, eyelids drooping over yellow eyes. "Not for a turn, not for a breath." She cast an orb, lighting the tunnel within which they stood.

"*Sleep?*" asked J'arn, tossing Lucan's wrist shackles aside. "Ain't no time for sleep, damn ye! We gotta save Aria!"

"What we gotta do first is heal Luc," Shyla said. "An' then we gotta *hide*. This tunnel ain't far enough from that tower, and I don't trust that... that *thing* to give us a day. Wolf needs a rest, or he ain't gonna make it."

Wolf whined.

"He'll give us the day," mumbled Lucan through cracked lips and a swollen jaw.

"And how do ye know that?" demanded J'arn, hacking down with his axe, busting the second set of shackles from Lucan's ankles. "And what's this impostor business?"

Lucan shook his head and opened his mouth to answer. Cindra interrupted.

"He lies," she said, laying a hand on Lucan's shoulder. "Nothin' but lies, ye canna believe a thing he says. Now help me."

"Just the knee," Lucan said, shifting. He winced. "And maybe the jaw."

Shyla and J'arn grasped Lady Cindra's shoulders as she sent waves of healing into Lucan. Lucan wept silently as the pain intensified. He and Cindra shared a long, knowing look. After a time, he nodded.

"Better," he said.

Cindra fell backwards, stumbling in exhaustion. She went to a knee.

"Lady!" said Shyla, rushing to catch her grandmother.

Cindra took Shyla's hand and came to her feet. "I'm all right," she said. "Ain't ready for the long nap just yet. And yer right, Shyla. Let's get yer Wolf somewhere safe."

"Nowhere is safe," said Lucan plainly.

"Oh, no ye don't," said J'arn. "We might die down here, but it ain't gonna be from despair. We gotta try! We ain't gonna just lie down—"

"No, J'arn, you don't understand. *Nowhere* is safe. Aria and I... we saw it. All of it."

No one spoke for a moment. Cindra broke the silence.

"Yeh best explain."

Lucan nodded and explained as best he could.

He and Aria had burned a wave of beasts and retreated back into their tunnel, careful to keep their feelings muted. After a time, they were left alone, and they set themselves free, melting the bars of their prison. They listened, and ran, and hid, and listened some more. They followed the path they had discovered through Aria's sonic magic, only to discover that it led to the great cavern where the spire lay. They doubled back, occasionally forced into fights when they could not evade detection, Lucan holding back foes as Aria sensed a new route. They found many and followed most, some to equally large caverns, some to dead ends, but an inescapable fact soon became clear. There was no door out of Fury, anywhere. Eventually, they found themselves with their backs to the cavern where the spire stood, pressed towards an opening high above its floor. A horde had them cornered—there was nowhere to go but to jump headlong into the pit. Lucan prepared the magic to do just that, hoping he might float their way to an empty tunnel, when, suddenly, inexplicably, the horde withdrew a dozen paces and held their position. The demons came from behind, from the opening of the cavern. There was no escape. He and Aria were separated, and Lucan would not relate what happened next. He did not need to; the truth was clear on his battered body. All he could say for sure was that what the Hand had said seemed to ring true: one could not come to this domain save through death.

"But *we* came," argued J'arn. "We found a way in. So did Lady Cindra."

"And I came by death," Cindra said. "Not my own, mind, but death all the same. The magic that brought yeh to me must be powerful indeed, but yeh came through the rip in the world I left behind me, right there in that hollow, right where I came in. And yeh can believe me when I tell yeh—that door didn't swing two ways."

"That don't make sense," said Shyla.

"Might not, but it's what is," said Cindra.

"Nope. Can't be. Breaks all the rules."

Lucan eyed Shyla. "I'm not so sure that rules—"

"Stop talkin' to me like I don't know what I'm sayin'!" Shyla shouted. "Were yeh not listenin' when Lady Lor gave us all that knowledge 'bout magic? There's *always* a balance! There can't *be* a way in without a way out! Life an' death, good an' bad, in an' out..." Shyla turned to Cindra. "What'd yeh say about a rip in the world?"

Cindra shook her head. "Ain't but an expression, child. Not a material thing."

"Well, sounds to me like it might be," said Shyla. "The rest of yeh came here before me, right? By how long?"

"Ten turns, at least," said J'arn. "Thought we'd lost yeh, and I was glad for it, if yeh get my meaning."

Shyla nodded and reached for J'arn's hand. "I do. But there was some sorta... curtain, I guess. And it was ripped, like yeh say... like... like it was blowin' in the wind. I dunno what it was, but it was sure enough real, and I didn't wanna go through."

"But you did," said Lucan.

"Had no choice," said Shyla. "Fought as hard as I could an' it slurped me up like soup. But..." Shyla shook her head, thinking. "But I guess it did close behind me, now that I think about it. At least it felt like it did. Dammit, dammit, dammit!" Shyla pounded her fist into the iron floor on each "dammit." The impacts echoed through the tunnels. Wolf edged closer to his friend and gave her face a lick.

"Well, that's something," said Lucan after a moment.

"Aye? And what is it?" asked J'arn.

"We know there's a veil, or whatever we might want to call it. And we know it can be opened, and we know it can be shut. But that begs another question. Why didn't it close after you, Cindra?"

Cindra shook her head.

"Well, ain't it obvious?" asked J'arn. "It didn't want to. Or *somebody* didn't want it to."

"Ah," said Cindra, nodding. "Now *that* makes sense."

"What does?" asked Shyla.

Cindra sighed. "It ain't good. Can only mean one thing."

The others waited.

"He knew yeh were comin'."

"And why's that not good?" asked J'arn. "Aside from the fact that we were comin' at all?"

"Because it means the Hand's gettin' his power from somewhere else. Some*thing* else, somethin' powerful enough to tell the future."

"Nah. I ain't buyin'. Nobody can tell the future," said J'arn.

"It's said that one can," Cindra said, her voice something between frightened and reverent. "The god of death itself."

"Kal," breathed Lucan.

Cindra's eyes seemed to glow at Lucan's utterance of the name. Her hands trembled. Wolf shifted closer to Shyla, whining.

"You all right, Lady?" asked J'arn.

Cindra looked away. "No, Prince J'arn. Don't think I am."

"Took too much," J'arn said, his tone grave.

"Too much," Cindra agreed. She bent to sit. The orb she had lit began to dim. She lifted her hand to her mouth and bit down on her palm, hard. "Gotta stay awake," she said.

"Lady... what'll happen if yeh fall asleep?"

Cindra looked at her granddaughter. "I s'pose I gotta say this now, 'fore it's too late. Yeh let me fall asleep, I ain't gonna wake up like yeh remember me."

"What's that mean?" pressed J'arn.

Lucan understood. "It means she might not be a friend."

Cindra nodded. "No 'might' about it."

"We gotta get outta here!" Shyla said with more than a hint of panic. "We gotta get Aria and get *out*!"

"I don't think we'll be gettin' Aria, child," said Cindra. "He won't let her go."

"Horse dung," said J'arn. "We ain't leavin' her."

"We might have to," said Lucan.

All eyes turned to the man. He lit another orb to replace Cindra's.

"Ye know something," J'arn said.

Lucan did not reply.

"He called ye an impostor. Think it's about time ye explain that."

Lucan met J'arn's gaze. "It may be, but I'm not going to. You'll have to let that go, J'arn."

"Why?" said Shyla. "If yer not who you say yeh are, I think that's something we all oughta know."

"Agreed," said J'arn. "Out with it."

"No," Lucan said firmly. "It's not your business, and it has nothing to do with any of this. Let it go."

"Hmph. And ye wonder why Mikallis didn't trust ye."

"Shut your mouth, J'arn. You don't know what you're talking about."

"You gonna shut it for me?"

Lucan glared at the prince of Belgorne. "I'd rather not. But I will if I have to."

"Lucan," said Cindra gently.

He turned.

"Tell us what yeh can."

"Me?" he asked. "Why not you? He called *you* his slave. Second only to Kalashagon. If there's a threat in our midst, it damned well isn't me."

"Fine!" Cindra answered, her eyes aglow. "Then I'll say it! Aria is not to be trusted! She's got secrets, he says—"

"Cindra, don't—"

"—and he's been tellin' me for as long as I been down here! The elves are to blame for all this, and don't ask me how 'cause I don't know, but the Evanti family is right smack in the middle of it!"

"You said yourself he's a liar!" Lucan argued. "You can't believe a word—"

"Then why won't he let her go?" demanded J'arn. "Tell me *that*! And why'd he cut the *impostor* loose?"

"Stop," Shyla said.

"If you call me that again, J'arn, prince or no, we're gonna have a problem—"

"Please, stop," said Shyla again. "Both of yeh."

Cindra turned to Shyla. "Oh, shut up, Shyla! Let 'em have at one another! I could use a bit o' entertainment!"

Wolf came to his feet, snarling. Shyla, Lucan, and J'arn turned to Cindra, aghast.

"Lady?" Shyla asked.

Cindra glared at Shyla. A hungry look flashed across her face. Shyla took a step back. The look faded.

"Oh... oh Shyla! I'm so sorry." She held out a hand.

"Lady," J'arn said, moving protectively between Shyla and her grandmother. "Might be ye need a turn alone."

"No," said Cindra. "I'm... I'm fine. We just... we canna be fightin' amongst ourselves. Understand? He wants it. We canna let him win, not like that."

J'arn moved closer to Cindra. He put an around her shoulder and moved her off a few paces from the others.

"Aye. Not like that. But ye ain't square in the head right now Lady, are ye?"

Cindra stopped. "Not all the way. I'm so tired... dunno when I slept last. And, well..."

"Ye took too much."

"I took too much."

"Lady," he whispered. "If ye start to... to go bad—"

"Then yeh take that axe and lop my head off," she whispered in return, leveling a solemn look at the dwarf. "Make it clean, if yeh please, but don't hesitate."

"I like ye, Lady. Shyla loves ye, more'n anything. But I'll do it, no mistake."

"I know yeh will. And yeh must. Same if I fall asleep. Don't let me wake up."

J'arn nodded.

"Do I need to worry 'bout Lucan?"

Cindra glanced over J'arn's shoulder. Lucan stood off from Shyla, gazing into the dark. They were speaking, but Cindra could not make out their words. Shyla scratched the fur beneath Wolf's enormous sagging ear.

"He's got secrets, and more'n one," she said. "But I think yeh can trust 'im. Don't really matter anyways."

"It don't?"

"If yeh don't make it out of here in a day, yeh won't never have to worry 'bout a silly thing like trust again."

J'arn nodded. "We'll make it out. But... ye say that like ye ain't comin' along."

Cindra patted J'arn's arm, the gesture oddly parental for a gnome who looked to be no older than twenty years.

"We'll just have to see, I s'pose."

Cindra turned to walk back to the others. J'arn hesitated.

"How will I know?" he asked.

Cindra met his eyes, understanding the question. "Yeh'll know. And if yer a bit early, I guess I won't have much to say on the matter. But be quick about it, and don't yeh miss. Yeh won't wanna face me as an enemy."

XXVI: THE GROVE

OU ARE RESTLESS, Mistress," said Petahr. The elf poured himself and Pheonaris another cup of tea.

"Observant as ever," she replied, slumping into a chair across from Petahr. The untidy cabin left little room to pace, but she had been doing her best for an hour.

"Still nothing?" he asked.

Pheonaris cast the initiate an annoyed glance. "You would know as soon as I did, or have you given up your habit of eavesdropping?"

Petahr handed her a cup and looked away. "No need to be fractious."

Pheonaris took the cup. "I am not *fractious*," she replied. "I am worried."

And she was. She had received word on the Winds from Marchion of the trouble in the Maw, two messages now, which she had relayed to Thornwood, her most recent missive sent the night before. The queen had yet to send reply. Neither had she heard from Aria. Her Speechstone had been silent for several days.

"It may be time to send someone north," Petahr said. "If our queen—"

"Our queen will send orders when she decides what to do," Pheonaris said, less sure of her declaration than her tone implied. *What if she is not well?*

"Very well," said Petahr. "South, then?"

"To whom? And to what end?"

"Some news from Mor would be helpful—"

"You saw the light in the sky, just as I did. Mor has its hands full with the dragon. No, all we can do is wait. And you need not wait here with me. Haven't you something to do?"

Petahr shrugged, sipping his tea. "Not especially."

Pheonaris sighed. The young elf was nothing if not devoted.

"What do you think she will do?"

Pheonaris understood the question. "She will not commit us to war, not now."

Petahr's expression was unsure. "If she does not respond soon—"

"She will."

Turns of silence passed. Pheonaris stared out her small, dingy window, watching the light of day fade to grey. Petahr stood to cast orbs of light into her lanterns.

"Can you not contact Nishali? To counsel patience, at least, until we—"

Pheonaris held up a hand. "Quiet."

The Winds whispered, carrying the First Knight's words .

~You must come, Mistress. Please, it is Phantom. Come now.~

Pheonaris stood.

"How many horses are in the stables?"

"Boot and Garlan took all but two, Virtue and Gale."

"Which?" Pheonaris asked, rummaging through the clutter, tossing vials and bundles of herbs into a bag.

"Well, Virtue is compliant enough, though not very fast. Gale still defies the bridle a bit—"

"Bring me Gale. Saddle him only; forgo the bridle. Quickly, now!"

Petahr raced from the cabin as Pheonaris finished packing and pulled on a pair of riding pants. By the time she had laced her boots and tied her cloak, Petahr called from outside. She thought for a moment before reaching behind the door for a spare cloak. She flew out the door.

Petahr stood patting a restive, stamping dun stallion. "He is a bit nervous, Mist—"

"Petahr," she said solemnly. "Would that I could honor you properly, but there is not time." She threw the second cloak over his shoulders.

"Mistress! I—"

"I ordain thee into the Order of the Society of the Grove, Petahr Heartwood, honorable elf of the Wood and my devoted friend. I furthermore name thee my Third, second only to Trellia Evanti, and charge thee to act in my stead." Pheonaris tied the clasp. "I leave you the Grove."

Petahr stood in shock as his mistress alighted the saddle.

"Be my ears, Petahr, and be my lips. Listen, and convey the queen's messages to Marchion," she paused for a moment, "and to Nishali." Pheonaris leaned over the saddle, placing a hand on either side of Gale's neck. She closed her eyes. In a breath, the two were Bonded.

"Ride, Gale!"

~

Gale and Pheonaris flung the miles behind them, Gale

galloping without complaint though occasionally challenging Pheonaris' suggestions regarding their course. The headstrong stallion, bored by the Northern Road, seemed to prefer every branching trail they crossed, insatiably curious to know what lay to the east and west. The Mistress remained vigilant and kept them to the road, occasionally needing more than her knees to hold their route, but her Bond with Gale grew quickly fierce, their temperaments naturally attuned to one another. The ride might have been a joy had its purpose not been so dire.

Barris would not call for Pheonaris were the situation not grim. His pride would not allow it. And to call on behalf of Phantom... Pheonaris shuddered.

It was dawn when the two came across Spirit, Sera, and Hope. A brief query of Spirit's mind told the awful tale of the cargo they carried. The Mistress fell to tears, but there was no time to break stride.

~Go, my friends. On to the Grove. Petahr will tend to you. I am so sorry.~

Oh, these terrible times. It was only then that Pheonaris remembered just how cold she was, how dismal was the dawn, how bleak and desolate the world had become. She indulged the feeling for hours, her surrender to general melancholy somehow easier than considering the more specific losses of Trellia and Mikallis. When their pace began to flag, Gale would have none of it. He whinnied urgently and threw his head, as if to call her from despair.

~Thank you. Ride on, great stallion. They are not far, now.~

They were not. They rode at speed for another hour. Pheonaris and Gale rounded a wide bend at a near gallop, and topping the next rise they saw Barris leading Phantom on foot. Two horses followed. An old man rode one. An ashen lump lay atop the other.

"Mistress!" Barris called. "Oh, thank the Father!" Barris moved Phantom off the road and helped the old man from the saddle. The man landed on unsteady feet and fell to his knees. Barris appeared no stronger.

Pheonaris slowed Gale to a walk and jumped from the saddle, careful to maintain contact with the snorting, frothing horse as they approached Barris' company.

"This is Gale," she said to Barris. She then spoke into Gale's mind. *~And this is Barris. Trust him. He is a friend.~*

Gale huffed his assent as Barris placed a hand on the saddle horn. "Easy, friend. Easy." Barris turned his attention to Pheonaris. "There is not much time. Can you withdraw from Gale?"

Pheonaris nodded, releasing the Bond. Her knees unlocked briefly. "I am fine. We are not yet spent. Who is this?"

"Gerald Longstock, ma'am. My friend..." Gerald's voice faltered.

Pheonaris turned from the man and looked over Phantom, frowning. She spoke to Barris. "These scars. He seems... well, but..."

"Phantom will be fine. It is this man, now, that needs you." Barris pointed to the younger man draped over a bay mare.

Pheonaris crossed quickly to the man and lay a hand on his head. Alarm crossed her features. She quickly lifted him from the saddle and laid him in the snow. His hood fell open, exposing a tortured and torn face. Pheonaris gasped.

"Barris! What happened to this man?"

"You must save him. Please," Barris begged. "He has given himself. You must."

Pheonaris shrugged off her sack and began to rummage through it. She pulled out a waterskin and popped the cork. She held it to the man's mangled lips.

"Here, sir. Drink."

Vincent lifted his head feebly as Pheonaris poured the Spring water into his mouth. The man swallowed.

"Not wine," he said meekly. "Hoped it might be wine."

"This is better," said Pheonaris.

"Unlikely."

"More, now, just a bit."

She held the skin again up to his mouth. Vincent coughed and pushed her hand away. Pink froth bubbled from his lips.

"Gerald."

"I'm here, Vincent." Gerald turned to the Mistress. "Spring water, yes? How long for it to work?"

Pheonaris frowned. "It... it should be helping already."

Vincent grimaced, some internal pain gripping him anew.

"Well, *is it?*" Gerald demanded, his face a mask of desperation. "Is it working, dammit?"

Pheonaris shook her head.

"Gerald," Vincent repeated, his tone soft, resigned.

Gerald took his friend's hand.

Pheonaris looked on as the younger man looked into the older man's eyes. "Tell the others—" he coughed again "—I'll be keeping an eye on them."

"Oh, Vincent." Gerald began to weep.

"An *eye*, get it?" Vincent tried a smile. "Just the one."

The Merchant of Mor took a long, trembling breath—

"Anie."

—and died on the Northern Road beside the Mistress of the Grove, the First Knight of Thornwood and his storied steed Phantom, and his dearest, oldest friend, Gerald Longstock, who drenched his hand in tears.

XXVII: HIGHMORLAND

LOUDS OF STEAM emitted from Kalashagon's black maw with each foul, gurgling breath. The stench induced a heave from the sorceress, her body rejecting the wholesome stew given her by the Mancheles. She wiped her mouth and forced herself to stare at the black beast who towered before her.

Kalashagon bent his head towards Mila. He sniffed at the diamond clutched in her hand.

~Such power,~ Kalashagon conveyed. *~But would it be enough, I wonder?~*

Mila answered aloud, her words far braver than her tone. "Only one way to find out."

Kalashagon curled his black lips back, exposing equally black fangs, the longest as tall as Mila, these jutting from crimson gums which pulsed in time with the vile monster's heart. The sight proved the beast must *have* a heart, an idea which Mila found abhorrent. The dragon paced around Mila, his long, serpentine neck weaving around trunks of trees, his barn-sized body slicing saplings in two where razor-sharp scales scraped against them. Mila turned with the dragon, her hand outthrust, knuckles whitened with strain as she grasped the gem as tightly as she might, careful, always careful, to remain facing him whichever way he turned. If he were to strike, she would have only a moment to ignite the gem, and she would not hesitate. If she were to die this day, her last act would be to obliterate her killer.

~Foolish witch. You cannot stay my wrath forever. Soon you will freeze.~

"I have more magic than this, slave."

~Then you will starve. Or sleep. I have gone decades without food, years without sleep. I will outlast you, witch. My master has prepared me well.~

"Not well enough to save your eye," Mila sniped.

Kalashagon snarled. *~I have another.~*

"But only the one. Maybe I should wait until you are distracted and pluck it out for you. Bring some balance to that disaster of a face."

~And you, so very beautiful.~ The dragon's black tongue extended forward. Mila took a step back. *~Yet with all your beauty, you are but mortal. Soon you will rot. As all things do.~*

Mila smirked. "And what are you, then? Immortal? Unlikely, if you cannot even survive a cycle on Tahr without being blinded."

~I am *immortal!~* Kalashagon thrashed his tail, roaring, felling a half dozen trees. Mila let out a yelp. The copse within which she had been hiding was quickly becoming a clearing. *~This body will fail perhaps, one day. Many years from now, long after your wretched people are long forgotten. And I will return to my master, who will make me another.~*

Mila remained quiet for a moment, steeling herself, willing her mind clear. This parlay would go on for some time, she knew, and if she were to gain any advantage, she would need to set aside her terror and sharpen her mind.

"And if you fail him?"

~I will not.~

"And if you do?"

It was the dragon's turn to remain silent. Mila knew she had struck a chord.

"All I have to do is ignite this gem," she said, "and he will punish you, won't he? More decades spent in hunger, more years in pain."

~There is no pain I cannot withstand, witch.~

Mila laughed aloud. "So what? So you withstand it. Is that the end you seek? Is that to be your great rebirth? How long did you suffer at his hands, I wonder, to become what you are?"

Kalashagon thrust his head forward. Mila prepared to ignite the gem, but the dragon's jaws did not open. He stopped within a hand of her face, baring his fangs.

~Millenia.~

Mila blanched. A thing far removed from pity sparked within her, but not wholly unlike it; the feeling tiny, remote, buried by rage and terror and the horrors of her own life, but it was there, begging her heart's attention.

Kalashagon withdrew a half dozen paces back and settled onto his haunches. His immediate fury had waned; a game of waiting would now begin. Mila sat, settling against one of the few trees remaining nearby. The two did not speak for an hour. It was Mila to rekindle their parley.

"You should defy him."

Kalashagon lifted his head, turning to his right, squinting his black eye at the sorceress.

~You are a fool.~

"Am I? You said it yourself. I cannot outlast you. I will tire. I will grow hungry. I will freeze. I will not die within your mouth."

~Then you will die by my flames. Or I will pick at your frozen carcass. It matters not.~ The dragon lowered his head again.

"I swear to you, Kalashagon, before I do, I will ignite this gem. I will not wait until the end."

Kalashagon bared his fangs.

"And if by some chance you survive, a chance I would not count on, there are others you are bidden to slay, are there not?"

~There are.~

"And when you are wounded, when your scales are blasted from your body, when your remaining eye is obliterated and your limbs are shattered, how then will you carry out your task?"

~So, then, witch, that is your ploy here? You would have me leave to pursue my other prey?~

"No. I would have you defy him, dragon. Defy your master. To spite him, if nothing else."

~ You are a coward, Mila Felsin. And you bargain poorly.~

"I am not afraid to die," Mila lied. "But *you* should be."

Kalashagon looked intently at Mila for a long turn.

~Of what consequence is my fate to you?~

Mila stood and approached the beast, moving but a step closer. She spoke her next words into the dragon's mind, where he might sense their truth.

~I have suffered much. I have caused suffering in return, much of it in the name of the one who took everything from me. You have endured more, far more, and yet you also do the will of the one who has harmed you most.~

A quiet moment passed. An insane urge to draw nearer, to reach out and touch the dragon, nearly overwhelmed Mila's good sense. She resisted, barely.

~*Perhaps,*~ conveyed Mila, ~*it is time we choose our own paths.*~

Kalashagon rose. Mila shuddered. The edges of the diamond pressed gouges into her palm. The great dragon unfurled his wings, the immense black sails clearing the area of snow and ash. The orange glow in his throat returned as he towered over the sorceress, his great and terrible magnificence on display.

~*You have played well this day, Mila Felsin. I will kill you in the end. Upon that you can rely.*~

Kalashagon flapped his mighty wings and launched himself into the air.

~*But I believe I will save you for last.*~

XXVIII: THE MAW

ELL? OUT WITH it. How many'd we get?"

"At least twenty," Martle replied. "There were four others, Sire... they still lived, but their burns—"

"An' ye put 'em down?"

Martle nodded. "Aye."

"Good work. No point in havin' em suffer, elves or no."

"They weren't elves, Sire."

Dohr looked up from the table, meeting Martle's stare. He popped the cork on a skin of ale and drained it, his fourth for the day. It was not yet noon. Dohr blinked as he tried to focus on his cousin's face. He was sure he saw an accusation in the dwarf's eyes. He narrowed his own.

"Ye must not think on it, Martle. They were volunteers. This be war."

"Sire, they weren't soldiers—"

"Fury they weren't! We're all soldiers now. Every last one. Ain't enough dwarves left to make such distinctions. I'll hear no more on it. Where are we on supplies?"

A grey-bearded dwarf spoke up. "Twenty tents, including this one. We saved the grain and wagons and such, but we're outta pitch, and—"

"Whadda they call ye, old-timer?"

"Name's Kimber, Sire. Farrion Kim—"

"We don't need pitch to march, Kimble. I wanna hear about food. Don't give a hot heap o' dung about the rest. Understand?"

"I understand, Sire, but a bit o' pitch mighta helped light some fires for folk. Hard to find dry wood this time o'—"

"And we're outta pitch, ye said?"

"Aye."

Dohr slammed a fist on the table. *"Then what in Fury good is a report about what we* ain't *got?"*

Kimber lowered his head. Dohr motioned for Martle to pass his own skin over. Martle took it from his belt, popped the cork, and turned it upside down. "Sorry, Sire. Empty." Dohr muttered a curse.

"Sire," Martle said, "I know ye don't wanna hear it, but we're gonna have to do somethin' about shelter. We got thousands o' dwarves slept outside last night. Weren't the coldest, but today's shapin' up—"

Dohr leveled a gaze at his cousin.

"Listen up, Martle. An' listen good. You, too, Kibbler—"

"Kimber, Sire."

Dohr flashed a fiery look at the old dwarf.

"Sorry."

Dohr continued. "As I was sayin'. We're gonna be fightin' the elves here in a day or three. They might be marchin' on us right now. They tried to arrest yer *king*, damn ye! A *Silverstone*, like... like some common thug! Arrogant bastards thought I'd just go off with 'em, quiet-like into the night. And ye know then what they'da done after? They'da slaughtered the rest of ye, sure as stone."

Kimber tugged at his beard. "Sire, I dunno about—"

"Kimble, if ye say one more word outta turn I'mma have Martle here gut ye. Right here. *One more word.* Now I was sayin'. They'da slaughtered what's left o' Belgorne. Why else arrest your king? So ye'd be leaderless, that's why! So ye can't put up a fight! Ye think they give one turn's thought to that gnome wench? Was a pretense, is all. And before ye ask, I dunno why they want war with us, but if I were to lay a guess, it'll be the same reason anybody ever goes to war. Food's scarce everywhere. Hungry folk go to war. Mor's gonna march north, or Thornwood's gonna march south, and pickin' off what's left o' Belgorne afore we can choose a side is just cold strategy. They'll get our grain. They'll get our iron and steel. Better them than Mor, is what they figure, and ye can bet a bag on it." Dohr reached again for his skin, forgetting it was empty. He threw it at Kimber. "Dammit! Can a king not get a bit o' ale, for Fury's sake?"

"I'll go fill it, Sire," said Kimber, bowing.

"See that ye do! And rustle up a bottle o' nightnectar, while ye're at it. Go on, now, move yer old sorry arse!"

"Aye, me king."

Dohr turned to Martle. "Now, what was I sayin'?"

"The elves, Sire."

"Aye. The bleedin' elves. Ye know they're gonna wipe us out, don't ye? Every last one of us, young and old. This is the end, cousin." He pounded his fist on the table. "The." Pound. "Bleedin'." Pound. "*End.* So when I ask Kimble there about supplies, I ain't askin' about any damned thing but what we can take with us to the Sapphire."

Martle frowned. "But, if the elves are gonna attack—"

"*We ain't gonna be here!* Leastways not me an' you. When that old geezer comes back, I want the two of ye to get a wagon or two filled with whatever supplies ye can, enough for a couple dozen dwarves to make the trip south. Ye can pick the dwarves ye like, but ye make damned sure ye pick ones that can fight. And ones ye can trust to keep quiet." Dohr thought for a moment. "Make sure ye grab a few she-dwarves, too."

Martle's jaw dropped.

"Bah, close yer trap afore ye catch a mouth o' midges." Dohr motioned for Martle to sit across from him. The dwarf slumped into the chair.

Dohr regarded him for a moment before speaking. "Ye knew this was comin'."

Martle shook his head. "Can't say as I did, cousin."

"Then ye be a fool. Soon as them elves came creepin' I saw it. Saw it like I see ye standin' there. Ah, for Fury's sake, wipe that miserable look off yer face, soldier. I got plenty o' reason to weep an' whine myself. Had the Sovereign for what, half a cycle? King o' Belgorne I was! Hmph. Try havin' *that* taken from ye, see how ye feel. Don't see me cryin' about it. Then there's the shame o' bein' me father's son. Coward, he was, now that I think on it. Ain't nobody but a coward gonna take his own life. Oh, I hear 'em talkin', the great Garne Silverstone, heart o' grief for his people, sorrow for the ages, blah blah blah. They're already singin' songs about 'im, can ye believe that? Like he was some bleedin' hero. Then there's my fool of a brother. Gonna go to the elves for help! Ha! Good idea, ye damned buffoon. Woulda made one dung-drippin' king, that one. But ye can bet a bag he's dead, too, soon as the elves got hands on 'im. Well, Fury take 'em both. There's one

Silverstone gonna survive this mess. Ain't no reason for us all to die. You, neither. We go south, wait out this mess. Maybe we come back, but more likely we don't. Ain't gonna be no food for least a year, all this ash. Farms west o' Mor'll go barren. Livestock'll die. Gonna be nothin' but war and famine from here on out, cousin. Only place might give a few of us a chance is down by the sea, and better a few dwarves survive than none. Ye follow my lead, keep our company from tearin' itself apart, and we might just have ourselves some families a few years hence. Fury, if ye like I'll name ye general. And don't ye feel a bit bad about it! Any other o' those out there'd do the same thing if they had a few soldiers to order around."

Kimber returned with two full skins. He placed them on the table. Dohr shot him a look.

"I'm sorry, Sire. Nobody seems to have any nightnectar, or at least they ain't sharin'."

Dohr popped a cork and took a long swig.

"See what I mean? Won't even spare a bottle for their king. Rotten, ungrateful lot. Kimby, I want ye to go with Martle. He has orders."

"Aye, Sire," he replied. Both Martle and Kimber glanced at the second skin. Dohr snatched it from the table and tucked it under his chair.

"Well, go on then! *Move!*"

~

"Sire."

Dohr continued to snore. Martle kicked the cot.

"*Sire.*"

"Huh? Wha... oh, Martle." Dohr glanced at the lantern his cousin held. "Dark yet?"

Martle nodded. "We're ready."

"Wait outside while I dress. Leave the light."

"Aye, Sire."

Dohr's head rang like an iron bell. He grabbed a pair of dirty leggings from the foot of the bed and stood to pull them on. He fell over before he could get a foot in. *Gah. Still drunk. Just as well.*

He managed to dress eventually, though he mislaced a boot twice before getting it right. He tied his dagger to his waist and slung his axe over his back. His armor sat on the ground, leaning against the center tent pole. He stared at his father's breastplate for a long while, the decision whether to take it somehow striking him as a crucial one. No one on the Sapphire shores would recognize it; the storied steel armor would mean nothing to anyone but the dwarves of Belgorne. Only those who came along would know it for what it was. Dohr considered whether wearing the distinguished piece might enhance his authority among the soldiers he led south. He decided it would, and that in all likelihood his kingly influence would be tested more than once on the journey, and that such a visible reminder of his station might serve to stave off disloyalty, but he could not bring himself to reach for it. Some part of himself, some long-neglected fragment of honor cried out within him, against him, demanding that he leave the breastplate behind, this the battle-dented heirloom of his father, and his father's father, and his father before him, and try as he might, his arm would not obey his mind's command.

Martle stuck his head into the tent.

"Sire? Need help with anything?"

Dohr glanced one final time at the breastplate. He reached down, taking only his helm.

"Grab the lantern." Dohr stomped from the tent, his gait unsteady.

He and Martle snuck to the far edge of the encampment, if it could even be called such a thing. Dohr crept past glowing fires, quiet families huddled around them. Most simply sat in silence. Those he did hear spoke in what he imagined were hushed, despondent tones. He saw only one tent as he skulked south, keeping to the shadows and out of the sight of his people.

Scant twinlight illuminated two wagons, each strapped to a team of two, sitting at the base of a hill. Perhaps a dozen horses huffed clouds of steam, their riders holding the reins. Dohr peered around, beginning a head count. Martle saved him the trouble.

"Eighteen," he said, "including us. Ten male, eight female."

"Fighters?" asked Dohr.

Martle shrugged. "They can all work a crossbow and wield an axe. Ain't a one seen battle, though. Best maybe we don't look for trouble."

Dohr stepped forward into the middle of the small company. He opened his mouth to speak, imagining that he should say something, but nothing came to mind. His head throbbed. He stood silent for an uncomfortably long time.

"Ready on your order, Sire," prompted Martle.

On my order.

Dohr turned and looked back, towards the fires. Still far from sober, he saw twice as many as were there to see. He squinted, trying to bring his eyes into singular focus, but could not. He looked back again to the assembled soldiers whose faces he could no longer make out after staring into the firelight. Seventeen expressionless, orange ghosts looked back at him.

"Mount up," he said finally. Dohr reached for the saddle horn of a nearby horse. He stepped into the stirrup and pulled himself up. He clumsily tried to throw a leg over, but only managed to kick the horse in the flank. The horse stamped and shied, throwing its head. Dohr Silverstone, King of Belgorne, fell flat on his back with a thud and a moan.

"Oh, for Fury's sake," said a female dwarf. "Somebody toss 'im in a bleedin' wagon and let's get outta here."

XXIX: DÓMUR ARUNDIR

A.Y. Evanti, 864, The Tenth Cycle

 IKALLIS WAITED, watching, scanning the eastern sky as he had each clear dusk for the past thirteen cycles. This evening he lay atop the new roof of his cabin, the humble home built hastily a year before to survive the winter but made sturdier each season. Kallar had not quite warmed to Mikallis throughout the past year, but on his last visit, he had taken enough pity on him to spend a day teaching the art of pulping marywood bark and casting tiles. Heavy rains and violent storms would soon herald autumn's arrival, Kallar had promised, and if Mikallis did not want to "drown in ugly coffin", he must pay close attention, as Kallar would show him only once. Half a cycle of failure duplicating Kallar's efforts had finally yielded an example of tile resilient enough to use for a roof, but Mikallis' tiles came out far thicker than Kallar's—and heavier. When the boughs Mikallis had selected for new trusses began to bow, he was faced with a choice: learn to make thinner tiles or reinforce his roof and walls. He chose the latter, and this very afternoon, the day before Kallar, or perhaps Shem, were due to visit, he had affixed the final tile, completing his prodigious task. Mikallis imagined his home could now withstand anything, save perhaps Kalashagon himself landing atop it, a risk that would not exist for fifty years. Thus, now, he lay proudly across his roof, hands folded behind his head. From this vantage point, he would

soon again see Kal breach the horizon in the east just as Lor dipped below in the west.

The exercise had become a ritual near the end of winter, when the idea first came to mind. Each day, when the sky was clear enough, Mikallis marked the door of his cabin with a white rock, imagining the left and right jambs to be the east and west horizons, and upon these he drew a line marking each day. Above these lines he drew the Twins as they appeared at dusk, careful to represent their positions relative to the chalk-line horizons in the best scale he could depict. At the end of the cycle, if he had made his marks well, he could see the progress of time, each day bringing him closer to the day of his birth, of Aria's birth, and, eventually, to the day when he would return to Greater Tahr and replace the Mikallis he had once been.

The method by which his re-entry into his world might be accomplished was still a mystery... would that other Mikallis cease to exist upon meeting him? Would he? Would it be best to wait until the dragon killed the other Mikallis, and then re-enter his world? Could he allow his other self to die? Should he? Would it be too late by then to save Aria from her fate? If for no other reason, Mikallis was grateful for the time between this year and that far-off one, for he imagined it would take quite a long time to puzzle out such answers.

Mikallis swatted a nibbling insect from his sunburnt arm. The sun had now withdrawn, its blistering work done for the day, though tenacious pastel strokes persisted across the sky. A ghostly white thumbnail emerged over the eastern horizon to contrast against a cloudless blueberry backdrop. Bright, twinkling acolytes to the god of death began also to emerge, pinheads of light in white, blue, and red, gleaming in anticipation of another opportunity to guard their master's pursuit across the sky—or so Mikallis had come to imagine. Opposite, to Mikallis' right, Lor had just begun to shy, seeking haven beneath the greying hedge of the distant range, hastening now to escape fiery fingers of pink and yellow and orange, these hues displayed haphazardly, each vying for the contested right to paint the few scattered clouds which separated east from west, and day from night.

Mikallis slid from the roof and retrieved the chalk stone from its resting place in a misshapen wooden bowl beside the door. He went to a knee and made his markings. This, the last day of the cycle, was always bittersweet. The top- and bottom-most depictions would on such days be most contrasting, their distances between the Twins and their respective horizons least similar, and thus the depiction of time's passage was most well-illustrated. The twenty-ninth mark also meant that he would be visited the next day by either Kallar or Shem, or perhaps both as they once had, and their company, however brusque and brief, kept Mikallis from feeling as if he had faded into nothingness. They would trade; Mikallis would have a dozen gourds to offer tomorrow, these now finally ripened, and two full sacks of dried venison. He also had cured the skin of the young buck from which the venison came, a debt which he owed against the advance of two dozen arrows and a bow given him in the second cycle of that year, when the snows were high and the wolves were plenty. In exchange he would be receiving portions of milled flour, salt, and cheese, perhaps a candle or two, and, if Kallar kept his promise to consider the matter, he may also receive a few ingots of iron from which he might attempt to cast spearheads and nails.

These mundanities were pleasant to consider, but the night before the first day of a cycle also meant he would be wiping clean his marks the next day. On the wall inside his cabin he would duplicate only the last mark of the cycle. Now there would be eight, one for each cycle since the first he had made in the Spring, but before he could leave his timeless, doorless prison, there would need to be over six hundred.

Mikallis stood, squinting as he tried to compare his poor drawings of the Twins on the jambs, but the light of day had faded. He turned to face the fire pit which sat between his two gardens, then back to the scant pile of wood which sat beside his door. He decided against a fire; he had gathered very little wood this cycle, busied with the task of reinforcing his roof, and there was no telling when the rains might come. He would forgo his nightly fireside conversation with the as-yet-unborn princess of Thornwood and retire early this night. He stepped through his door and lay upon his bed of hay, which had begun to reek. Perhaps his visitors would bring a bale to trade.

Only at these times, only when the day had been spent and no light remained under which he might busy himself, did Mikallis allow himself to consider The Question.

What is the truth?

The question had been an enemy the previous winter, a teasing cruelty, taunting him as he shivered and starved and fought his instincts to use his magic for a bit of comfort, or to manage a meal. By spring it had become an annoyance, a resented thing he preferred to keep at bay. By summer, as sweltering boredom and loneliness sank in, it had become a welcome distraction, one he realized he had begun to indulge far too often when he might have instead been improving his homestead. So, he established a policy: he would restrict its consideration to these quietest of times, when no other task called to him. Now, knowing that Ronun might come at any time expecting an answer, the question had again become a worry, and he regretted not giving it more attention. What might Ronun do if his answer was incorrect? What might he think of Mikallis' failure? Failure was certain. He had not settled on an answer. He did not even truly understand the question. The truth about what? The truth about himself? About Ronun? About time, or life? Perhaps righteousness? Good? Evil? And who decided what was true, in any case, on any of these subjects? Who was the arbiter of truth and falsehood? Did such a one exist? Certainly, Mikallis would fail this test. In his failure, would he forever lose the chance to ask Ronun for his own answers?

Mikallis kept returning to the idea that the answer to The Question was in some way tied to his own question of why the Stone Elves punished the use of magic as they did, but try as he might, night after sleepless night, he could trace no thread between the two.

Mikallis' eyes began to droop.

Goodnight, Aria.

~

Mikallis awoke before dawn to the sound of a whinnying horse. *So early?* he wondered. *They usually come at noontime...*

He stood and stretched quickly, rushing to pull on his one fresh pair of pants and lace his sandals. He emerged from his cabin as his grey woolen tunic fell to his waist. The bright flames of a fire in his pit greeted him, a pot boiling in its center, its orange light revealing the silhouette of a horse and wagon. He turned to see Ronun sitting on the stump beside his door, sipping tea.

"You have grown lean, Mikallis of Thornwood. It has been a difficult year, no doubt."

Mikallis stammered. "I... um, welcome, Ronun—"

"Have Shem and Kallar not traded generously with you?"

"Ah, no, I mean, they have traded fairly—"

"Fairly? Hmm. Tea?" Ronun handed Mikallis a cup.

"Yes, thank you. Please, forgive my stuttering. I did not expect you this morning."

"I can see that. One could surmise also that you did not expect Shem nor Kallar today."

"Oh, no, I did, but they usually—"

"Do the Alvi of Thornwood no longer practice the honor of Sif Rhai?"

Mikallis tilted his head, confused.

"The Gift of the Chair," said Ronun. "Has this practice fallen out of favor?"

"Oh... no, it has not—"

"Do you not honor Shem and Kallar, then?"

Mikallis' shoulders slumped. He thought for a moment before responding, examining his feelings on the matter before answering. He had promised himself to choose his words carefully with Ronun, to speak the whole and honest truth.

"I am grateful to them, Ronun. But also resentful. I did not think to honor them—"

"Why resentful?"

Mikallis sat on the ground before Ronun. "I am not sure I can put it into words. It is a selfish thing to feel, I know. It.... it is envy, I suppose. That they should have freedom while I—"

"I can see this is difficult for you to admit."

Mikallis nodded. "It is."

Ronun sighed. "It should not be. It is how you feel, no more. Though, you are unwise to feel as you do. Or perhaps only ignorant. May I enlighten you?"

"Please do."

Ronun bent and moved from the stump to the ground, an action Mikallis saw to be generous. He offered a hand to assist, which Ronun accepted. The old elf sat cross legged beside Mikallis, facing out from the cabin. The two sat in silence for a few turns, Ronun in no hurry to begin his sermon, content watching the tops of the trees brighten from charcoal black to dull grey as the first diffuse light of day pushed aside the night.

"Do you recall the things I said to you in our last meeting?"

Mikallis nodded. "I do. Every word, I think."

"I imagine you have searched your memory of those words for clues, yes? Clues to the question I asked you?"

"Yes. Exactly that. More times than I can count."

Ronun nodded. "Because you wish to ask things of me. And you believe that you must first answer my question of you."

Mikallis nodded.

"I am..." Ronun paused, "a bit disappointed. Though not altogether surprised. You have spent a year alone, visited only by two others, once per cycle, and you have overlooked the most important thing I told you in our last conversation, in favor of wasting your attention in service of your own ends."

Mikallis looked up, shame and shock etched on his face. He moved to speak.

"Be still," Ronun urged, "and listen. In our last meeting, I told you that you would be visited each cycle by a sentry, and that he or she would make a great sacrifice to ensure your well-being. Tell me truly. How much time have you spent considering what sacrifice Shem and Kallar have made for you?"

Mikallis shook his head. "Almost none. I..."

The realization struck Mikallis like a falling boulder.

"Oh, dear Father. I just assumed they were inconvenienced. But... the threads... the reason I am here, secluded..."

"Go on."

The boulder settled in Mikallis' belly. "They have isolated themselves, haven't they?"

Ronun nodded.

"To protect me. To protect your people from what harm my presence here might—oh, Ronun, I am a fool. I did not—"

"I do not think you a fool, Mikallis, for whatever value my assessment is worth. Nor do I think you wicked. I can see that this realization is profound to you. But you must be truthful with yourself, now, if you are to gain wisdom. One's heart is only as true and pure as the mind which controls it. When we think only of ourselves, of those we care about, of our own challenges and griefs and heartaches, we can bring no good to the world. It is the conscious act of setting aside our own worries in deference to the well-being of strangers—enemies, even—that brightens one's heart. There was once an adage taught within the ranks of the elven knighthood. 'Honor cannot be but for sacrifice, and sacrifice—'"

Mikallis completed the axiom. "—cannot be but for love. It is still taught in the knighthood." A pang of longing struck as the former elven captain thought of Barris.

"Very good," said Ronun. "I am pleased that the old wisdoms still pervade among your people. But there is more to ponder in such timeworn words than their obvious meanings. To sacrifice for one that you love is a noble thing. It is no great thing, however. Even the most craven among us may find the strength needed in a chaotic, fearful moment to martyr oneself for someone they love. The terrible prospect of facing grief and loss may propel any to heroism. But true honor—the sort that goes unnoticed, unheralded, the sort that will never be sung about in taverns or in great laments—is found in the quiet sacrifice we make in our own minds when we choose to consider the perspective of another. This is the truest love, Mikallis, for it is selfless and pure."

Mikallis did not realize he had been weeping until a tear crept into the corner of his mouth. He wiped it away.

Ronun placed a hand on Mikallis' shoulder, using it to brace himself as he stood. Mikallis helped the old elf to his feet.

"I will cook breakfast." Ronun said, "if you will unhitch the wagon from Magsilla. Her hip troubles her; she will be glad to be rid of it."

"I... you intend to leave it here?"

"I have no use for it. And as I say, Mags despises the thing. Bring me the sack in her left saddlebag. With luck the eggs have not broken, and I can make you a proper meal—"

"Please, Ronun, you need not—"

"Mikallis."

Mikallis fell silent.

"I wish to cook you breakfast."

Mikallis nodded. "Thank you, sir. I will get the sack."

Ronun hummed a tune as dawn brightened the clearing, cooking eggs and fatty meat and small green potatoes as Mikallis worked to unhitch the wagon from Mags. The mare made to nip at Mikallis a time or two. He imagined she might be hungry. He jumped into the wagon to see if there was anything she might eat. There Mikallis found a veritable bounty: baskets upon baskets of fruit, huge bags of flour, large, wax-dipped wheels of cheese, enough salt to last a season... he nearly wept again.

Mikallis took three of the apples and jumped from the wagon. He fed them to Mags, grinning ear to ear. The old mare gobbled them eagerly; she might have bit off Mikallis' finger had he not snatched it back in time. He turned to see Ronun watching him, smiling.

The two lingered long over breakfast, talking of weather and food and simple things only. Mikallis had tried to thank Ronun for the wagon repeatedly, but the elf droned over him, refusing to acknowledge the gift. A lull fell in their conversation. After a few turns, Mikallis broke the silence.

"I am sorry I did not make you a chair, Ronun. I did not see it at the time, but you honored me when I arrived here. Nü glahr ni."

Ronun nodded. "I can see that you are sorry. And I know that when I return, you will have made up for the slight."

"You will return, then?" Mikallis asked hopefully.

"Mustn't I? You have not answered my question, and I have not answered yours."

Mikallis smiled.

"You are welcome to try at it, if you like," said Ronun.

Mikallis sat in silence for a turn. Finally, he shook his head. "No. It would not be an honest answer. Only a guess."

Ronun moved to stand. Mikallis rushed to help him.

"Then I will see you next autumn, Mikallis of Thornwood. I pray that you fare well."

"I pray the same for you, Ronun."

"I will suppose that your next visits with Shem and Kallar will be more fulfilling to you both. I ask that you be as kind to them as you are able. As you know, they have sacrificed much. They are as lonely as you."

"They will be treated with all the honor due them, Ronun, and more. I swear it."

Ronun smiled. "As least offer them a place to sit. That would be a start. Would you help me to my horse?"

~

When Ronun returned the following year, he was treated to a morning spent in blissful repose, breakfast simmering in a pan upon his arrival, this served with steaming tea as he rocked gently in an ugly beast of a chair, this, Ronun had said, as comfortable as any he had ever sat in. Mikallis asked only one thing of him then, which Ronun promised to consider. He left when it began to rain.

On his third visit, the chair had been moved to beneath a grand awning attached to what was now far more than a humble cabin. They cooked and ate their breakfast together, indoors. Ronun commented how healthy Mikallis looked, but suggested he begin to train with a staff. It would not do for a friend of his to be incapable of sparring with him on his next visit. Ronun left his own grey staff behind, along with the box Mikallis had requested the year before. "You must keep these secreted, Mikallis, for as long as you remain here. Be careful what you—"

"I understand, Ronun. You have my promise."

Ronun nodded. "A thing which I trust."

Mikallis watched as Ronun and Mags rode off that afternoon, sad to notice that Mags' gait had worsened, but glad to know she had Ronun on whom she could rely. When the two had made it out of sight, Mikallis entered his home and opened the box. Within he found one hundred pages of blank parchment, four feather pens, and three large bottles of greenish ink.

He went to his hearth and lit a long piece of hay, which he used to light a candle. He used that candle to light another. Soon his home was well-lit. He sat at his dining table and took out a sheet of parchment. He uncorked a bottle of ink and dipped a pen.

Dearest Aria,

It is the year of Evanti, 866, the first day of the tenth cycle, and you will not be born yet for another twenty-five years. I will not be born for another fifteen. But I will begin this first letter as I shall end every other:

I love you, and I miss you...

XXX: THE GRAND BARRACKS

ENERAL," SAID CAPTAIN Varyl, "You're gonna wanna hear this."

Slater ignored the captain and barked at a young corporal. "Tighten those straps, soldier, or you're gonna fall right off the saddle! And get yourself a helmet that fits! Who's your sergeant? Well, tell him to get his sorry arse over here! *Move!*" Slater turned to Varyl and Nia.

"Make it quick, Captain. A bit busy at the moment."

"Ah, I'll let her explain it, Sir, if you please."

Slater glared at Nia. She spoke quietly. "Maybe you'll want to hear this in private, General."

"Did you find what you were looking for or not?"

She nodded. "I did. Forty or more."

"Then why in Fury are you still here? Varyl, my orders—"

"Sir," said Varyl. "Private might be better."

"Dammit, follow me," he snapped. The general led the two to an empty stable stall.

"Out with it."

Nia took a breath. "Ah, the thing is, I don't think I can get to them in time."

"You sure as sunrise can't by standing here yapping at me, young lady."

"She won't make it on horse, General," said the captain. "Not soon enough, at least. If her intelligence is accurate, the Mother is already stationing spellcasters around Tahr. We won't have surprise."

Slater sighed. "That's a problem. If we take to the streets and they're ready for us—"

"You'll be slaughtered, General," said Nia. "Without question."

Slater eyed Varyl.

"I agree with that assessment, Sir. And if we do nothing—"

"They'll come burn us where we stand. So, what then? We can't march, we can't hole up." Slater faced Nia. "I assume you've got something in mind."

"You won't like it," said Nia.

"That much I worked out on my own."

"There is a spell..." Nia began.

"Of course there is."

"Yes. Well, if I can get my hands on some gemstones, and figure out a way to power them, I might be able to transport myself to where these Incantors are gathered. I might even be able to bring them back."

"Transport yourself? You mean, like, *poof*, there you go?"

"Roughly."

Slater shook his head, disbelieving. "And you can *poof* them right back? All of them?"

Nia nodded. "If they'll come."

"Well, that was gonna be the rub all along. So, what do you need, some gems? I can make that happen."

"There's more," said Varyl.

"The part I won't like," said Slater.

"Ah, the thing is, it takes a whole lot of power to manage this spell," said Nia. "And I mean a *whole* lot."

"Go on."

"I can…" Nia hesitated, seeking words. "Ah, I'll just say it. I can siphon it from your army."

"You can *what*?"

"Siphon it. I can use my magic to funnel strength from your soldiers—"

"Over my dead arse you can."

Varyl snorted. "Told you he wouldn't like it."

Nia held up her hands. "Just hear me out."

"No. Find another way."

"General, there really isn't one."

"Too bad. We'll figure something else out."

"Sir," said Varyl. "There isn't time."

"You're *backing* her on this? Are you out of your mind?"

The captain shrugged. "Probably. Better crazy and alive than sane and dead, though. Just hear her out, Sir. Doesn't sound all that bad."

Slater chewed his cheek and turned to Nia.

"The more of your soldiers I siphon from, the less, um, uncomfortable it will be. You have plenty of soldiers—"

"Uncomfortable? You mean they'd feel it?"

Nia nodded. "Understand, General, the Daughters do this all the time, but they do it without people's consent. You remember the days before the battle at the bridge? Maybe remember your troops being a bit, ah—"

"Stumbling around like drunkards for a day and a half? Yeah, I remember that. That was *you* lot?"

Nia nodded, reddening.

"And you think this is a *good* idea, Captain? Weakening your own troops before battle?"

"This is different, General," said Nia. "The power we needed for that... well, we powered an amulet. It was all supposed to help defeat the dragon."

Slater's jaw fell open.

"Anyhow, that was far more power than what I need for this. A hundred times as much. What I need for this... if even half of those here in the barracks volunteered—"

"Volunteered?"

Nia nodded. "I won't do this without the consent of everyone involved, General. I told you. I do not serve Kal."

"Anymore."

Nia shrugged.

"Well, go on, then. How sick would it make these men and women?"

"It's hard to tell for sure. But I'd say maybe they'll be a bit nauseous for a few hours."

"A few hours. And what if it goes wrong?"

"Goes wrong?"

"Listen, I might know bugger-all about magic, but I know it can go wrong. I've lived in the shadow of that tower all my life. Accidents happen. People die."

Nia nodded. "Ah. That does happen. This spell, though... with enough volunteers, I think the risk of that is very low."

"Low, but not zero." Slater glowered at Nia. "You know what I'm asking. Could this... this siphoning, could it kill my soldiers?"

Nia thought for a moment. "If something were to distract me while I'm casting, then yes, anything is possible. It is powerful magic."

"But you deem the risk low."

"Very low. It would be far more likely for the spell to kill me."

"But you're willing to do it."

Nia nodded. "I am."

"You'd die for this fight."

"Not ideally, no. But we're all dead if we don't act."

"Can't argue with that. All right, good enough for me. If you're willing to risk your neck for us, I'd bet my men and women would do the same. How many would you need?"

"How many do you have?"

"Here in the barracks? Four thousand. Another battalion stationed at the palace, which is where I need to be directly."

"A thousand would do."

"And some gems," Slater added.

"Bigger the better. Emeralds and sapphires, if you can get them."

"How many?"

"Forty of each would be a great start. Fifty would be better."

"Two for each Incantor?"

Nia nodded. "Roughly."

"You say 'roughly' a lot."

Nia shrugged. "Magic is an imperfect science, General."

"You don't say?" Slater frowned, thinking. "Only one person I can think of would have that much treasure lying around, but he's on his way north. There might be another rock we can turn over, though. Follow me."

The general marched quickly out into the square and grabbed the first horseman he could find.

"You know where the Languid Lady is?"

The young captain blushed. "Um, well, I think I've seen it…"

"Uh huh. Take a horse up there and tell Eriks Lane I need to see him."

"How soon?"

"How *soon?* Aw, for Fury's sake, get off that horse. Come on, now. Go find yourself another." Slater mounted the grey warhorse in a single, smooth leap. He lowered an arm for Nia.

"Um, I'm not much of a rider—"

"Good. This isn't much of a horse. Get on up here."

It took Nia several tries, but the horse was patient. On the fourth try she tucked in behind Slater.

The general turned to face Varyl. "Get me two thousand soldiers into formation. Tell them nothing. Send the rest inside. I'll be back in ten turns."

~

"Open up, Lane, I know you're in there." Slater knocked again.

"General?"

"Yes, *General.* Now open up. Need your help and I'm a bit pressed for time."

Two bars were thrown. Lane opened the door to the Lady. Kalindra, Maris, and Chaneela stood a pace behind him.

"Wow. Uh, forgive me Sir, I didn't expect—"

"You don't have to 'Sir' me, Lane, unless you're regular army now."

"Maybe a bit irregular, if you please."

"All the same. Ladies, I need a word with you."

"Who's this with you?" asked Maris, suspicious.

"Nia, ma'am."

"And what do you want?"

"Are you going to invite us in," Slater asked, looking around, "or are we just hoping to invite a few neighbors over for afternoon tea and a bit of ransacking?"

"Come on in," said Chaneela. "Wipe your feet. Been sweeping ash all afternoon."

The two entered. Slater wasted no time. "Ladies, I have to ask for a donation to the army."

"Ask?" pressed Kalindra.

"Yep, just asking. You can say no if you like. But I hope you won't."

"What can we do for you, General?" asked Maris, her tone milder than her sister's.

"Gems," said Nia. "As many as you can spare. Emeralds and sapphires."

Both Maris and Kalindra put their hands to their necks, each well bejeweled.

"You'll get them back, if all goes as planned."

"And what exactly do you need them for, Miss Nia?" demanded Chaneela.

Nia shared a look with the house wizard. "One Fury of a spell."

Chaneela frowned. "We don't keep our gems charged in this house. Not sure how much good... wait. Are you a Daughter?"

"I was."

"Was? There is no 'was' once you take your oaths."

"I might have skipped those," Nia said, offering a shy smile.

"You can trust her," said Slater. "I do, and that's saying quite a lot."

Lane's eyes widened. "You bet your arse it is."

"How do you plan to charge these?" asked Chaneela, her tone a poorly veiled accusation.

"As you'd expect," said Nia. "But with volunteers."

"Volunteers? No one in their right mind would—"

"Let me worry about that, ma'am," said Slater. "Can you help us?"

"How many?" asked Kalindra. "What size?"

"Call it fifty of each," sad Nia. "Big as you've got."

"A *hundred* precious gems?" protested Maris. "What do you think we are, a bank?"

The general leveled a gaze at Maris. "You're better than a bank, and we both know it. Question is, do you keep them here?"

Maris and Kalindra shared a look, communicating in the silent way twin sisters can. After a turn Maris shrugged her shoulders. "Fury's sake, wait here. Lane, if they try to follow me, gut 'em."

"Will I need to gut you, General?" asked Lane with a wink.

"No, but I'll open you up stem to stern if you ask me that again."

"Oh, you boys," Kalindra said. "You get a girl all aflutter with your talk of steel and guts."

Nia laughed.

Lane shot her a look. "She's not kidding."

"Yeah? We could be friends, you and I." Nia shot Kalindra her own wink.

"Sorry darlin', she's off the market," said Lane.

"Don't take it too hard, dear," said Kalindra. "You're lovely enough, but you magic folks are into some weird stuff."

"You have *no* idea."

"I'm gonna throw up," said Chaneela. "You ever cast a thing like this before?" she asked.

"Like it? Sure," said Nia.

"Hmph. Maybe you could use an extra pair of hands. Make sure you don't blow yourself up."

"Oh, I'll take the help if you can give it. I'll assume you have experience with the process?"

"Not the way you blood and bone types do it, but yes."

"Solo magic, then?"

"Solos or circles."

"Circles? *Kalian* circles?"

"Oh, Fury no. I'm not suicidal. Lorian."

"There are *Lorian* circles?"

Chaneela frowned. "I thought you were a Daughter. They don't teach you about Lorian circles?"

Nia shook her head.

"Huh. Well, dear, we'll need to be expanding your education. Will she be with you long, General?"

"That, ma'am, is a question I don't yet know the answer to."

"Why's that?"

"Because I don't know if I'll be around long myself, this doesn't work."

"Well," Maris said, returning, "you're in luck. Just so happens I'm holding a few things for a friend right now."

"A friend?" Nia asked.

"A dear one. Myself. Now look here." Maris set the box on an end table and opened it up. "Will these do?"

"Sweet stars in the sky!" cried Nia. "Yes, that will do fine! How many is that?"

"Fifty of each, as you asked. A few could use a polish, but you'll find they are of exquisite quality."

Nia moved to touch one, a thumb-sized, intricately cut yellow sapphire. Maris slapped at her hand.

"When do I get these back?" she asked.

"Well, either a few days, or never."

"Which is more likely?"

Nia shrugged. "I can tell you, though, that we might just save Mor with them."

"You might."

The general interjected. "Or we might all be dead in a few days, you included. It's all gone pear-shaped, ladies. It's this or we all run north, fast as horses can take us, and throw ourselves on the mercy of the elves."

"Which isn't a terrible idea, really," said Nia.

Maris and Kalindra exchanged another look.

"Fine. Take them. Don't muck it up."

"*I'll* take them," said Chaneela.

"Chaneela," said Lane. "It would be good to have your magic here protecting the girls—"

"*Girls?* Shut up, Lane," said Kalindra. "I could gut you faster than Slater."

"That true?" Slater asked Lane, smiling.

Lane shrugged. "Probably."

"Then, my lethal friends, I shall endeavor to return these to you forthwith." Slater bowed dramatically. "Now can we get on with it? No offense, but this ain't a social call."

~

"All right you crazy bastards," Slater shouted to the men and women assembled in the square. "I need some volunteers. A thousand at least. All of you, if you've got the nerve. Do I have any soldiers with nerve in my army?"

Two thousand cheering soldiers answered with exuberance.

"Good! You're gonna need it. So what's gonna happen here is that these two fine ladies here are going to do some creepy nasty magic, and you're all gonna stand there and feed her a bit of yourselves so she can pull it off. She might die, she says, but you probably won't. Gonna be puking on your boots for a few hours, though. This works, we'll have a damned good chance of taking the Temple. We don't do it, well, I'm sorry to say it, but there's a better chance this next battle will be our last. That's the whole truth of it. Any soldier who wants to back out, you just slide out of formation and won't anyone ever say anything to you about it, or I'll personally kick their arses up and down this square. But if you stay, you'll be giving your families half a chance to make it through winter. Questions?"

A chorus of mumbles came in reply as soldiers turned to one another, some expressing more than a little fear, others disbelief. Slater let them mumble. After a turn passed, a soldier raised a hand in the middle of the formation.

"All right, quiet down!" ordered Slater. "That you, corporal Bricks?"

"Yes, Sir. Just one question, Sir."

"Well, out with it then."

"Do I have to puke on my own boots? I'd rather puke on my Sarge's. She's been a real pain in the arse all day."

A female hand came from behind and cuffed the corporal. The battalion fell into laughter.

"You go ahead and puke wherever you like, Bricks," said the general. "So long as it's not on my boots. Any more questions?"

No one spoke or raised a hand.

"All right. Volunteers, one step forward. Those who wish to bow out—"

Two thousand soldiers took a step forward—some nudged from behind—but none left formation.

Slater turned to Nia and Chaneela. "Don't muck this up."

"We won't, General," said Nia. "You might want to go inside—"

"Cast your spell, Nia of the sea. I'll be right here with my battalion. Boots needed a polish anyways."

XXXI: THE TEMPLE OF KAL

OUR REMAINED, AS the Mother had expected. She glanced at the two dead Daughters.

"Hmm. Glena and Zara," she said. "I might have guessed. Gifted, but never quite ruthless enough." The Mother glanced at the two bone earrings on the table and turned to face a weary, bloodied Jaila. "It is done?"

Jaila nodded. The Mother returned the nod silently and took the earrings from the table, hooking them into her ears with as much ceremony as tying one's shoes.

"The Unordained can clean this mess. We must hurry to the altar room."

"Now?" demanded Clarien, youngest of the four.

The Mother glared. "Yes, now. Or are you too weary, poor dear?"

"It's not that Mother," said Jaila, hesitant, " it's only, we thought we would begin tomorrow—"

"We do not have until tomorrow. While you four have been... busy... I have been listening for Kal's voice."

"He spoke to you?" asked Teena, the oldest, dubious.

The Mother scowled at Teena. "No, Teena, he did not *speak* to me. But I heard what was there to hear. Your sister Nia has been a busy girl today. It must be tonight. Take a few turns to wash yourselves. Heal what injuries you must. We begin in a quarter of an hour."

"Mother," said Dinah, the least vocal of all her Daughters.

"Yes?"

"Your earrings are stunning."

The Mother curled a lip in appreciation of the callous observation. Seldom did Dinah speak, but when she did, what fell from her lips was invariably twisted. *Ah, dear Dinah, you I will miss most.* The Mother slid from the dining hall and walked the fifty paces to the altar room, stopping to light fresh incense along the way. She recalled her annoyance at the task when she was yet but an Unordained Daughter. Now, she completed the duty with reverence and no small amount of nostalgia. She reached the door of the chamber and turned, glancing back down the dimly lit hall, taking in the ever-unquiet ambience of the Temple. The Mother did not believe ghosts a common thing, for in all her many years she had only ever seen one, but it was known that when a person passed between worlds, something more than a lifeless body was left behind. When such transitions were brought about through violence, the essences that remained might vary in power, but they were *always* restless. The Temple of Kal had collected far more than its share of these essences over the course of centuries; the very spirit of the place thrummed with angst and agitation. Most found the Temple terribly unsettling, but the Mother recalled the day she had first walked its halls. It had felt like coming home.

She removed her shoes, feeling the cold, familiar stone on her bare feet. With a long sigh, she entered the altar room and pulled her gilded dagger, placing it on the altar. She knelt slowly. Age brought a degree of pain to the act of obeisance, the Mother considered just then, but also a profundity which no young Daughter could appreciate. Looking back, she supposed she had not truly begun to see Kal's greatness and gain his wisdom until her joints began to creak. *Perhaps that is the trick of it*, she mused. *Wisdom must be stored in the knees.* The Mother shifted position. *And perhaps the hips.*

It was not wisdom she would need in the coming moments; what she needed was strength, courage, and a great deal of attention to detail.

"Sharpen my blade, sharpen my wits," she whispered. "Let not this circle fail, lest thy will go undone."

She repeated the prayer, again and again, her pace deliberate, the cadence of the words falling into a rhythm to match her slowing breath. The Mother felt her mind begin to settle. The pain in her knees and hips began to fade. Her spine gradually untightened; her shoulders slumped. In time she fell wholly into a trance, aware only of her own intent and the words of her whispered prayer.

Something like a bell sounded within her mind, telling the Mother it was time.

I am ready.

The Mother stood and turned. There behind her stood the four surviving Daughters of her coterie: Clarien, young and fair, but extraordinarily cunning, and a brilliant wizard. Jaila: strong-willed, occasionally disobedient, never anything but cruel. Teena: irascible and shrewd; a true master of Kalian magic. And, of course, Dinah: ever silent, ever dangerous, ravenous and devastating as a matron spider.

The mother reached for the dagger with her right hand. She extended her left hand, palm facing inward. Dinah knelt before her, bowl at the ready. Clarien began to cast, sealing off the altar room from all outside sounds and interruptions. Jaila approached with a quiver of five brushes, these carved from bone and fletched with human hair. Dinah reached into the quiver and selected the first, the widest of the five. She knelt to Dinah's right; Jaila to her left.

"Our lord Kal gives to those who ask, but never without recompense, and he will extract his price. We do your will, Kal. The time is at hand for you to lay claim to this world. Send us your great servant, he who has always been yours, he who has been transformed."

The Mother sliced deeply into her palm. Her prayer had indeed been heard; the knife was quite sharp, far keener than what any whetstone could accomplish, though this only delayed the onset of pain. Veins and nerves soon realized they had been severed, and when they cried out, the Mother's tears flowed—not, however, as freely as her blood.

The bowl began to fill. Clarien dipped her brush. Jaila withdrew another.

The Mother lifted her head and cried out, her voice a trembling blend of agony and fanaticism. "Guide your Daughters' hands, oh Kal! Make your circle perfect, and on this day, great debts shall be repaid!"

XXXII: THE NORTHERN ROAD

HEONARIS CAST THE spell, filling over the grave with cold, snowy dirt.

Barris kneeled to lay a hand upon the mound. "We could have taken him home, Mister Longstock." The knight found his burial unfitting, ignoble. "His sacrifice—"

"His sacrifice was to earn your faith, Sir Barris. And your trust, so maybe you'd want to unite our people. You want to honor him? Dragging his corpse back to Mor won't do that. Time is short. Vincent knew that." Gerald wiped a tear from his eye.

Barris shook his head. "He deserved better than this."

"You think I don't know that?" shot Gerald. "But he wouldn't want it. If you knew him... the thought of his friends sobbing over a dead body when there are things that need doing... ah, you stubborn bastard. I will miss you."

Gerald choked back a sob and stood. Barris put a hand on his shoulder in sympathy. Gerald nodded sadly at the gesture.

"What do you need of us, Mister Longstock?" asked Pheonaris.

"Gerald. Just Gerald is fine. What I need—what Vincent wanted—is for our people to unite. We face the same storm. I assume your people are hungry these days, as mine are?"

Pheonaris nodded. "Many are without homes. I have not been to Thornwood in some time, but I know they will be struggling, if not now, then soon."

"That we can solve. But I am going to need all the magic of the elves to do it."

"How?" asked Barris.

"Farming by magic. No need to get into the details of it here and now, but it can be done, and I know how to do it. What we need first is an alliance, and a strong one. A new treaty, maybe."

"But with whom?" asked Barris. "Halsen is dead, not that Thornwood could ally with that glutton in any case, no matter our heart on the matter."

"With our people. Doesn't matter who signs the parchment or sits on the throne. Doesn't matter if there *is* a throne. There are those of us who hold a bit of sway in Mor, and if Thornwood would offer a hand in friendship, maybe we could extend one to Belgorne as well. Even G'naath, even Eyreloch, if they'll join us. As for formalizing an agreement, we have a general, Slater—"

"I know this man," said Barris. He glanced to Pheonaris. "He is honorable." He turned back to Gerald. "But he does not command the armies of Mor."

"He does now. More than half went south under Fallon. Slater commands those who stayed behind."

Barris nodded. "The better portion."

"Exactly. Good riddance to Fallon and the rest. Cowards to a one."

"What of the Sapphire?" asked Pheonaris. "I have heard no report—"

"Fallon will sack every village he marches over. There will be war in the south, and nothing you or I can do will stop it. But we can deal with that later. Listen..." Gerald glanced at the mound of dirt. "Can you give me a turn, here, and we can continue this on the road?"

Pheonaris nodded. She and Barris withdrew a few dozen paces away, giving Gerald some time alone.

"What exactly did this man do for you, Barris?" asked Pheonaris. "For Phantom?"

Barris looked into Pheonaris' eyes, his gaze direct, his words plain.

"He gave his life that Phantom may live."

"A spell?"

Barris nodded. He explained in brief detail.

"That is a dark magic, Barris."

Barris shook his head. "I thought so as well. But you must understand, I was desperate. Forgive me, but after losing Mikallis, and Trellia—"

Pheonaris pulled Barris near and held him. "I know."

"It was not as you might think. It was not dark. There was love in it."

"But he did not know Phantom. Nor you."

Barris released Pheonaris. "A love for his people. I sensed it. And... not only for his own people. Ah, it is such a loss. He would have made a great king."

"A king?"

Barris nodded. "Gerald and I spoke of it. His friends, they have long been an underground sect of... of protectors, I think you might say. A power beneath the notice of the throne."

"What sort of power?"

"The sort that offers justice when none can be otherwise found."

Pheonaris considered Barris' words. "Justice has long been

dead in Mor."

"Not dead. Hidden."

"Ah. I see. Kept alive by this sect."

Barris nodded. "Led by Vincent Thomison. He is... was... a powerful man. If Gerald speaks the truth, and I cannot doubt him, he was also a good man, and a fair man. They all wanted him to lead. Even Slater might have followed him."

Pheonaris sighed. "And he is gone. And Mor is adrift."

"Worse than adrift. There is a vacuum there, and I fear who might fill it."

"Who is left to?"

Barris shrugged. "I cannot tell. But in dark times are born dark kings."

"As in the Strife."

Barris nodded, thinking of Neral and Halsen the First. "Just so."

"You know we cannot promise what Gerald asks without speaking to Terrias."

"I know no such thing," said Barris. "He asks for my promise to try. I cannot withhold it."

"A promise is no small thing."

"It is not. I have made few and asked for fewer."

Pheonaris reached up to touch Barris' face.

"Would that you had made me a promise."

Barris took her hand. "Would that I had. There is none other with whom I would have wished to share this life, none save—"

"None save her."

Barris sighed. Pheonaris brought his hand to her lips, placing a delicate kiss between his knuckles before letting go.

"All will be as it must be. Time is a playful thing, Barris. Like love."

"But a promise is not. I will give this man my promise, and forgive me for saying so, but—"

"You need not ask. I will share this honor with you."

Gerald approached. Barris and Pheonaris exchanged a look. Barris nodded.

"Gerald. I vow to you that I will do what I can to unite the people of Tahr, in the name of your Vincent Thomison. I cannot speak for my queen, nor for any other, but I will honor the sacrifice you and your friend have made for Thornwood this day."

Gerald nodded and looked to Pheonaris.

"I, too," she began, "will join this cause—"

The Mistress' eyes widened at the sound of her queen's voice.

~Mistress Pheonaris. Forgive my delay. I have been searching day and night for the texts of Ya Di beneath the Citadel. They are lost! Burned! Tell Barris, if you can. Convey this order to Nishali and Marchion: we must avoid war, at all costs!~

Pheonaris listened intently. Nothing followed.

"Did you hear?"

Barris nodded. "If the texts are lost..."

Pheonaris finished the thought. "We cannot delay," said Pheonaris.

"Texts?" asked Gerald. "What are you two babbling about?"

Barris led his friend to his horse. "It is a most terrible day, my friend. Most terrible. I will tell you on the road to the Grove."

"Tell me what?"

Barris helped Gerald atop his saddle. "On the road. Please, we must hurry."

"Why? What happened? What's the rush?"

"Ya Di is the rush, friend," said Pheonaris, mounting Gale. "We have committed a great sin, perhaps the greatest ever committed, and now Ya Di is upon us."

"Ya Di?"

"The Day," said Barris.

A most terrible day.

XXXIII: THE MAW

HAT I DON'T UNDERSTAND," Hatchet said to Oort, stroking his scraggly grey beard, "is how ye became king o' G'naath. I don't mean to say I disbelieve ye, mind—"

"The Wolfslayer didn't wanna be king," said Rak before Oort could answer. "But the Elders were gone, and everyone was fearful, then Argl told everyone 'bout Oort and Mama and then they all started tellin' each other and then next thing, they're all bowin' an' scrapin' and such. Was Argl here suggested it. Didn't one of us disagree."

"I been huntin' the Maw all my life," Argl said. "We gnomes don't have much trouble in the mountains. We see better than you folk at night, we're too small an' quiet for much to take notice of us, and we know the ground. But Mama..." Argl shivered visibly. "She'll just walk up on yeh, all sneaky-like, and then yer screamin', and then yer dead."

"Aye, ye ain't just singin' hymns, there," agreed Captain Flint. "We Scouts ain't been afraid o' nothin' for long as we been Scouts. 'Cept Mama."

"'Cept Mama," said Rak.

Oort remained silent, sitting beside Thinsel. They had unwrapped her and set her beside the fire. She still could not speak but could now sit. She listened intently, sipping what remained of the elves Spring tea, watching her husband with adoration and pride as Rak and Argl went on. After a time, however, he had enough.

"So they named me Wolfslayer, Argl named me king, a bunch o' the rest nodded and ain't no one said otherwise, so I s'pose I'm king. And I had the idea to let Belgorne shelter in G'naath for the winter, 'cause I know it was the Elders done this terrible thing to everyone, and G'naath owes a debt. Then your putrid bastard of a king did what he done to Thinny, then all the rest to the elf folk, and now I'm a mind to drop the tunnels and leave yeh all to freeze, truth be told."

Hatchet eyed Oort. "Bold thing to say, sittin' here smack in the middle o' the Belgorne army."

"Bold my arse," said Flint. "Ye can't blame him and ye know it, Hatchet. If King Greykin here says he's of a mind to drop the tunnels, then ye best stand down an' let 'im, 'cause wont a one o' my Scouts let a dwarf raise a hand to stop 'im."

Colonel Onyx had been listening quietly. "Damn ye Flint, Brandaxe is the general here. S'posed to be him sayin' such things."

"Hmph. Was takin' too long."

Not even Oort could suppress a chuckle at Flint. He turned to Thinsel, her grey eyes alive in the firelight. He saw her heart there. She would have him act with mercy.

He addressed Hacthet. "Yeh gotta put yer king down, General. Won't be no talk o' me changing my mind 'bout the tunnels long as he lives."

"Well," said Hatchet, "I can see why ye'd say so, but I ain't no kingkiller. He's the brother o' the true king, who may yet live, and it ain't for me to end 'im. We'll bring 'im to justice, though, on that ye have me oath. There'll be a trial."

"What's to try?" demanded Oort. "Ain't no question what he's done."

Flint stood and walked around the fire, taking a seat beside Oort.

"I know ye be a king, now. Maybe I got no right to tell ye how to be one. I ain't a general, as Onyx here keeps remindin' me. I ain't but a captain. But I'm old, an' I've led people all me long years, an' that's worth somethin'. I'll ask ye let an' old dwarf say a few things."

Oort took a breath and nodded.

"A king is just. A king follows the law. We got a treaty, all of us. Thornwood, Mor, Belgorne, an' G'naath. Law says we try a person for such things. If ye wish to let us all freeze here in the Maw, that be a decision ye'll have to make, and ye be free to. But ye ain't free to break treaties, not if ye ever want the world to be put right again. Oh, sure, ye can do as ye like. But we got where we are 'cause Dohr ain't got the wisdom to tell his arse from an anthill. Don't ye make the same mistake. The acts of a few, no matter how awful, can't condemn the heart of a people."

Oort held his tongue for a long while, staring at his feet. A squeeze of his fingers lifted his gaze to Thinsel. She gazed back at him. Her expression said she would stand by him, no matter his decision.

Oort turned to Hatchet. "Are your dwarves of a mind on this, then? Takin' Dohr to trial? Do all yer men and women see it such?"

Hatchet nodded. "Those that understand what he's done? By and large, aye. Word broke quick around camp when Lux here showed up, and all the whispers come back to me are all o' the same mind. I won't lie to ye, though. Might be a few in my army'll take a bit to come around. I set out to take G'naath by force. These dwarves set out with me, set out without any food but what we could carry in our own sacks, and that'll be about gone. Wasn't ever any question if we'd take G'naath—can't be done, and we all know it. We left partway so the rest could go on to seek refuge with the Shorefolk, so maybe they'd have enough food that at least some'd make the journey. But we left partway to die a fightin' death, and fight we woulda, to the last dwarf, least til those tunnels came down on our brainbuckets. These dwarves... they've lost everything, Wolfslayer. *Everything.* But, truth be as it is, a few days out here settled us down. Now, most'd just as soon lay down an' die out here in the Maw. Most don't give a damn no more about kings and wars an' all the rest. But here be what matters: Garne Silverstone made me general. The way we do it in *my* army, every dwarf chooses to serve or not, every day they wake up. They show up to work, they be mine for the day, body and soul. I'm their conscience. They act on my orders, whatever they do falls on me. But I can't tell ye what tomorrow will bring, 'cause tomorrow they all gotta make that choice again. All I can tell ye is that these dwarves chose to follow me when they woke up this mornin', and so what we do about G'naath an' Dohr an' all the rest today be my decision. As this be yours."

Oort thought of Shyla just then, of her own trial not two cycles gone. Even with all the wicked Elders presiding over her fate, it took one, only one, to grant her mercy. Now, on the word of one Scout and three gnomes, this general would grant his own people mercy. Oort was decided.

"I'll keep the tunnels up. I'll trust yer oath and trust yer dwarves to keep it. Yeh get that done, yeh'll find shelter in G'naath. Best as we can manage, at least."

Hatchet nodded. "Ye won't regret it. We'll name us a regent 'til J'arn comes back or we find his body. Not all the way sure on how we'll do that, but I s'pose once we get settled, if we get settled, we'll have us a vote. As o' right now, it'll be me. Flint," he said, turning to the captain. "Spread the word among the captains. Looks like we might survive this nightmare a bit longer. Ye tell 'em it be thanks to King Greykin, and ye make 'em understand. And tell 'em to stretch whatever rations they got left. We march at dawn to arrest Dohr Silverstone, and it'll be one hungry march."

~

Nishali watched.

"Forty fires," whispered Lanna. "Maybe more."

"More," Nishali said. She shifted on her knees, pointing out across the overlook. "Look there, over the second ridge. See the shadow against the horizon?"

"Ah, I thought that was a fog."

Nishali shook her head. "No. The air is too dry, now at least. That will change at dusk. Those clouds, there..." Nishali pointed east. "A snow comes. But there..." she pointed north again, "that is smoke. There are over a thousand here. Perhaps two thousand."

"Why do they not march? The dwarf captain, what was his name?"

"Kalder," replied Nishali.

"Him. He said they had set out for G'naath. It is daylight, but they camp—"

"Cowards," Nishali said. "Like their king."

A ranger approached from behind.

"My Tenth is in position, First Ranger."

"Good. What do they see?"

Palla Longshadow, now Second Ranger of Thornwood, displayed a frown. "Little you would call good. We can cut off perhaps an eighth of their forces if we attack from the canyon, even defeat them soundly, but once we do, all surprise is gone."

"We can do no better?" Nishali asked.

"Not by my estimation. But..."

Nishali sensed hesitation.

"Speak your mind."

"Very well. I am not sure that we must attack. They seem... wasted, to me. My rangers sense a melancholy within their ranks, and hunger. I am not sure how much of a threat—"

"Thank you for your assessment," Nishali clipped. "They will be less of a threat if we cut their forces by an eighth. How many will we lose?"

Palla shrugged. "None, if we wait until dark and are cautious. We can rain arrows down from above. We would need only silence, and a bit of light."

Nishali smiled darkly. "These we have in abundance, Second Ranger. You have done well. Would you have us take up position now?"

Palla shook her head. "I would counsel that we wait until dusk. Let me hunt a bit more for scouts and lookouts, though I expect to find none. They make no effort at even a most basic defense. Their camp—"

"Haphazard," said Nishali. "They are oblivious to our

presence and assume they are under no threat. Poor discipline. But I agree. My lack of caution has already cost us dearly."

Lanna extended a hand to the First Ranger.

"Nishali—"

"No, Lanna. You must never disregard your failures, nor underestimate them. Swallow them whole, or they will return to swallow you."

"Yes, First Ranger."

"Make what preparations you deem appropriate, Palla. Do not hesitate to alert me to any concerns."

"Yes, First Ranger," said Palla. "I have only the one, which I have stated."

Nishali leveled a look at Palla. "Military concerns, Ranger. Our course is decided."

"Very well." Palla turned away.

Nishali pulled her bow and sat back against a stone. She inspected the ash-carved weapon closely, caressing its limbs, seeking blemishes or gouges. She found none. She examined its wrapped leather grip, ran a finger along the worn rest. Finding no flaw, she withdrew its string from her cloak pocket and notched it into the tip, pulling it taut. She bent the bow by the strength of her own arms, a feat none but an elf of the Wood could accomplish, and one which Nishali did with ease. She set the loop in the bottom limb notch and gently released the tension. She watched as Lanna did the same with her own bow, noticing the shake in her arms as she strung the weapon.

"You should practice more," said Nishali, inspecting her linen string for frays. She cast a silent enchantment into the threads, then another into the wood. She pulled the string and pressed her ear to the ancient wood, listening for creaks and cracks. The bow sang like an instrument.

"I suppose I will get plenty of practice in the days to come," said Lanna.

"Surely. But a Ranger builds her strength before it is needed."

Lanna nodded. Nishali had expected a reply.

"What is it, Lanna?"

Lanna shook her head. "I wish... ah, forgive me. It is nothing."

"If it were nothing, saying it aloud would cause you no grief."

Lanna faced Nishali. "I have never killed. I do not wish to."

Nishali thought for a moment before replying. "Yet you were first to voice your support for me."

"My support for you is undying, Nishali Windwillow. You are my First. The Rangers are my family."

"These dwarves have killed your family, Lanna."

"Not these," Lanna corrected. "But I agree with your strategy, for whatever that is worth."

"It is worth much."

"I am glad. But I have spent my years nurturing life, short as they may be compared to your own. I have hunted only to eat, or to grant mercy to a wounded animal. I have not—"

"Hear me, Lanna. Hear me well. Sometimes, in order to preserve one life, another must end. It is the way of nature. Why should it be less so when the lives of elves are taken? Why should we not preserve our own kin, as a wolf might its cubs?"

Lanna set her bow in her lap. Nishali had asked the question rhetorically but could see Lanna was chasing an answer. She remained silent, allowing the young ranger to work out her reply.

"Because we are not animals," she said finally.

Nishali stood. She offered Lanna a hand to rise.

"That, Lanna Arbarri, is where you are mistaken. And if you are not, if humanity and the animals are not the same, then we are certainly the lesser of the two." Nishali turned to join the rest of her Tenth. "Were that not true, my Kade would still be alive."

~

Dusk fell swiftly but lingered long over the dwarven encampment, the sun diving abruptly below the peaks to the west but taking its time to find the far horizon. An odd, yellow-green light reflected off the thinning plumes emitting from Fang; the wind had shifted westerly, an approaching storm from the east extending its blustery reach through and over the Maw, shredding the clouds of ash before it.

The unsettled silence that had besieged General Brandaxe's army had evolved into hope as the afternoon wore on and Flint spread the word. Hope! Flint had nearly forgotten such a thing ever existed. The rosy banter between his fellow captains and their sergeants felt foreign, or at least premature, but he would say nothing to discourage faith.

And that's all it is, he decided. *Faith. Same as the faith that me Kari will find her way to the elves and deliver that axe. Same as the faith that J'arn might pop out from under a rock one o' these days. Same as the faith he'd be any better than his brother.* He crossed through a narrow canyon, stopping to speak with a young captain he found at the far end. Thump, they called him, a fitting moniker for the brutish-looking dwarf, though Flint could not quite remember his proper name. Thump offered a rare grin through his coal-black beard on hearing the news.

"Aye, it be good news," said Flint. "But ye keep sharp, Cap." Flint looked to the ridges on either side of the canyon. Dark had fallen. He could see nothing out of place, but something *felt* lopsided. He tried to dismiss it as no more than the sense of the coming storm, but the hairs on the nape of his neck would not concede the argument. "Can't say as I like ye campin' here in the canyon."

"Ah, we're just tryna stay outta the wind, Cap. Don't ye worry. Thanks to that Wolfslayer, ain't no Mama anymore to come an' take a bite—"

Blinding light came from everywhere. An arrow silenced Thump, his sentence forever unfinished.

"*Cover!*" Flint screamed. "*Take cover!*"

Cries came from all sides. Flint desperately sought cover of his own but could see nothing. All was white. He covered his eyes and fell to all fours, scrambling, listening, his hearing his only reliable sense, but his ears heard only the slicing, ripping sound of arrows through the air, through trees, through dwarves, and the terrible, hopeless screams.

Something exploded through his back, something else through his calf. The pain was lightning. He could not draw breath to scream again. A third arrow pierced his shoulder, pinning him to the ground. He opened his eyes, squinting against the cursed light to catch one last glimpse of anything. He could not.

His last thought was one of relief, that at least there were some dwarves left, here on the far side of the canyon, who would die before he had delivered to them the lie of hope.

XXXIV: FURY

HIS IS THE PLACE," Cindra said, collapsing to her knees. "I remember these black rocks here, juttin' out." Cindra ran a hand along the iron wall behind her. "It's different in here."

"Different how?" asked J'arn. "Do ye feel somethin'? Maybe the door is here somehow, maybe it's—"

"It's not here," said Lucan, breathing heavily. He cast another orb, setting the cavern alight. "It might have been, but it's gone."

"Well ye don't need to quit that easy!" said J'arn. "Shyla, can ye sense anything? Anything at all?"

Shyla wandered the cavern, looking. J'arn noticed her gait; she was unsteady like the rest. Exhaustion was taking its toll. He watched as she placed a hand on Wolf's shoulder and closed her eyes. After a moment, she spoke.

"Wolf senses somethin'," Shyla said. "But... it's like Luc says. Whatever it was, it's gone."

J'arn closed his own eyes and tried. He still struggled with his magic; he understood it—Lady Lor had seen to that—but while his mind could conceive of how to do a thing, some barrier remained between thought and execution. He concentrated nonetheless but was rewarded with only a headache. His own discomfort, however, was nothing compared to the fatigue he knew the others were experiencing. He still felt some strength within himself, his dwarven endurance not yet ready to fail him, but as they had walked the tunnels these past hours, searching desperately for this place, it became clear the others were running out of time—Cindra most of all.

"Ye gotta get up, Lady," he urged. "Come on now, take me hand. There ye go. Let's just walk a bit. Maybe somethin'll come."

"I don't wanna walk anymore, dwarf," she said, letting J'arn lift her upright despite the assertion. When J'arn had led her a few steps away from the others, she whispered.

"It's time," she said.

"My arse it's time," said J'arn. "Ain't time 'til I say so."

"Let me sleep, J'arn. Please. All I ask is yeh gimme one turn o' rest, real rest, before yeh do it."

"Ain't gonna happen, Lady. Not yet, not until—"

"*Stop!*" Cindra hollered.

J'arn stopped. Cindra glared at him, her yellowing eyes not quite aglow, but close. J'arn sensed both her growing depravity and her shame at her inability to keep it at bay. It broke his heart.

"Lady?" asked Shyla. "What is it? Do yeh sense something?"

Cindra kept J'arn's gaze. He nodded.

"No, Shyla. Lady just needs a rest is all." J'arn helped her to the floor of the cavern.

"But yeh said—"

"Just a rest, Shyla," said Cindra. "Don't ye fret, now."

An agonized scream sounded from somewhere in Fury. A human scream. Not Aria.

A small hand pulled at J'arn's sleeve. "What was *that*?" whispered Shyla. Her fear made J'arn shudder.

"Came from this way," said Lucan, his voice hoarse. "Back the way we came."

J'arn turned. Lucan cast an orb down the tunnel to the right. He, Lucan, and Shyla peered into the tunnel as the orb cast aside the darkness. J'arn could see nothing out of the ordinary. Wolf moved between them, snarling, hair standing upright along his spine.

"What is it, Wolf?" asked J'arn. "Whaddya hear, boy?"

Another scream. Longer. Louder. The cackles and mewls of the horde returned, following the shriek through the tunnels. Wolf pawed once at the air. He backed away, whining.

J'arn nearly reached for his axe, an instinct to fight rising within him. *Dammit. All me life I train with an axe. Now it's no use.* He clenched his fists. A third scream resounded, its pitch terrible and tortured.

A whiff of sulfur curled J'arn's lip. "Ye smell that?" Wolf whined behind him. "Same as when we got here."

Shyla and Lucan sniffed the air. Shyla coughed. "It's getting' hard to breathe again."

J'arn grimaced, the thought of Shyla's pain somehow worse to him than all the horrors of Fury. "Use the magic, Shyla. Like I first showed ye."

Shyla struggled. J'arn placed a hand on the small of her back, ready to help her breathe again if he must.

Shyla turned, her pink eyes moist. "I don't think I... *Wolf! Get back!*"

J'arn spun around. In the center of the cavern, just beyond the now sleeping Lady Cindra, a thin, shimmering yellow glow stretched from floor to ceiling. Wolf whimpered at it, a desperate edge to his whine. He crept around Cindra, towards the glow, his head low.

"Wolf!" cried Shyla again, louder. Wolf obeyed, padding to her side, but J'arn could see he did not want to. The yellow crack grew wider, its edges afire. A rumbling, whooshing sound from the crack grew in intensity as another scream echoed though the tunnels.

"The door!" J'arn shouted. He turned to Lucan and Shyla. "It be the door!"

"How?" Lucan's eyes widened, his pupils dilating in the growing light. "We didn't do anything—"

J'arn reached for Shyla's hand. "Who gives a damn? Come on! We gotta—"

Shyla gasped. J'arn turned back around.

Lady Cindra's eyes had come alive, matching the mustard hue of the rip behind her. She lifted her head and gazed directly at J'arn. He took a half step back. No hint of the Lady Sandshingle that was remained in those awful eyes.

This was not Cindra.

A hopeless, menacing female voice filled J'arn's mind. Its character matched Cindra's own; the dialect did not.

~*You waited too long, Prince-that-was.*~

Cindra floated to her feet.

Shyla cried out in panic. "Lady! Grandmama! It's me! It's yer Shyla!"

~My *Shyla? Yes, I suppose you* are *mine.*~

The bare, cold intent in the statement nearly unnerved J'arn. His courage began to fray yet still he jumped in front of Shyla, placing himself between her and the once-Cindra. He held out his hands. The tips of his fingers shone red. "Don't make me fight ye, Lady."

~You will not reach this door.~

"We don't have to!" shouted Lucan. A hand from behind grasped J'arn by the neck. Lucan pulled him into an embrace with one arm, Shyla with the other.

The demonlady began to cast. A silver sphere of lightning formed between her hands, spitting and crackling. Her hair grew wild, her eyes more so. She pulled her hands back, past her waist, turning, preparing to launch the deadly orb.

Shyla keened, a pitiful, unintelligible cry of despair. She struggled against Lucan's grasp.

Lucan held her fast. "Grab Wolf, *now!*"

J'arn felt the ring on Lucan's hand begin to warm against his own throat and understood. He grabbed the snarling Wolf by the tail.

As the sphere of lightning shot forth from the demonlady's hands, as Shyla wailed, as another, somewhere, cried out in greatest agony, J'arn only just heard Lucan's ear-splitting cry:

"Barris!"

XXXV: THE TEMPLE OF KAL

ELL DONE, MY DAUGHTERS. Let us begin."

The Mother shrugged the sheer violet gown from her shoulders. The fine garment slithered down the Mother's thin form like a living thing, pausing briefly to caress her hips before drifting lazily to the stone floor, the ceremonial raiment now a lifeless bundle at her feet.

Penance D'Avers, daughter of fishmonger Deahma and Lorian Prior Crago, once-wife of Samean, once-mother of Sartean, now mother of the Temple of Kal, stepped out from the pile of linen and into the Kalian circle.

She lifted her thin arms, closed her black eyes and threw back her head. Long, fine ribbons of hair fell to the small of her back, silver wisps brushing against exposed flesh. She took a slow breath, her nostrils filling with the sweet, pungent blend of burned incense and her own acrid sweat. It was not warm in the altar room; hers was a different sort of sweat, the sort that beads at one's pores when dread takes hold.

The spell would require no complex incantation, no wild, arduous gesticulations. This was no spell of Kehrlia, no intellectual feat. Nor was it a mere prayer; nothing so common could call forth such power. It was a thing of utter devotion requiring three components: intent, supplication, and sacrifice. The sacrifices to be offered this day had been stored in bone; the awful artifacts now dangled from the Mother's ears, dancing in time with her heartbeat. Supplication would come soon, and painfully. As for intent, only two words would be required, these chanted as the Mother meditated on her plea:

"Use me."

A Kalian circle often displayed no outward evidence that a spell had been initiated, not for several turns at least, often for hours. Kal was said to ignore his petitioners until their devotion was laid utterly bare. The Mother knew otherwise. Kal responded as Kal would. It came down to this: if a spell did not serve his ends, he might ignore it completely. The orcs, when they had lived in Greater Tahr, experienced this regularly, for they failed to understand Kal's true nature. They attributed their failed circles to a technical failure of their spiritdoctors. Many an orc had been slain by their own tribe when a petition for rain or bounty ended in failure. Such was naught but arrogance, the Mother knew, an arrogance that persisted among many Daughters, and even the Mother before her. No, the favor of Kal could not be obliged by something so banal as proper procedure. The technique was a test of devotion, no more, no less, for to form a perfect circle was to demonstrate the care to do so. If, however, the petition itself pleased Kal, errors in its composition were forgiven, and his favor was displayed in splendor. On this day, before the Mother could utter her chant a third time, none bearing witness could deny: *Kal was pleased.*

A darkness burst outward from the Mother's earrings like flashes of black lightning. All light in the room was extinguished, replaced by a violet glow emanating from the painted strokes of the bloody circle. Unlike lightning, however, the flash was accompanied by no thunderous report; rather it absorbed all noise, vacuuming every sliver of sound into a hungry void.

The Mother screamed—

"Now!"

—but no one heard.

Teena had not needed to hear. Black stains darkened the Mother in places, these the faults of her flesh. Teena cast her dark fire into the Mother's still-bleeding palm. Clarien, Jaila, and Dinah followed her lead, cauterizing cuts and blemishes on the Mother's body which would have been otherwise invisible to the naked eye. The Mother cried out at the pain, but it was not the sound of her own scream which returned to her ears.

Another screamed. A man's voice, distant and tortured. Again, longer, louder.

The circle began to pulse in time with the Mother's pounding heart, rays of anti-light darkening the altar room in an ever-increasing pace. Again, the Mother screamed. Again, the sound of another's wailing misery sounded from the void, closer now, louder. The Daughters withdrew their magic; her wounds had been closed. The pain did not recede. It amplified, stabbing deeply into her flesh in time with the pulsing circle, her heart drumming now, its beats now more predominant than the rests between them. Time slowed, bent, snapped...

The door was open.

The Mother fell to her knees. She lifted her eyes to the altar, it now quickening, its once-living rings of maple now throbbing like veins. Dried, crimson stains in the ancient wood began to liquify anew, pigmented memories of terrible moments when it had drunk the essence of supplicants willing and unwilling.

Soon, now.

~

Sartean screamed.

~I HAVE NOT FINISHED WITH YOU, MAGICIAN!~

Something tore at his soul, stretching it, shredding it.

He screamed again. Longer, louder.

~NO! HE IS STILL MINE!~

A single word sounded in Sartean's mind, whispered in dark chorus by a thousand voices. It did not come from The Hand.

~...indebted...~

A crushing, tearing grasp seized Sartean from within his chest... and then relented. For the span of a breath, no more, there was release. It was not to last. A new thing pressed at him, bending him, breaking him. He screamed again, a shaking, panicked scream like the ones he used to offer The Hand in the days before he had been broken. Something crushed him, compressed his mind within his own skull. Cold fingers tore at his flesh, clutching, clawing their way into his battered body to reach what remained of his spirit.

I know these hands.

Sartean traveled then, dragged body and soul through an emptiness by his very heart. He slammed against some barrier, over and over, his whole self pounding against it, again and again in awful rhythm like an angry child might bang a doll against a wall. The barrier softened, dissolved, and he was through it, but what lay beyond was fire.

Sartean wailed again as the outer part of himself was burned away. He smelled it. Smelled his old self crisping. Then, suddenly, as if what he had just endured never happened, he lay in darkness upon a cold, hard slab.

He gasped. His mind was in disarray. The room strobed between utter darkness and dim violet. He blinked, shocked to discover he had eyes. He turned his head to the right, away from the pulsing. A stone wall faced him. He turned to the left...

Of course. He knew those hands.

"Hello, Mother."

Penance D'Avers stood and faced her son.

"The second debt is paid," she declared, her voice little more than a tremulous croak.

Sartean did not need a clear head to understand what he saw. This was a Kalian circle, his mother its supplicant. It still thrummed with life.

Only a prick...

Sartean lifted a finger, pointing it at his mother's cheek. A droplet of blood bubbled its way through the tiny perforation.

The mother wiped at the droplet. She licked her finger as she met Sartean's gaze, forcing a smile. She bowed her head, shutting her eyes tight against what was to come.

"And now, I pay the first."

END OF VOLUME FOUR

FROM ME TO YOU

Two books to go.

First things first—please shoot me an email so I can make sure to let you know when #5 comes out: sean@seanhinn.com Go ahead, do it now before you forget. I'll busy myself here writing for a bit. (Mention "Book 5" in the subject so I know to look for your note.)

~

Good, you're back. Thank you for the email—I will write you back, I promise. I return every email from fans, each and every one without exception, because I am truly, madly, completely in love with you peeps.

If you've picked this book up on its launch day, it's been exactly three years—to the day—since I released the first book into the wild on July 25th, 2016. It was called *Tahr* back then, as many of you know, not *Omens of Fury*, but as it turns out, a tahr is a Himalayan goat, and when you googled the book, all these goat pics popped up—which is cool, if you're into goats, and now I *am* into goats, a fact which many of you have also learned by now—but it wasn't exactly great marketing. What were we talking about? Oh yeah, how much I love you. Three years, four books, and if you lovely humans hadn't shown me so much love when #1 came out, it would have taken me a Fury of a lot longer. I'd probably be working the buckets on some goat farm somewhere by now, sneaking into the stables to hammer out a paragraph here and there. Instead, I now can eek out a living at this whole thing, give or take, so I get to live in Tahr all day, every day—thanks to you. Hence, the heart-pounding, butterfly-inducing love I have for you all.

Which brings me to the question you're (hopefully) brimming with—when will #5 come out? When will the series be complete? I've been saying all along that I expect to be done with this series in 2019, and I am going to *just* miss that deadline, methinks, but only by a couple of months. Unless something catastrophic happens, #5 will be in your grubby little hands this fall. I'm in the *zone* over here, writing my tail off, and now that the conclusion is getting near, I'm *burning* to get this story onto paper.

(OK, if you were waiting to email me until you got that answer, I get it. But please go do it now. You know how you're clamoring to know what happens next? I'm clamoring to hear what you thought of #4. You scratch my back, I'll scratch yours, deal?)

About the story... you'll notice that this book was the shortest of the four to this point, and I know how many of you like a big honkin' doorstop to read. Here's the thing about that: I made a calculated decision while writing *Descent* that I was going to focus very specifically on certain threads in the story. Those threads took thirty-five chapters to explore. It just is what it is. You can bet a bag on this, though: there's a big doorstop on the way.

Another thing that might be worth addressing is the dark turn the books are taking. If you compare #4 to #1... yeah, night and day. (Well, "day and night" is probably more accurate.) For those of you who like your fantasy on the lighter side, stay with me. Not because the books are necessarily going to brighten up like sunrise over the great falls of Eyreloch, but because, as you well know, light casts a shadow, and to leave those shadows unexplored would be to understate the brilliance of light itself. If there's anything at all you might glean from the books about me, it's that I believe in the power of light, and with a bit of luck and no small amount of magic, our heroes just might throw back the shadows before it's all said and done. I'm certainly rooting for them.

Thank you, brave and noble friend, for undertaking this quest with our champions. You've followed them—and me—into Fury, and for that I am *indebted...* but do not fear. I know where the door is.

-Sean

P.S. Another quick note... if you find a typographical or formatting error in this volume, please email me and let me know. I will send you a signed thank-you note for your trouble.

APPRECIATION

First, last, and always... my Emily. More than ever, your encouragement helped me get these words onto the page.

My children, kind and brave and loving, stronger than I ever was at your age. Smarter. *Better*, in every way one could measure. I admire each of you more than I can put into words.

My author friends in The Secret Order... you know who you are. You know what you did. Muahahahahaha...

The Epic Fantasy Fanatics crew! Long live the goats!

My Typo Troopers... without wmoh this boko wld loko lyke tihs.

You, my dear reader, for your steadfast companionship on this quest.

Magpie, Fred Bobdog, and Louie, for all the fuzziness a man could possible stand.

My snails, Jack Sparrow, Turbo, and Gary, for reminding me I don't always need to be in such a damned hurry. Also, I hope you haven't escaped again, Turbo. If you have, please come home. You're not as fast as you think you are. If Louie finds you... *shudder*

And again, my Emily, because it all begins and ends with you.

APPENDIX A: CAST OF CHARACTERS

Anie Thomison *(AY-nee TOM-is-sun)*: Wife of Vincent Thomison. Deceased.

Aria Evanti *(AH-ree-uh ee-VON-tee)*: Elven Princess of Thornwood, daughter to Terrias Evanti, heir to the Seat of Thornwood. Unmarried.

Argl *(AR-gul)*: G'naari hunter, personal guard to King Oort Greykin.

Barris *(BEAR-iss)*: Sir Barris, First Knight of Thornwood. Parentage unknown, no known heir nor kin.

Blythe Kalder *(BLYTH KAL-der)*: Captain of the Gate of Belgorne.

Chaneela (sha-NEE-lah): Unendorsed house wizard to sisters Maris and Kalindra

Clarien *(KLEH-ree-en)*: Ordained Priestess Daughter of the Temple of Kal.

Cindra Sandshingle *(SIN-druh SAND-sheen-gul)*: Gnomish witch, descendant of the Sandshingle and Claywart bloodlines. Maternal grandmother to Shyla Greykin.

Colonel Onyx *(KER-nel ON-ix)*: Second in the dwarven army to General Brandaxe.

Cloudia *(CLOW-dee-yah)*: Elven ranger, healer.

Dohr Silverstone *(DOR SIL-ver-stōn)*: Secondson of Belgorne, brother to J'arn.

Dell Brightwater *(DELL BRITE-waw-ter)*: Ranger of Thornwood, spouse to Janna.

Dinah (*DY-nah*): Ordained Priestess Daughter of the Temple of Kal.

Earl *(ER-ul)*: Citizen of Mor. Wagon loader.

Emma Manchele (*EM-muh man-SHEL*): Wife of Fillip, purveyor of fine candles, honey, and honey-baked goods.

Eriks Lane *(ERIKS LAYN)*: Former Defender of Mor. Member of the secret society of the Merchants.

Fillip Manchele (*FIL-lip man-SHEL*): Husband of Emma, purveyor of fine candles, honey, and honey-baked goods.

Freya Brennan (*FRAY-uh BREN-nan*): Birth name of sorceress Mila Felsin.

Gale (*GAYL*): Dun stallion, community mount of the Grove.

Garne Silverstone *(GARN SIL-ver-stōn)*: King of Belgorne, direct descendant of Brenn Silverstone. Widower. Father to J'arn, Dohr.

General Brandaxe *(BRAND-axe)*: Leader of the dwarven army. Second to Dohr Silverstone. Nickname "Hatchet."

General Fallon (*FAL-lin*): General in the Army of Mor. Departed south with most of the army when Halsen fell.

General Slater (SLAY-ter): Head of the army remaining in Mor. Former beneficiary of the Merchant's services. to Kari Flint, deceased

Gerald Longstock *(JEH-ruld LONG-stok)*: Housemaster to Vincent Thomison, wizard. Member of the secret society of the Merchants.

Glena (*GLEE-nah*): Ordained Priestess Daughter of the Temple of Kal. Now an earring.

Gritson (Laine Gritson, Jr.) *(GRIT-sun)*: Dwarven engineer, second to Kelgarr (Boot). Father to Laine III, husband of Gennae, brother-in-law to Kari Flint.

Halsen *(HAHL-sen)*: King of Mor, direct descendent of Jons Halsen, of the days of the Strife. Unmarried. No known heir.

Hope *(HOPE)*: Chestnut mare, mount to Lucan Thorne. Taken from Samuel Thomison in Lucan's escape from Mor.

Jaila (JAY-lah): Ordained Priestess Daughter of the Temple of Kal.

Janna Brightwater *(JAN-na BRITE-waw-ter)*: Knight of Thornwood, spouse to Dell.

J'arn Silverstone *(YARN SIL-ver-stōn)*: Dwarven Firstson of Belgorne, heir to the Sovereign. Son of Garne, brother to Dohr. Unmarried.

Jarriah *(jeh-RYE-uh)*: Apprentice of Kehrlia

Jaysen Theel *(JAY-sen THEEL)*: Private in the Army of Mor.

Kade Calayaan *(KADE CAL-aye-yan)*: Second Ranger of Thornwood

Kal *(KAL)*: Nearest of the two moons of Tahr, smallest of the Twins. Believed by some to be the Lord of Death, harbinger of death and decay.

Kallar *(KAL-ar)*: Stone elf.

Kalindra *(kah-LIN-dra)*: Mistress of the brothel's guild of Mor. Twin sister to Maris.

Kari Flint *(KEH-ree flint)*: Dwarven barkeep of the Hammer Niece to Latimer Flint, scout captain of Belgorne. Sister to Gennae Flint. Unmarried.

Kalashagon (kah-LASH-a-gon): Great winged beast, Dragon, Slave of the Hand of Disorder.

Kimber (KIM-ber): Elderly advisor to Dohr Silverstone.

Lady Lor *(LOR)*: Lady of Eyreloch, servant to the powers of Life

Lady Kal *(KAL)*: Lady of Eyreloch, servant to the powers of Death.

Lanna Arbarri *(LAN-nah ar-BAR-ree)*: Ranger of Thornwood

Lor *(LOR)*: Furthest of the two moons of Tahr, largest of the

Twins. Believed by some to be the Lord or Lady of Life.

Lucan Thorne *(LOO-can THORN)*: Also "Lucan not-Thorne." Erstwhile tavern hustler and orphan. Unmarried. No known heir or kin.

Lux *(LUX)*: Dwarven Scout. Member of Flint's Five.

Lyan (*LY-an*): Ranger Captain of Thornwood.

Mama *(MAH-muh)*: Legendary dire wolf once known to prowl the foothills between Belgorne and G'naath, slain by Oort Greykin.

Macon (Kyle Macon, "Mac") (*MAY-son*): Sergeant of Belgorne.

Magsilla (*mag-ZIL-la*): Mount to Ronun.

Maris *(MEH-ris)*: Mistress of the brothel's guild of Mor. Twin sister to Kalindra.

Mikallis Elmshadow *(mik-A-lis ELM-sha-do)*: Currently serving a cyclical stint as Captain of the Guard, protector of the Evanti family. Close family friend to Aria and kin. Unmarried.

Mila Felsin *(MY-la FEL-sin)*: Citizen of Mor. Incantor of Kehrlia. Inventor of Flightfluid.

Neral Evanti *(neh-RAL e-VON-tee)*: Elven Goodfather of Thornwood. Widowed husband of Elisia, father to deceased son Banor. Lifelong Captain of the Elven Cavalry. Great grand-uncle of Terrias Evanti.

Nia (*NEE-ah*): Unordained Priestess Daughter of the Temple of Kal

Nikalus *(NIH-ka-lis)*: Stableboy, assistant to Master Argus. Friend to Sir Barris and Phantom.

Nishali Windwillow *(nih-SHA-lee)*: First Ranger of Thornwood, councilor to Queen Evanti.

Nova *(NO-vuh)*: Dwarven Scout. Member of Flint's Five.

Oort Greykin *(OORT - GREY-kin)*: Father to Shyla Greykin, husband to Thinsel Greykin.

Osraed: (OZ-rye-ed): Grey mare. Mount to Vicaris Trellia Evanti.

Penance D'Avers (PEN-nanse dee-AV-ers): Daughter of fishmonger Deahma and Lorian Prior Crago, once-wife of Samean, once-mother of Sartean, now mother of the Temple of Kal.

Petahr *(PAY-tar)*: Brother of the Grove.

Phantom *(FAN-tom)*: Black stallion, mount to Sir Barris of Thornwood

Pheonaris *(fee-oh-NAR-is)*: Elven Mistress of the Society of the Grove. Mentor to Aria Evanti.

Rak *(RAK)*: Once gatemaster of G'naath; King Oort Greykin's personal guard

Ronun (*RO-nun*): Eldest of the Stone Elves.

Sartean D'Avers *(SAR-tee-ann dee-A-vers)*: The Master of the Keep of Kehrlia in the kingdom of Mor. Head of the Fraternity of Incantors. Adviser to King Halsen. Unmarried. No known heir.

Sera *(SEH-ra)*: White filly, mount to Princess Aria Evanti.

Shem (SHEM): Stone elf.

Shyla Greykin *(SHY-la GREY-kin)*: Gnomish outcast of G'naath, daughter to Oort and Thinsel Greykin, granddaughter to Cindra Sandshingle. Unmarried.

Sienni *(see-EH-nee)*: Young Incantor of Kehrlia. Former assistant to Mila Felsin.

Simmon Heartwood (*SIM-mun HART-wood*): Eldest Ranger of Thornwood.

Sir Marchion *(MAR-chee-on)*: Second Knight of Thornwood. Councilor to Queen Evanti in Sir Barris' absence.

Spirit *(SPI-rit)*: Sorrel-coated colt, mount to Mistress Pheonaris.

Slater (*SLAY-tur*): General in the Army of Mor.

Smit: (*SMIT*) Corporal in the Army of Mor.

Teena (*TEE-nah*): Ordained Priestess Daughter of the Temple of

Kal.

Terrias Evanti *(te-RYE-us e-VON-ti)*: Elven queen of Thornwood. Mother to Aria. Gret grand-niece of Neral Evanti.

Thinsel Greykin *(THIN-sel GREY-kin)*: Mother to Shyla Grekyin, wife to Oort Grekyin.

Trellia Evanti *(TREH-lee-uh ee-VON-tee)*: Vicaris of the Society of the Grove, paternal aunt of Queen Terrias Evanti. Unmarried, no heir.

Triumph *(TRY-umf)*: Steel-grey stallion. Mount to Mikallis Elmshadow.

Varyl *(VEH-ril)*: Captain in the Army of Mor.

Vincent Thomison *(VIN-sent TOM-ih-sun)*: A wealthy citizen of Mor, leader of the secret society of Merchants. Widowed. No known heir.

Wolf *(wulf)*: Canine companion to Shyla Greykin

Yano *(YAH-no)*: Incantor of Kehrlia. Deceased former assistant to Mila Felsin, killed by Kalashagon at the Morline Bridge

Zara *(ZAH-rah)*: Ordained Priestess Daughter of the Temple of Kal. Now an earring.

www.seanhinn.com